The U

THE L

An Anthology for Cancer Relief

EDITED BY WILLIAM MEIKLE

KAROSHI
BOOKS

Karōshi Books

Copyright © 2013 Karōshi Books

All rights reserved. No part of this publication may be reproduced, stored in a retrieval system, rebound or transmitted in any form or by any means, electronic, mechanical, photocopying, recording or otherwise, without the prior written permission of the author and publisher.

This book is sold subject to the condition that it shall not by way of trade or otherwise be lent, resold, hired out or otherwise circulated without the publisher's prior consent in any form of binding or cover other than that in which it is published.

1st Paperback Edition

Cover design: Simon Marshall-Jones

Published by:
Karōshi Books

ISBN: 978-1490480237

The Unspoken

CONTENTS

Foreword. Signs in the Air ~Ramsey Campbell
5
Just Breathe ~ Tim Lebbon
7
Photographs of Boden ~ Simon Kurt Unsworth
25
The Last Gift ~ Steve Lockley and Steven Savile
47
Where the Market's Hottest ~ John Shirley
59
Pages of Promises ~ Stephen James Price
73
Underbelly ~ Anna Taborska
93
Heal Thyself ~ Scott Nicholson
125
Harbinger ~ Stephen Laws
141
The Unfinished Basement ~ William Meikle
159
Alien Love ~ Nancy Kilpatrick
175
A Girl, a Toad and a Cask ~ David A. Riley
185
Polyp ~ Barbie Wilde
205
The Cure ~ Johnny Mains
223

Karōshi Books

The Big One ~ Guy N Smith
231
Cankerman ~ Peter Crowther
247
X for Henrietta ~ Steve Duffy
261
Bitter Soup ~ Gary McMahon
283

Ramsey Campbell

FOREWORD. SIGNS IN THE AIR BY RAMSEY CAMPBELL

January 2009 my wife Jenny's sister Penny died. She'd been treated for cancer some years earlier. While it wasn't the direct cause of her death, we suspect it was a factor. In my little eulogy at her funeral I said this:

"I've been a skeptic for much of my life, but I do at least believe we all pass into the fabric of the universe. On the morning Penny died I was up in my workroom as usual by dawn. It's on the third floor of a Victorian semi, and I have a view across the river to Liverpool. What I mostly see from my desk is the sky. That morning, all the time that the sun was visible beyond my window it was surrounded by an enormous rainbow halo, the like of which I've never seen. I thought it might be Penny.

"Like all the family I've kept being overtaken by surges of grief these last few weeks. Whenever I am I hear Penny's voice comforting me - saying 'Oh Ramsey' as only she could, with sympathy and humour as well. I don't mean an actual physical voice, but it might as well be; it sounds exactly like her. It certainly feels like her presence, as if in some sense she's still here. I hope she is for as long as she wants to be."

Signs In The Air

As is the way these days Lum'Rhin Dharvu, the LifeRites Celebrant/Officiant, asked to be sent the eulogies in advance for inclusion in Penny's memorial book. While I was typing this piece to send, the rainbow once again appeared around the sun.

I offer all this as consolation without attempting to interpret it. One way we keep our loved ones with us even once they're gone is by talking about them. We writers have the great gift of being able to pass on memories or elements of our lives to people who don't know us or those who were dear to us. I know that some of the stories in this anthology are based on actual experience, but I won't presume to speculate how many of the others are. I believe it needn't matter. What counts is that the authors have engaged their considerable imaginations with their themes and contributed stories worthy of the book. Perhaps some of them have the ability to heal, at least emotionally. Meanwhile science builds up its own healing power, and our hopes.

I have a last anecdote to share, and once again I'll leave it uninterpreted, though I know what I would like it to mean. Earlier this month we had another death in the family, alas; Jenny's brother's partner Doris died of cancer. I was already booked on the day of the funeral, and so Jenny took the train to Newton Abbot on her own. As she stepped off the train she saw Penny waving to her from the far end of the platform. In a moment Penny was gone but not, I think, for ever. Perhaps my writing this will help her to be here.

JUST BREATHE BY TIM LEBBON

Nia was walking in the woods with her father when she saw the dead squirrel. It was hunkered down against the base of a tree, its tail curled around its head like a bushy grey hat. She froze, her father walked on ahead of her—swishing ferns with his stick, he said you *always* needed a stick when you were walking in the woods—and waited for the squirrel to notice her presence.

It was moving slightly in the late afternoon sun. Nia frowned. It didn't look like normal movement, and she was used to seeing someone moving wrong because of how her mummy sometimes twisted around in bed. She took a few steps closer.

"Nia?" her father asked. His voice was weaker than it used to be, sadder.

"There's a squirrel," she said. She walked across the carpet of dried leaves and fallen twigs, her footfalls crackling and cracking, and the squirrel barely moved.

"Covered in ants," her dad said. He'd come to stand behind her without her noticing. His shadow went the other way, and the tree held the squirrel in its own.

Just Breathe

"Why doesn't it run away?" Nia asked. The thought of being smothered in wood ants like that was horrible. She'd gone through a stage of having bad dreams about it, and her mummy had told off her dad for bringing her here. Big ants, the length of her thumbnail, dark with reddish legs, millions and millions of them making nests from pine needles and sometimes, if there was no wind and you stood quiet and still, you could hear them crawling all through the woods, as if the whole pace was alive and whispering.

"It's dead," her dad said. "Look." He nudged the squirrel. It tipped onto its back and its tail shifted from its face, showing an open, toothed mouth and one glazed eye. Her dad's stick stirred up the ants, and hundreds of them moved faster, hurrying in their tasks.

"Poor thing," Nia said. She hated dead things. They looked all wrong. They looked too motionless and broken, and she wished she could fix them.

"Can't see much wrong with it," her dad said. He turned it onto its front with his stick. She'd once seen him lifting a dead cat with his foot, looking for its collar so he could take it home to its owner. Aren't you going to do something with it first? she'd asked, and her father had frowned at what she meant. He'd know now. But she wasn't going to say anything, because he'd probably tell her off. Mummy said she had a strange view of death, but she always sounded a bit pleased when she said it. Admiring, Nia thought.

"Can I have a look?" Nia asked, taking a step closer.

"Nothing to fix here," her dad said. He shoved the creature with his foot. It was stiff and still, and did not bend.

Nia saw no wounds, no signs of why or how it had died. If it had been a fox or a buzzard, there would have been blood, and bits of meat gone from it. The fur would have been broken, instead of simply dirty and clotted with dirt. *If it's just something gone wrong inside, I should be able to put it right*, she thought. *I should be able to open it and make things better, like Daddy did with my radio last Christmas. Take the back off, find the loose wire or the bit of brain that's gone wrong, make it all work again.*

"Come on," her dad said. "Let's walk all the way around today. The nurse will be with your mum for another hour, at least."

Nia left the dead thing reluctantly. She knew it would remain dead, but still she wished she could look closer.

*

"It's called cancer, Sweetie. It started in my boob, here. And because cancer is nasty, it tries to spread to other places to ruin them as well. So even though the doctors gave me some drugs, and put special x-rays in me to try and stop it, they didn't work."

Nia cannot answer, or ask questions. This is the first time her mummy has told her what's wrong, and though Nia has known for a while—Mummy is looking poorly, and thin, and she and her dad have been going off for days and leaving Nia with Nanny much more often than usual—to know for certain, to be told, is something she suddenly doesn't want.

"But the doctors are still looking after me. And there's going to be a nurse coming in to see me every day from now on." Her mother seems flustered, upset. "For a little while."

"What for?" Nia asks.

"To give me some medicine."

"Can't Daddy do that? Or me?"

Her mother smiles. She looked more tired than ever. "This is special medicine that goes in a machine. And every few minutes, the machine will put a bit of the medicine into me." She shifts slightly. Sitting at the dining table is uncomfortable for her, Nia can see that. But even though she's a little girl, she knows her mummy has done it for her. Got out of bed, showered, dressed, and come to sit here to tell her stuff about what's happening.

"And that medicine will make you better," Nia says. She's tapping her fingers on a table mat, making a tune that's been in her head for a while.

Her mummy doesn't answer. Nia glances up, smiling, uncertain. Her mummy is looking at her in a strange way, and Nia doesn't like it at all. It's almost as if her mummy can't see her, and she's seeing something a lot further away.

"Yes, Sweetie," she says.

"Good," Nia says. "Tell the nurse I'll help her if she wants. I know how to fix you."

She taps again, watching her fingers, trying to repeat the same tune. She hears her breathe heavily, and doesn't look up at her again. Nia is only eight, but she is already a clever, wise girl. She knows that seeing her mummy's tears will change how things are right now. She knows that seeing them will make everything more real.

*

"It's just not that easy," her dad said as they left the woods and walked home across the fields. "If it was, I'd do it myself. I'd put things right myself."

It surprised Nia, because he didn't like talking about things like that in front of her. When she glanced up at him, she *knew* he was talking about Mummy. His face had gone that way it always went when her illness was mentioned with the nurse, or Nanny. He looked lost and afraid, as if it was actually him who was sick. As if it was him who was going through all the pain.

"I just think it *should* be that easy," Nia said. "If the cancer's in her boob, just take it out. Why can't they just take it out?"

"Because it's not only there," he said. Nia knew this was difficult for him. He leaned against the last stile they had to climb over before home and prevented her from passing. Maybe he wanted to stay away from the house, in the woods and field where things were out of sight.

"Where else?" she asked. She already knew some of it. She'd heard the nurse talking on her phone once.

"Her bones," her dad breathed. "Spine, hips, skull. It's eating her, and—" He glanced back at Nia, as if forgetting she was there. "Mummy's very poorly."

"I know," she said, shrugging. Her mummy often fell asleep now when Nia was chatting to her, and then Nia would fall silent and watch her thin face, or read, listening to the regular whirring of the machine that gave her medicine. A driver, they called it. "But the nurse will make her better."

Nia looked away from her dad as his face changed. She had seen the same change in her mother's expression, felt the same loaded silence that was a response to her utterance of faith in the nurse, and Nia was becoming afraid of it. She looked back towards the woods and imagined the squirrel racing out from beneath the fence, bushy tail high, glazed eye glittering once again. Perhaps it would follow them home.

"Mummy's very poorly," her dad said again, and he climbed the stile and led them home.

*

Nia had never told anyone—especially her mummy and dad—but before her mother became ill, Nia had tried.

She found the dead bird behind their garage, in the spread of soil, weeds and cat poop that her dad sometimes called the vegetable patch. Mummy would laugh at that, and ask him when his spuds would be ready for pulling. He'd say something quietly, and his mother's laughing would turn into a giggle that Nia knew she shouldn't be hearing. There was kids' talk, and adults' talk, and she was already becoming receptive to differences between the two.

The bird was a robin, its cheery red breast ruffled and dulled in death. The first time she saw the bird she stared at it for a while—maybe all afternoon—before her mum called her and she went in for tea. She dreamed about it that night, then next day she returned to the vegetable patch and the robin was still there. She thought the neighbour's cat might have eaten it, or it would have got better and flown away. But it stared back as it had the day before, misshapen head turned to one side, its little black eye regarding her with quiet solemnity.

She thought it must have flown into something and banged its head. It was amazingly light when she picked it up, almost as if it wasn't there. It was stiff as well, like a model bird her mum put on the Christmas tree and which her dad laughed at.

She used the knife she'd brought from the kitchen to cut its head. Inside wasn't wet as she'd feared, but she could see nothing wrong. She touched one bit, then another, and tried pushing the cut back together again.

"Just breathe," she whispered, realising that she couldn't remember what song a robin sang.

The sides of the cut didn't fit together. Her heart started pumping quicker and she breathed faster, suddenly afraid that she'd hurt the robin more than it had been hurting before.

"Sorry, sorry," she said.

"What's wrong, Sweetie?" her mummy asked from behind her.

Just Breathe

Nia pushed the knife into a clump of leaves and then stood, holding out the little bird. She started crying. It looked so still and dead, not as it should, and she told it how sorry she was again.

Her mum's face fell, and she said something about a cat having got it, and she took it from Nia and said she'd go and bury it where the cats couldn't touch it anymore.

"You go in and wash your hands," she said. Nia did as she was told. As the soapy water swilled down the sink, she thought of the robin sitting behind her on the shower rail. She believed, she believed, she'd touched its bad bits and fixed what had killed it. But when she looked in the mirror, the robin wasn't there.

*

They walked home the long way around the village, and her dad went into the little shop to buy a bottle of wine. Today was Wednesday, and Nanny came to stay every Wednesday. She would sit with Nia's mummy, get her drinks, talk to her, and her dad would sit in the conservatory and listen to music. The wine would go quickly, and sometimes he'd fall asleep there before the tears came, and sometimes he'd cry himself to sleep. Nia often crept into the kitchen and looked through the back door at her dad, but she had never gone out there to talk to him. She knew that this was his private time.

She had her own private times, too.

*

After the robin had been the curled up spider she'd found behind her old dollhouse. She didn't really play with her dolls anymore, and they'd been shut into their house for some months without her giving them another thought. Then she moved the house, and found the dead spider.

Lifting it gently into her palm by one leg, she heard her mother groaning in the bedroom next door. It was the middle of the day. She'd come home from school at the beginning of that week to find her mummy in bed, and she had barely got up since. That's what had shocked and upset Nia more—the fact that her mummy was always in bed now, not how ill she was looking.

Nia held her breath, listening as her mother settled into sleep again.

As she exhaled, the spider rose from her palm and drifted to the floor. It was a big one, but so dry, so light. She stared at it for a long time, balanced on the edge of her pink rug. Maybe if she added water it would come alive again. Spiders can't have been that complicated inside, something so small. A bit of water, and maybe she could use a pin to just remove whatever bug had killed it, or slip a piece inside away from another piece inside...

It seemed just so wrong that something alive could suddenly not be.

After the spider, she spent some days watching out for roadkill. There was a flattened hedgehog close to the railway bridge, dry and recognisable only from its spines. Obviously too dead and gone, with some bits missing. But then she and her dad passed a badger on the way to town, and it was there on the way back, too. She asked her dad about it, and he said a car must have hit it and knocked it onto the grass verge.

"Can we stop to see if it's all right?" she asked, and her dad said no. "Why?"

"Because it's dead, Nia."

"How do you know?"

"It's been run over."

"How do you know if you don't stop to see? Maybe it's just stunned. Injured."

"No, it's dead. Probably crawling with maggots, and the council will come along soon and scrape it up."

She didn't like the sound of that. *Scrape it up*. It inspired horrible images, and the sound of a shovel against Tarmac.

Her dad drove on, passing the fields full of miniature horses, the local garden centre where dozens of cars were parked and people were eating in the cafe as if everything was normal, and then they turned into the village past the pub. There were four people sitting in the pub's small front garden, drinking beer and laughing in the sun. Nia wanted to tell them that her mummy was sick, at home in bed. And thinking of that, a fear that she had never felt before gripped her. She started shaking, then crying.

Her dad noticed and pulled over at the side of the road.

"Hey, hey," he said. He undid his belt and leaned across the seats, hugging her to his shoulder. He'd let her sit in the front seat, which she knew wasn't really allowed. Nia loved her dad.

"The badger shouldn't be dead," she said. "It's just not fair. And I ... I don't understand."

Her dad sighed, and she felt his heavy breath against her head, shifting her hair. She adored the smell of him; it was comfort, and a familiarity that made her safe.

"It's just a thing," he said. "The badger ... imagine you and I could make a model of a badger, using meat and bones and fur, and all the parts that go to make a real one. And imagine we were very, very good at making models. We'd get all the parts in the right places, and sew them up, and connect them exactly as they should be. It'd have the right number of legs and eyes and teeth, and claws. The fur would be coloured and patterned just right."

"What about its blood?" Nia asked. She stayed cuddled up to her dad, her eyes closed. It was easier to imagine that way.

"We'd use proper badger's blood and fill its veins," he continued. "Seal it up so it didn't bleed. Then we'd warm it up to the right temperature. And you know what would happen?"

"The badger would come alive."

"No, Sweetie. It wouldn't come alive. It'd be a model we'd made, that looked very much like a badger, but wouldn't be one. The badger isn't what it's made from. It's what makes it alive." He leaned back and eased her back into her seat. "When the car hit the badger, it took away its life and left just the model behind. Understand?"

Nia nodded.

"You're sure?"

"Yes, Dad."

Just Breathe

"Good. Right." He started the car again, sighed. "How about an ice cream before we go home?"

Nia nodded. But she didn't speak, because she was afraid of what she would say. Her dad didn't understand at all.

*

The squirrel was on Nia's mind as they walked back along their street to the house. She watched birds foraging on lawns, the speck of countless flies floating on the summer afternoon air, and the day seemed loaded. She could not explain it better than that. The village had held its breath, and when it breathed again everything would change.

Nanny was waiting for them at their front gate, Nia's dad's mobile phone in her hand. She looked strange. She held up the phone as they approached, glanced at Nia, smiled like she was in pain.

"I tried to call," she said to Nia's dad, "but your phone was in the conservatory." Then she started crying, and the village breathed.

That late afternoon was a blur, and Nia felt removed from what was happening in her house. There was always someone with her, talking in quiet tones, comforting and soothing—Nanny, the nurse, Mrs Andrews from next door—but Nia was alone, and some distance from them.

A doctor came and went into her mummy's room. He stayed for a while, then left again.

Her dad was crying. She heard him, but never saw, because around her he managed to hold it back. His face was puffy, and his looked ready to pop.

Nia knew what had happened before they told her. The life had gone from her mummy, and now there was only the model of her left behind. All the bits were there and in the right places, but the thing that made them work together was gone. That was because there was more in her than there should have been. There was cancer, and somehow it had made her die.

Nia couldn't understand how or why. So what if it was in her bones, her skull, her hips, her boob? So what? Why should that make her die? Why?

This was why Nia cried. When she sat with her dad on the sofa, she asked what needed to be asked.

"Can't we fix her, Dad?"

"No, Sweetie. No one can fix Mummy now."

I can, Nia thought, but she did not say it out loud. *I've been practising for this forever. I'll take all the bad out, and Mummy will work again. She'll smile like she used to, and enjoy dried ginger, and reading, and love making plant pots in the spring, and sit in her chair in the garden with a cup of tea every evening after dinner.*

Everyone cried some more, but for Nia it was not quite over.

*

Nia's dad took her upstairs. Nanny objected, but he insisted, and asked Nia. She nodded and said yes. There was someone coming to get Mummy soon, and Nia had to see her one more time. There was something she had to do.

Just Breathe

It was very quiet and still, and when Nia pushed the door open into her parents' bedroom she saw her mummy lying in the bed. She looked different. Still thin and pale, but where new lines had so recently etched themselves in her face, her skin was smooth again. It was as if in dying, she had aged backwards.

"Mummy," Nia said, standing in the doorway. Her dad stood behind her, hands on her shoulders.

"Beautiful," he said. "She's at peace now, Sweetie. No more pain." His voice was soft and smooth, loaded with love.

"Can I...?" Nia asked, and when her dad didn't respond, she walked across the bedroom and stood beside the bed.

She remembered standing here before when she was smaller and had been woken by a nightmare, gently prodding until her mummy woke and took her into her warm, cuddling the bad dreams away. She wished this was a nightmare. Holding her hand up, moving in to prod at her mummy, her dad spoke up from the doorway.

"Sweetie, no!"

But Nia was not finished.

She touched her mother's face, and it was cool. Nia gasped. Then she moved her hand up to her mummy's forehead, where she knew the cancer had grown, and tried to squeeze her fingers closed around it.

Big hands lifted her away and did not put her down again.

"She's cold," Nia said, and her tears flowed.

"Yes," Daddy said. He hugged her close. "Come on. Time for bed."

Nia let him carry her from the room and get her ready for bed, and she went downstairs to kiss Nanny, and then back up to her bedroom where Daddy sat on her bed and tried singing her to sleep. But his voice kept breaking, so Nia held his hand and squeezed. She drifted off to sleep searching for whatever it was inside that made her Nia.

*

Something tickled her awake. A caress on her cheek. She rubbed at it and felt something small between her fingers. It moved.

Nia sat up in the darkness, window framed by moonlight, the night-light on the landing casting a warm glow across her half-open door. Her fingers felt strong, her knowledge deep, and as she held her breath she heard a gentle whisper from all around her bedroom. *You can hear them in the woods*, she thought.

Standing, walking across her carpet, every few steps she trod on fallen leaves that crackled against her heels and toes.

She crossed the landing and opened her parents' bedroom door. It was still daylight in there, as if night refused to fall unless everything was finished, and things were changed.

"Good," Nia said, her voice surprisingly loud. "Good," she said again. It was nice that her voice kept her company.

Just Breathe

She entered the day-lit room and crossed to the bed, where her mummy still lay dead. She looked even more different now, even younger, as if she had simply fallen asleep and lay ready to be woken up.

And that was it. Her mummy was asleep, a deep sleep that set the model of her still and cold. The cancer things in her had made her sleep, and it was up to Nia to take them out and wake her up.

A wood ant crawled across her mummy's face and paused at her left nostril. Nia reached for it, and the ant reared on its back legs. She picked it away and dropped it on the carpet at her feet. There were more ants on the bed, and several crawling across her mother's nightie. Nia pushed them all gently aside.

Perhaps the squirrel followed us home, too, Nia thought, and she glanced at the window. But the creature was not there. Of course not; it was a wild animal, and would not show itself so easily.

She leaned against the bed, and the mattress springs creaked a little.

Nia, a voice said. It was very far away.

Nia reached out and touched her mother's face, and her fingers sank inside. She would not need a knife. She delved deep, watching her mummy's eyes in case she stirred, and then her fingers brushed something rough and alien that made her shiver with revulsion. Here was the first one, and she moved her hand deeper into her mummy's head as she sought a good grip on the growth.

Nia, babe.

Nia gripped and pulled. There was no blood, but her mother's head lifted slightly from the pillow as Nia tugged the horrid growth from her head. *Fixing the model*, Nia thought, and somewhere in the body before her lay the mother she had always loved and so wanted back. There were growths and imperfections marring the model right now, but Nia was the one to put things right. Remove the bad and leave the good, and everything would be fine once again. *Beautiful*, her dad had said, and he had been right. Mummy was beautiful.

Whining softly, Nia moved her hand down towards her mother's chest, and the voice came in again.

Nia, babe, come on back.

"Just breathe," Nia said, and there was something wrong with her voice. She frowned, because instead of young and full of hope, it sounded older and stricken with grief.

She pressed her hand against her mother's chest, and Mummy opened her eyes.

*

"Nia, hey, here, come here." He hugged her close.

"Mum," Nia breathed. She let herself be hugged, and smelled Max's comforting scents of sweat and stale breath, all the man she loved. He leaned back against the headboard and she pressed her head to his chest, arm across his stomach. She was sticky with sweat, heart thudding.

"Same dream," he said, but there was no accusation.

Just Breathe

"Yeah." Each time she came close to finished a new sculpture, her mother came to visit. Nia welcomed the dreams, and supposed it was a large part of what drove her to uncover new shapes in stone. Her dear old dad always came to see, and always commented on how proud her mum would be.

"Going to finish it today?" Max asked.

Nia breathed gently a few times, enjoying the sound of his incredible heartbeat. She loved the mystery of him.

"No," she said. "It's just a sculpture. Nothing's ever finished."

Max slept, but Nia stayed awake until dawn, when the sun beamed across their bedroom and birds sang nature's miraculous, unknowable song.

Simon Kurt Unsworth

PHOTOGRAPHS OF BODEN BY SIMON KURT UNSWORTH

Boden was searching through the old photo albums in the loft for pictures of his dad when he first found it. There was a particular image he remembered from his childhood, of Dad pulling a face at the camera with Boden and Sally and mum standing behind him, that he wanted for the wall of shame. He knew it had ended up boxed in the loft, and finally came across it in an album with a maroon cover and a curling sticker on it that read '1977- 1979'. *One album for three years worth of photos,* he thought as he brought it down the ladder, *Christ, we could fill an album with the photos we take during one day out now, if we printed them all.* He had thousands, literally thousands, of pictures of him and Chrissie, far less of his parents and very few of his grandparents, who hadn't died that long ago. There was only one existing picture of his great grandparents, a stiffly formal thing showing two people who weren't even memories to him.

He couldn't use the picture in the end. His dad was clear enough in it, tongue out and hands forming comedy horns at his temples; no, the problem was the image of Boden himself. It had darkened, a blurred cloud of mould or damp-affected chemicals obliterating his face and neck. Rubbing the patch did

Photographs Of Boden

nothing to help; if anything, it was larger when Boden lifted his thumb. Flicking through the rest of the album revealed that another couple of nearby pictures had been affected in the same way, one of Boden sitting on a bench in a park somewhere and the other of Boden on a beach holding a plastic bucket. In both, his face had gone, lost to a dirty smear that looked greasy even though, when Boden touched it, it was dry.

Eventually, he found another picture of dad looking stupid, this time asleep in a chair one Christmas day with a pint balanced on his belly, and the wall was complete.

"How many pictures is it?" asked Chrissie that night as Boden scanned and printed the last of them before sticking it to the long strip of card.

"Sixty," he replied. "One picture of dad looking like an idiot for each year of his life."

"It's a lovely idea," said Chrissie. "I'm sure he'll be very grateful."

"He won't, he'll be embarrassed," replied Boden. "But it'll make him smile and he's supposed to smile on his sixtieth."

"Speaking of smiling, have you heard from Sally? Is she coming?" asked Chrissie.

"No, and I don't know," said Boden, and he could hear the chill in his voice even as he didn't want it to be there, especially not with Chrissie. His sister had caused enough family tensions and arguments over the years and he was determined she wasn't going to spoil dad's big day.

"Where is she?" asked Chrissie. "Can you ring her?"

"Still in London, I think, and I'm not ringing her. I've sent her messages and emails, and she knows when the party is. She knows she's welcome to come if she behaves. Hell, I *want* her to come and she knows that too, but I'm tired of chasing her, trying to get her to act like a decent human being and be a part of this family."

"I know," said Chrissie. "I just keep hoping that something'll change."

"Me too," said Boden and despite all of the anger and all of the disappointments and arguments, he meant it.

*

The party was a success, the wall of shame made everyone including Dad laugh, and by the time the last of the guests left he and Boden were both drunk. They, and Chrissie, were sitting at Dad's dining room table, and Dad had just mentioned Sally.

"I'm sorry, Dad," said Boden, "I did tell her, she knew about tonight. I hoped she'd come, but you know what she's like."

"I do," said Boden's dad, Roger, his voice laced with whisky and sadness and age. "She's like your mother was, hot-headed sure of herself, convinced she's right all the time."

"Hot headed? She's rude, self-centred and a liar," said Boden, unable to help himself. "She expects everyone to do things her way, the way she wants, and when they don't she sulks like a baby. She's not come tonight because it clashes with a night out with her friends, and I wouldn't rearrange it. After all, why should you be allowed to have your sixtieth birthday party on your actual birthday if it interrupts Sally's social life?"

"John," said Chrissie softly, warning.

"I'm sorry, Dad," said Boden, trying to let it go, to be calm. "But it annoys me. *She* annoys me. She never thinks about anyone but herself and she's never done anything for anyone if there wasn't something in it for her."

"She's young," his dad said. "She'll learn. Besides, you weren't so perfect, oh son of mine, not by a long way!" He proceeded to tell a story about Boden having a teenage tantrum because he'd been grounded after coming in from a concert late, and his telling had Chrissie laughing so hard she cried; Boden's dad's impression of a furious, teenage Boden was both affectionate and sharp and even Boden laughed.

It was a good story; the only problem was that Boden had no memory of it, and was sure it wasn't true.

It didn't matter in the end, not really, and Boden remembered the story only as a good part of the end of the evening, something his dad and him and Chrissie had shared, something private and special. So his dad was remembering something wrong, or making it up for the sake of being a raconteur and to impress Chrissie; Dad could be a smooth sod on the quiet, Boden knew, and tended to turn on the charm around attractive women. Besides, he also wouldn't have put it past Dad to make up something as a way of distracting Boden, of telling him *Don't judge, don't let other people's pettiness or smallness make you petty or small,* without actually telling him. After all, it was only a story.

The weekend following the party, Boden went to his dad's, this time without Chrissie. There was no real reason for the visit, just a pop-in to see how things were going, a quick coffee and then he'd be gone. He did it most weekends, and he usually enjoyed it. This time however, as he sat in the front room with Dad and caught up, something nagged at him, something subtle that drew his eye; not towards itself, no, but away, as though his vision was sliding off something that it should be able to grip. It was only as he stood to go that he realised what it was.

"Where's the picture?" he asked, surprised.

"What picture?" asked Dad.

"The one of us at the zoo," said Boden. It had stood on the mantelpiece as long as Boden could remember, an image of Boden and his mum and dad posing in front of a lion cage in a zoo somewhere, taken when Boden was perhaps four, a couple of years before Sally came along. Boden liked the photo because his mum was laughing in the image, wide and free, and both he and his dad were grinning broadly.

"Zoo?" asked his dad.

"When I was a kid," said Boden. "You and me and Mum. We had a good day. The zookeeper took the photo with that old Instamatic thing of yours that you had to wind on after taking each picture, remember?"

"No," said his dad after a moment. "I mean yes, I remember the camera and I remember a trip to the zoo about eighteen months before Sally was born, is

Photographs Of Boden

that the one you mean? Because I don't remember a photograph."

"That's the day out, yes," said Boden, and went to say more but stopped at the frown on his dad's normally placid face.

"That was a horrible day," his dad said. "You cried and cried all day, and refused to be cheered up. You did that a lot when we had days out. Your mum used to joke that you were determined that we shouldn't have a good time. We did take photos that day, but none of them were much good when we developed them. Your mum, she looked fit to explode in them, and you were crying or all puffy-faced from crying. I don't think we ever put any of them out on show, did we?"

Maybe it's behind the cards, thought Boden, going over and moving a few of the Sixtieth cards and peering behind them. There was a picture there, a small one in a plain wooden frame, smaller than he remembered the zoo photo being and differently oriented, portrait rather than landscape. He lifted it, not sure what he expected to see, hoping that it was his memory, or maybe dad's, at fault, and was faced with a picture he had never seen before. In it, his mum and dad were standing in a garden, their old garden he thought, the one at Highmore Terrace, smiling at the camera, and in front of them was Sally.

Boden was not in the picture.

"That's a nice photo," said Dad from behind him. "But it wasn't taken at the zoo."

"No," said Boden. "It's Highmore Terrace, isn't it?"

"That's right," said Dad. "I suppose I should change it really, it's been up years, but it was one of your mum's favourite photos and I haven't the heart to take it down. It'd be like I was, I don't know, disrespecting her or something. Silly, really."

"No," said Boden.

"We never did manage to get one of you and Sally and us all together that looked nice, you were always so grumpy, wouldn't ever smile."

"Yes," said Boden, putting the picture down, thinking, *No, that wasn't me that was like that. Not me. Sally.*

"You were a terror, son," said Boden's dad. "A real terror!" He laughed as he said this, patting Boden's shoulder in an *It's okay, that's what children do, I still love you* gesture.

"Yes," said Boden again, and then, "Dad, I have to go, Chrissie's expecting me." and even to him his voice sounded hollow and the lie obvious and brittle.

That night, under Chrissie's bemused gaze, he brought all of the photograph albums down from the loft and began looking through them carefully. He had inherited them from Dad after Mum died, when Dad had moved to the flat and when Sally had said she didn't want them because she had neither the space to store them nor any interest in looking at them. He was looking for the photos from the zoo; the one on Dad's mantelpiece, the one that *wasn't* on Dad's mantelpiece, wasn't the only one that had been taken that day, it was just the best. The rest were in the albums somewhere, in amongst the other pictures of him and his parents looking happy, sitting in gardens in summer or in rooms on Christmas day or

Photographs Of Boden

family birthdays. It was Sally who there were few photos of, Sally who never smiled, would deliberately turn away when someone pointed a camera at her, would grimace her way through family outings and events, not him. Not him.

Not him.

He found them eventually, the zoo photos. They were almost as he remembered them, pictures of mum in front of the elephant enclosure and dad drinking coffee from a Styrofoam cup at a table upon which half-eaten sandwiches were scattered, their greaseproof paper wrappings shed like snakeskin about them. There were fewer images of Boden himself than he remembered.

In each image, Boden's face was being obliterated by the blooming of something that looked like moss but which left no residue on his fingers when he rubbed it. The stains looked like clouds of ink billowing in water, and they weren't completely black; there were hints of rich, deep reds and purples in them, skeins of light and dark that looked like vines wrapped tight around suffocated branches. The stains were not limited to the images taken at the zoo, however; in some of the photographs placed around the zoo pictures in the album, Boden's face had also started to be lost.

There was a picture taken at his cousin James' fifth birthday, a day Boden remembered fondly as being good fun, in which his smiling, freckled face was already disappearing. A second, in a paddling pool at the age of perhaps seven, his smile spotted with flecks like oil spatters, while Sally looked on behind him, clean and untouched and smiling. A third, taken from somewhere in the audience of a school play, him on stage acting in the nativity, being Herod dressed in a robe made from an old blanket with big silver stars sewn on it; dabs of maroon and black already gathering across his exposed skin. Boden had the strangest feeling that they carried on under the costume, rippling patterns of spots, merging and blending, creeping across his flesh, invisible and stealthy. A fourth, in his school uniform. A fifth, running. A sixth playing football, a seventh, an eighth. A ninth, and more, and on and on.

The worst affected pictures were clustered around the first one he had found, as though that were the focal point and the stains were spreading out from there. Some of his happiest childhood memories were from around that period, and the images of them were being entirely obliterated. It wasn't simply a physical process, Boden found; a picture close to the others in the album from a much later period was unaffected, yet other pictures from the same occasions kept in other albums were showing signs of the telltale marks.

That wasn't the worst of it, though; no, the worst was when Boden tried to recall the occasions in the photographs, the zoo or James' birthday. His memories themselves seemed odd. It was as though there were two sets of things being recalled at the same time, the one that he *actually* remembered and another laid over the top, uneven and scablike, changing the shape of what lay under it, tightening it, puckering it into something new and alien.

Corrupting it.

Photographs Of Boden

Boden tried rubbing at one of the patches again, not liking the way it felt warm under his thumb, warmer than the surrounding paper, and liking less the way his rubbing achieved nothing. *Out, damned spot,* he thought to himself, and then *No, you're being stupid and over-dramatic, it's old chemicals reacting with damp or something. It's nothing.*

During the next few days Boden felt that he was permanently on the edge of something, although what he couldn't be exactly sure. He spent the time deliberately not looking at his old photographs and trying to not to recall memories that felt increasingly tender when he did accidentally probe them. He found himself more aware of how people spoke to him and the things they said. They angled their bodies towards him differently, hands folded across chests and stomachs as though protecting themselves. Surely this wasn't how people normally were with him? He prided himself on being relaxed, open and approachable, yet people were defensive around him, acting as though he was prickly, prone to aggression and attack. It made him uneasy, and he found himself over-analysing and over-reacting to things without knowing quite why. Even Chrissie noticed, accusing him of snapping at her after a conversation about some mundanity or other whilst they were lying in bed together.

"I'm not snapping," he said.

"Aren't you?" she asked. "Funny, you could've fooled me. What's wrong?"

"Nothing," Boden said, then paused. "Everything. Things feel like they're changing, *I* feel like I'm changing, and I don't know why nor how, and I don't like it."

"Is it us?" she asked.

"No," he said, surprised. "Christ, no. Why would it be? We're okay, aren't we?"

"I hope so," Chrissie said. "Really, I do. So, what is it?"

"I don't know," he said helplessly. "I don't."

"Have you argued with your dad again?" Chrissie asked. "You always get like this after you've argued with him, you know. I'm not sure you realise it, but you do, every time."

Boden didn't reply. Chrissie came over and lay with her head on his chest and soon fell asleep, but he remained awake. *Maybe what Chrissie said has some validity,* he thought. *She should know, I suppose, she's the one that lives with me and sees how I am after every argument I have with him. Maybe I'm just feeling bad after arguing with dad?*

Only, he hadn't argued with his dad, not recently. Not ever.

*

The blotches were worse, covering more of the photographs. No, covering more of *him* in photographs, his skin and smile and eyes and hair lost below a creeping, flecked darkness. Almost all of the pictures in the first album were affected now, all of the ones with him in anyway. Those furthest away from the picture of dad making the face, the furthest away in time, were the least affected, with only one of

Photographs Of Boden

two tiny blemishes appearing. *Like spots,* he thoughts, *like my photo has acne or a rash or something.*

There was one picture, of him in a family group with his mum and dad and auntie Jean and uncle Bill and Sally and their cousins Adrian and John. Boden's memories of the day were good; Sally hadn't been too tantrumy, Mum and Dad had been happy and had sat laughing with Jean and Bill most of the day. Jean was dead now, as was Bill, and Adrian lived somewhere in America, but John was still around. Boden rang him the evening after first seeing the photo, making small talk for a few minutes before saying, "John, do you remember an afternoon we all spent together when we were kids? In our back garden, I think? There are photos of us together?" His voice stumbled over the word *photos*; he hoped John didn't notice.

"I think so," said John after a moment. "It wasn't a birthday, was it, just a get-together?"

"That's the one," said Boden. "What do you remember about the day?"

"That's a strange question," said John. "You losing your memory or something?"

"Sort of," replied Boden, forcing a laugh that sounded, to his ears, hollow and flat. "Just humour me."

"Well," said John after a second's silence. "It was fun. We had a laugh. We played cricket, if I remember rightly. You were a bit of a whinge because your dad wouldn't get the paddling pool out, but that was pretty usual so we all ignored you."

Boden clenched, felt himself stiffen and then forced his tongue to loosen. "Thanks," he managed to say. He made small talk for another minute and then disconnected the call.

He didn't remember whinging, but as John had said it, something like a memory occurred to him, spongy and unreal. It overlaid the actual memory of a day in which it had been Sally who'd moaned about not being able to have the paddling pool out because the boys were playing cricket. In this new one, he was the one moaning, pleading with his dad to get the paddling pool out and his dad was refusing. Adrian and John played cricket in the garden while he whined, and eventually he rejoined them and every time he hit the ball he imagined he was hitting his dad with the bat and making him groan. No, that wasn't real, it wasn't what had happened. No.

Yes. Yes, because even though he was sure it wasn't real, he had a memory of it, a memory of how he felt and the smells and sounds of the day. The photo album was on his knee, but he didn't want to open it. Had to open it.

Couldn't.

Had to, and opened it. His fingers found the family photo quickly, leafing through pages of thick, coated card to find his face lost under a rippling, crusted stain. It had grown in, what, twenty-four hours? Swelling, spreading, completely covering him, making what had been his space in the picture a space for something else, something impenetrable and uncontrollable.

No, Boden told himself, *not uncontrollable. I will not be a slave to this.* The question was, what could he do about it? *Fight it,* he told himself, *fight it. It's changing everyone's memories of your childhood, so fight back, remind them of the reality,* your *reality and not the reality being made by that black growing thing.*

He rang his dad first, asking him the same question as he'd asked John. "God, you were a horror that day," his dad said. "Going on and on about the paddling pool even after we'd said you couldn't have it out."

"'A horror'?" Boden repeated. "No, dad, that was Sally."

"What?" asked Dad. "Sally? No."

"Yes," insisted Boden. "Sally, moaning about the paddling pool while I played cricket with Ade and John."

"It was you," said Dad. "You're my son and I love you, but it was always you, just like it's you now, blaming Sally when it's you. All those days out, those family events and trips and holidays that were spoiled, had to be changed, just because you didn't like something about them and made it impossible for anyone else to enjoy them until you got your own way."

"Christ, Dad, that was Sally, not me, can't you remember?"

"So now it's my fault? I'm going senile, perhaps?"

"No, that's not what I meant, Dad, but I never made things difficult, it was always Sally, that -".

"Enough," Boden's dad interrupted, and he sounded weary. "I'm not talking about this again. I'd hoped you might have grown up a bit by now, learned to take some responsibility for how you were and how you are, but clearly not. Fine, that's your choice, but I won't be a part of it." He finished talking, made a noise as though he was going to say something else but didn't, and then broke the call off.

By the time Boden had spoken to his dad and then tried to pull himself together after the call, the blackness had spread. It was now crawling across the photos in the albums either side of the '1977-1979' volume, darkening its way through 1976 and 1980, its tendrils already slipping into 1975 and '81. It was so *fast,* appearing to leap from image to image, from memory to memory, in the shortest of instants, corrupting them as it went. Now Boden could remember whining about the paddling pool as clearly as he could remember not whining about it, two layers of memory flapping like threads in his mind and waiting for one to achieve dominance, to take root. *It's not real*, he told himself, but knew that he was wrong, it *was* real because people remembered it, not just him but others as well, and people believed it. Whatever the black thing was, it wasn't just corrupting the photos, but his life as well, his past and his present and his future.

In the new reality, he thought, *I argue with dad, I've always been a whining bastard, Sally was a good girl and no trouble, I make people wary and they don't like me.* The question was, how far would it go? How much of his past could it affect, blight? His early years? His teens? Already, those new early memories had changed people's perceptions of him, changed how they reacted to him. What would happen if his entire past was changed? When would it stop? When it had eaten its way through his twenties?

Photographs Of Boden

His recollections of university? Work? Meeting Chrissie?

All of it?

Panicking, Boden set aside the old albums and went to the bedroom, pulling his and Chrissie's wedding album from its place in the wardrobe and rifling through it quickly. The pictures were unmarked, thank fuck, his face still smiling and clean, surrounded by people looking at him without a trace of tension or reserve.

Could it be reversed? Could he somehow turn it around by persuading people of the truth? Of *his* truth, rather than the truth be made by the blackness? His experiences with dad made him think that he couldn't, but perhaps he could stop it spreading. It was in the years 1974 through to 1985 now, from pretty much his eleventh birthday back to his birth. A thought suddenly struck him, rose up and refused to be ignored *If mum was alive, would her memory of the day I was born be affected? Changed from something that always made her teary and proud when she spoke about it and she'd had a drink, to something that she hated?* Boden had been an easy baby, she had always said, but would that truth be lost now? Would her memories of him be of a difficult labour? Of an unpleasant, hard-to-settle, graceless child, the way his memories were of Sally? And would the resentments and stresses that this new childhood caused back then have burned their way through the rest of his mum's memories, so that she reacted to him differently? He suspected probably so. *Thank fuck she's dead,* he thought, *I don't think I could cope with that.*

He started with the pictures closest to the affected ones, moving rapidly through 1985 and 1986 until he found one from 1987; it a group shot of him and a number of friends, taken on a school trip. The picture was as-yet unmarked, and he was still in touch with some of the people in it. Picking one at random, he rang them.

"Ollie? It's John, John Boden."

"Christ, John, hello! How're you? God, it must have been years."

"A few, yes. I'm sorry for ringing out of the blue like this, and this is going to sound strange, but I wanted to ask you something."

"Yes?"

"Well, ask and maybe remind you of something," Boden said, casually flicking back the photo album and then stopping. Black spots had already started appearing on the earliest photographs, tiny but noticeable. *It's speeding up,* he thought, *speeding up, growing, spreading out. I don't have much time.* "The school trip we took? To that castle in Wales? Do you remember it?"

"Bloody Hell, mate, that's going back a bit, isn't it? I do remember it, though, vaguely. Why?"

"Did we have fun? I mean, was I fun to be with, or a pain?" Closer now, he could see the blackness spreading through the album, watched it bloom across his flesh like some grimy flower.

"You were fine, mate. I mean, when we first met a couple of years earlier you weren't so good, but you were okay by then. Why?"

"I can't explain, Ollie, I'm sorry. I don't have time. Will you do me a favour?"

"If I can, I suppose."

"Try to remember that day, that I wasn't a pain, that I was okay, will you? Please?"

"John, you're worrying me now, what's going on?"

"Later, Ollie, I promise. Just remember."

"Yes."

"Remember."

He spent the rest of the day on the phone, ringing as many of the people in the photo that he could track down. All of the conversations were reflections of each other; yes, he'd been fun to be with that day, yes, they'd try and remember, what was going on, no he couldn't tell them but he would if he could, and all the while the blackness slipped it way through the photographs. Finally, when there was no one left to ring, he could only sit and watch as the black spots came closer and closer to the group photo, finally appearing on the same page, shadows gathering across his smile in the first picture and then the second, clustering around his eyes and disappearing below the neckline of his Bon Jovi T shirt. *Remember*, he thought, *all of you, remember.*

It came into the closest photo now, the one next to the group picture, blossomed and spread, taking the picture of him in a garden somewhere and drawing it into itself, unmaking him, recreating him as a changed and sour thing. The stain gleamed, rich blacks and maroons, warm when he touched it, the edges feathering out to absorb all of his picture skin. He turned his attention to the next image, and *remember and remember and please remember*

It got no further.

"Yes!" he cried, and actually punched at the air. He'd stopped it! Healthy memories, the actual memories of him and his friends, the ones they were holding in their heads, had stopped it, halted it in its tracks. He felt a rush of joy, but following on its heels was a realisation that brought it crashing down: how on earth could he stop it all? He'd have to go through every photograph, track everyone down, call them or email them or write to them, ask them to remember the good things about him. Jesus, it was a lifelong job!

Perhaps I don't need to, he thought. Perhaps if I can get one or two key people to remember me the way I am really, that might be enough. Perhaps the good memories can be set in, like an inoculation, and stop it getting any further. But who? Chrissie, for a start, but who else? Dad was already gone, infected by whatever this thing was, Mum was dead and there was no one else who he'd known for long enough, whose memories would have the strength to turn this thing aside, to fight it off.

Oh, no, God, wait, yes there was. There was one person, and he needed her now, much as he hated to admit it. Sighing, he reached for the phone.

"Sally?"

"Well, if it isn't big brother!"

"Sally, can I ask you something? Something important?"

"Of course, you can, Big Bro!" said Sally. She sounded happy, relaxed, not inclined to argue, to take umbrage at some imagined slight or at some message read into a tone of voice or word used. 'Doing a

Sally', he and Dad called it when she did that, when she found offense in things that weren't there. *Used to call it*, he amended sadly. *Now, Dad probably calls it 'doing a Steve'.*

"Sally, what was I like as a kid? As a teenage?"

"You were like most teenagers, and most big brothers, I suppose," she said. "Protective, a bit annoying, didn't like me pestering you. You were okay."

"Did we have good times?"

"John, what is this? Have you and Dad been at it again? Christ, can't you two leave it alone? You're like two walruses banging your fat together!"

"No, it's not that," Boden said. *It's got that, then, even with Sally,* he thought briefly, *me and Dad argue. That's a truth now. My past has altered.*

"Well what, then?"

"What were you like?"

"Me? What do you mean? John, what *is* this?"

"How do you get on with Dad?"

"Fine, John, we're fine. What's wrong? Please tell me."

"Fine? You're sure?"

" Of course I'm sure, John; Dad and I get on fine, just like we always have. Christ, is this another of your paranoid trips, another 'they love you more than me' days? I haven't got the energy for it, John."

"What paranoid trips?" he asked, but already he could feel new memories crusting over his own, ones where he rang up and screamed at Sally instead of her screaming at him, where he hated his parents and his sister rather than loved them, and he fought the memories, fought them but they rolled on, growing, smothering, wetly claustrophobic

"I'm not getting into this now, it was bad enough in the run-up to Dad's birthday," Sally said. "All the accusations and rants, and you know what John? None of it's necessary, it never has been. Mum and Dad love you, despite what you do to them, what you did to mum before she died, and I love you too. God help me, you're my brother and I love you even if I don't always like you a great deal. I'm going now. Try and ring Dad and make it up, please."

He couldn't fight it, it had got too far, had worked its dank fingers into too much of his past to be stopped, he saw that now. When he looked back at the school trip photo, it had started to blacken. *He* had started to blacken. *They're forgetting, or the weight of those other memories is corrupting this one,* Boden thought. He wondered about ringing them all again, but abandoned the idea. There seemed little point; he'd fought it and slowed it but not beaten it, and now that memory was infected, he'd never get it back. He remembered running across the grassy courtyard of the castle on that day, laughing furiously; and he remembered standing at the side of the courtyard sulking as his friends ran without him, one memory crowding and surrounding the other, thickening around it, replacing it.

Tired, Boden packed up the photo albums and put them back in the loft and then went and lay on his bed. After a few minutes, he picked up his wedding album, seeing with little surprise that black spots had started to pinprick their way across his skin in the earliest images in the album.

Photographs Of Boden

He thought about his and Chrissie's honeymoon, about the times they'd spent in bed together, about their laughter and the conversations and the future they'd planned and hoped for, and he wept. Already, new tendrils were worming their way into the memories, a raised voice on the honeymoon, a fist, flowers and apologies between the conversations and then more raised voices and fists. He tried to think about the good times, about the wedding and the love in his heart, felt it corrupting, swelling into something new and unwanted and tawdry, and he wept more.

When Chrissie arrived home from work, he had finished weeping, had nothing left to cry out. He greeted her with a kiss, and she flinched away from him, and in her eyes he could see the fear of the man he was newly become.

THE LAST GIFT BY
STEVE LOCKLEY AND STEVEN SAVILE

Simon walked out of the hospital. His head felt like it was in a thousand pieces but he was determined to stay in control. Breaking down wasn't an option. He was stronger than that.

Hearing the diagnosis had been like listening to his own death sentence, loathing the very sound of the word. *Cancer*. He had sat through the well-meaning consultant's lecture about the various treatments that were available, but it was the man's tone that sealed it. For all the talk of radiotherapy and chemotherapy and healthy eating hope wasn't something he should cling to. Wait out the inevitable; that was the message. Treatment would only be palliative.

Simon had heard it all before; his father had been diagnosed, and died, the disease stripping him of his humanity as surely as it peeled away fat and muscle. It left nothing but pain.

Simon wasn't going the same way. He had lived his life with dignity and would die with as much of it intact as the disease would allow, even if it meant there would be no treatment.

It hadn't been a difficult decision. He didn't want the slow lingering death. He didn't want his children to watch him waste away day by day before their eyes. He didn't want to live the lie, or perpetrate it.

The Last Gift

He didn't want to look at the faces of people who loved him and see them hoping that the next round of chemo would drive the disease into remission. So he made his decision, selfish as it was, he wasn't going to put them through it.

He was only 58. Knowing that he would never reach 60 was difficult. Thanks to the doctors he had enough painkillers in his pocket to end it right now. He understood how some people could do it. The thought of sitting at home, one last scotch, one last cigar, a good one, Cuban, hand rolled. It would be painless—unlike the alternative that waited for him.

It would take a few days to put his affairs in order—which in itself was depressing. How could the sum of his life be counted, and balanced out in a few days. He hadn't made the mark he had promised himself when he was younger. Or maybe he had, maybe his kids were his legacy, that was how it was supposed to work after all, wasn't it? The children were the future. His DNA or a strand of it at least, would be around for a long time to come. The thought occurred that even that was no guarantee. Perhaps the only gift he gave his children was treacherous DNA, his legacy the promise that their own flesh would turn on them before they were sixty. He didn't want to think about it.

One step at a time. Keep it manageable.

That first step was getting home; only he wasn't even ready for that. Not yet. Taking it would make everything so much more real. No, first he would sit on the bench outside the hospital and stare at the litter of cigarette butts and chewing gum wrappers, buying himself a few minutes.

That was a joke though, wasn't it? Buying himself a few minutes . . . there was no reprieve. No extra time.

"You all right son?"

He couldn't help but smile despite himself. Tears ran down his cheeks and he wiped them away with the back of his hand. He hadn't been called son for a long time. He looked up from the cigarette butts and saw the cadaverous face of a wizened old man stooping over him.

Simon's head swam and he found himself gripping the arm of the bench for support.

"You're not looking too good, if you don't mind me saying."

He struggled to shape some kind of word. His lips moved but nothing escaped. Nausea swept through him in a wave.

The old man placed a hand on Simon's shoulder as he sat down beside him. The world slipped away, sound fading into a distant drone of traffic and hospital noises, taking the old man's words with it.

In the space between heartbeats his world turned black.

"Is that better?"

It was the same voice, though as it filtered through Simon's brain it seemed muffled, fuzzy and distorted. He tried to open his eyes but found that all he could see were lonely grey shapes . . . shadows that lacked any kind of definition or form.

"What happened?" It was a fight to get the words out. His sense of terror was almost a physical thing. A thought leered blackly in his brain. He'd had a stroke. Not only was he dying on the inside, his damned

The Last Gift

traitorous body was determined to finish him off as crudely and brutally as it could. Fear turned his next few words into a mumble of meaningless syllables. The old man spoke over them.

"You collapsed."

Simon tried to open his eyes again. This time he found something he could focus on. He was no longer outside the hospital but instead was in some kind of small room with thin curtains against the window.

"Where am I?"

"Safe."

"That's not what I asked. Where *am* I? In the hospital?"

The old man shook his head. "They couldn't do anything for you in there, Simon."

"And you can?" He hadn't meant it to sound as harsh as it did. Ghosts haunted his mind whispering words like pain relief and palliative care. None of them mentioned getting better.

"How did I get here?"

"I brought you in a taxi. I'm afraid I had to pay the fare out of your wallet but I didn't think you would mind."

Instinctively Simon reached into his pocket. Fireworks of pain exploded inside his head.

Painkillers!

"Are you looking for these?"

Simon started to nod, instantly regretting it.

White light exploded behind his eyes. He bit back on the stab of pain. The cries that tore out of him were purely animalistic. He had never felt anything approaching this kind of pain in his life.

"Just lie back, try not to think about it. Thinking about it makes it worse, believe me." the old man said. "It'll be over soon. If it helps, think about this instead. While it hurts you are still alive. In that way pain is a gift. Now, I'll get us some tea"

The old man left the room.

Simon felt a moment of relief but it was short lived. Fear undermined it. He didn't know where he was. He didn't have a clue who the old man was. A cold pebble of doubt settled in his gut. Was he going to die here? Was this frail old man to be his killer, not the cancer after all? It was a ridiculous thought, but it was just the kind of irony he had come to expect. He didn't have the strength to escape if he needed to. Raising his head from the pillow was more than he could manage. And yet he was hard pressed to think of anything that was so desperate he needed to live for it; what he *really* wanted, more than anything was a day to see his grandchildren again, to say his goodbyes and give them one last day to remember him by.

So he prayed quietly to a god that had stopped believing in him, asking for one more day.

As he lay staring at the ceiling he noticed a number of strange undulations in the plaster. He traced them with his gaze, thinking they were simply shadows but each had a shadow of its own.

And they were moving.

The door swung open and the old man shuffled back in carrying a mug. Corkscrews of steam curled off it. He sat on the bed beside Simon and held the mug to his lips. The liquid was hot and bitter and quite unlike anything he had tasted before.

The Last Gift

"You'll feel a little better in a few moments. For a while at least."

"What do you want from me?"

"Want? I don't want anything."

"Then what are you going to do to me."

"That depends."

"On what?"

"On what you want me to do."

"Well unless you have the cure for cancer you might as well just take me home and let me die in peace." Simon laughed; this was something new for him, gallows humour.

The old man leaned forward intently. "Is that what you *really* want, Simon?"

"To go home?"

"To be cured of the cancer?"

"You might as well ask me if I intend to run in the Olympics or swim the Channel. It's all irrelevant anyway."

"Well, not really. It only becomes irrelevant if you have nothing left to live for. Believe it or not there are some people who are actually relieved to be diagnosed with a terminal illness. The disease makes sure their empty lives come to an end. They have nothing to live for but lack the courage end it by themselves."

"Wishes and fishes though isn't it? I mean, there's no cure, it's already too far gone."

"Stop thinking with your head, Simon. Some things don't fit with the way we think about the world but we know they are there. We always have known. But there's a price to pay."

"Oh, come on," said Simon. "If it was only a question of money, everyone would want to be cured."

The old man laughed.

"I didn't say anything about money."

"Right. Not about money. So what is this? Let me guess? Drag the helpless in and make them sell their souls to Jehovah?"

"God, in all of his guises, and the devil have nothing to do with it."

"So tell me."

"It's about taking the pain away."

The man danced around the truth, not lying, and not giving anything away. His words went round in circles, teasing without telling him anything.

Simon dragged himself up the bed. The pain was gone but moving took every ounce of strength the drink had restored.

The old man offered him the mug again. Simon drank greedily this time.

He fell back into the pillows. Something moved on the ceiling. The black shadowy shapes swayed slightly as though a breeze had touched them.

Were they cobwebs?

No. They were more substantial than that.

"I need to tell you a story, Simon." The old man said, laying the mug on the decrepit bedside table. "My story. I have wanted to tell someone for a long time but it never seems to be the right time, the right place. I make a thousand excuses. They aren't worthy, I'm not ready, but that is what they are, excuses. Now is the right time and you, Simon, are the right person, so I would guess that makes this the

The Last Gift

right place."

"Then tell me."

"Ah, so simple, so simple. But were do I start?"

"You could start by telling me your name."

"That's an easy one. Lazarus."

"What, like the guy in the bible?"

"No. Not like. I *am* the guy from the bible. Or I was, before."

Now Simon understood. He was a madman. It explained his hanging around the hospital. He had obviously just been to the psych ward and now Simon was wrapped up in his delusions.

"You know *part* of my story, Simon, but only a part. No one knows it all. I was dead. Tell me this—if a man is brought back from the dead, not by science but by a miracle, what does it *mean*? I was dead and then I wasn't. Do *you* know what that means, Simon?"

"No." Simon tried not to let his exasperation show. Suddenly he was very conscious of the fact that the rest of his life was measured out in hours and minutes, not months and years. "What does it mean?"

The old man looked at him with eyes that seemed to strip away the layers of his soul, delving deep into who he was, seeing things in him that Simon himself didn't recognise. "It means, Simon, that I have been given a gift, a gift that can never be returned. It means that I go on living even when I crave the blackness of nevermore, when I yearn for endless sleep. I cannot die. No matter how hard I try to end this wretched existence, I can't die. I age, although my skin has long since stopped reflecting it, there are only so many wrinkles a face can bear. I am old beyond years. I am old and I am tired. I look at you, and do you know what I see? I see a man that I would long to be. A dead man. Funny the things that can make you jealous, isn't it?"

"I'm sorry," said Simon, even though he knew he was feeding the old man's psychosis. There was nothing else he could say.

The shadows in the ceiling shifted again, writhed with dark life. This time Lazarus looked up too.

"They won't be long," he said. "Then it will be all over, for me at least. Maybe for you too."

Lazarus flicked a switch and turned the bedside lamp. The bare bulb shone harshly, throwing grotesque shadows across the ceiling.

The ceiling . . .

It was almost covered with amorphous black sacs, hundreds of them, in hundreds of different sizes, squirming and writhing with sick life. Whatever it was they harboured inside strained against the mucus membrane, desperate to break free.

"What . . . what the *hell* are they?"

"The fruits of my labours. An eternal life time spent paying for a gift I have long since come to hate."

"I still don't understand." Simon said, transfixed by the pulsating sacs.

"Do you have something to live for, Simon? Think about it, and tell me the truth. Do you *really* want that cancer to go away?"

Simon didn't hesitate. "Of course."

"I don't believe you, Simon. I have seen a lot of dying men during my time and you do not look like someone planning to fight for his life. You look dead

The Last Gift

already. Beaten. Isn't that the *truth*?"

"I'm dying. There's no cure. All I have left is to die with dignity. Why cling to the hope of something that is less than half a life?"

"And if you could have your life? Your full *normal* life?"

"Then," Simon said with a vehemence that surprised him. "I would grab it with both hands."

The old man nodded, understanding. "Give it to me then. Give me your sickness."

Lazarus laid his hands on either side of Simon's face. His skin was warm to the touch. Degree by degree the heat increased. Simon gave himself to it. Surrendered his flesh and in return felt the curious sensation of something being drawn from him. It was like a thorn being pulled from his heart.

There was pain but above that there was relief.

Lazarus screamed, drawing the cankers into his soul, feeding on them. The sacs on the ceiling writhed in a frenzy of turbulent motion, pulsing, throbbing, the mucus membrane stretching thin enough for Simon to see the faces of the sicknesses trapped within them. Lazarus' flesh mirrored the contortions of the gelatinous sacs, his face rippling and twisting as though his bones had lost form and become water. And still he drew more of the cancer into himself, screaming as the sacs stretched to breaking point, screaming as his face cracked and leaked, weeping for the life he was giving to Simon, for his own damnation.

He slumped on the floor, spent. Looked up at Simon. Looked above him at the ruined sacs of sickness already beginning to heal.

"Kill me," He begged. "Please. Take my life. End it."

Simon shook his head, pressed up hard against the wall.

"How can I? Even if it were possible, if what you say is true?" he said, something close to rapture on his face. "After what you've done for me . . . after . . . it's a miracle."

Lazarus wept.

The Last Gift

John Shirley

WHERE THE MARKET'S HOTTEST
BY JOHN SHIRLEY

"Air conditioner's broken again," Clarke observed, quite unnecessarily.

"Chalk up another deduction for Sherlock Holmes..." Eli Henderson was well aware that the air conditioning in the ChemiTex skyscraper was broken. His shirt was clinging to his back; his hair was pasted to his forehead as he walked beside Clarke Devreau down to the conference room. Sweat burned Eli's eyes, and so did the glare from the big panel window they passed, the picture window overlooking the city below. No movement of traffic down there. Just a kind of vague writhing through the haze, the murk...

Though the sun itself was hidden behind haze—the orb seeming smeared, blurred out by the scrim of clouds—its harshest radiance seemed to burn through, right into Eli's retinas. A mix of pollutants from the refineries, car exhaust, and evaporates from the Gulf produced the haze, and it seemed to him that the murk never quite cleared up in this part of town. He really needed a vacation, away from Houston, somewhere cool, and cleaner—Canada maybe.

They turned the corner, saw whited-haired Al Kerns, CEO of Chemitex, Texas's biggest chemicals manufacturer, at the other end of the hall. Kerns was heading for the same conference, looking vaguely

Where The Market's Hottest

depressed. The older man's tie was loosened, and he carried his blazer over his right shoulder.

Seeing Al, Eli experienced a rippling feeling, a strong sense of *déjà vu.* The long hallway, the tired older man hooking his coat over his shoulder, tie loosened, sweat marks under his arms...

Hadn't he seen that same thing, from here, countless times? No, that wasn't possible. Most days the air conditioner would be working, and Al would be cheerful, he'd be natty, wearing his jacket, very buttoned down. Eli shouldn't have seen him here, like this, before. It wasn't Al's style. Déjà vu was some kind of illusion in the brain...

But he felt it again when he stopped at the door to the conference room, facing Eli—who'd also come to a stop. Clarke, too, hesitated beside Eli, gently swinging the metal briefcase that seemed almost permanently attached to his hand. Clarke was never without that briefcase. Had he carried it on his honeymoon with Loraine?

They just stood there, the three of them a bit awkwardly. "After you," Eli said, smiling, mocking the curious awkwardness.

Al shrugged. He didn't move. He just kept staring at Eli.

Eli cleared his throat. "How about this air conditioning? I mean—how many hundreds of millions of bucks did this building cost? Only fifteen years ago—I remember when it opened. We were all at the ceremony. Well, except Clarke—he's just a kid."

He grinned at Clarke—a younger man, it was true, but not really young. Forty-one.

Clarke smiled pensively back at Eli and glanced nervously at Al. "So—" He licked his lips, and seemed to speak with great difficulty. "—so who's going in first?"

"Same as always," Al said, swallowing. There was a dull resignation in his voice.

"You..." Eli licked his lips, trying to remember what their meeting was about. Oh—the lawsuits. "Clarke you bring...bring those risk assessments?"

"Got 'em right here..."

Another ripple went through Eli. They'd had that precise exchange before, *exactly* the same, sometime, hadn't they?

Clarke you bring...bring those risk assessments?
Got em right here...

"Ha, whoa, what a feeling of..." Eli's voice trailed off when he saw the stricken look in Al's eyes.

"Don't say '*déjà vu*,'" Al said, almost pleadingly. "Just don't say it. They laugh when you say that."

Eli stared at him. "Who laughs?"

Al opened his mouth to reply—then a kind of dullness swept over his features. He shrugged. "I...can't remember." He cleared his throat again. He added dreamily, "Well. We'd better...head on in. To the meeting."

He led the way, Eli followed him, his heart sinking. It was even hotter in the rectangular conference room. The farther end had its own wide window on the city. The skyscrapers looked a little warped by the thick haze.

Eli reached up to loosen his own tie, then remembered he'd taken it off completely. "Gosh it's warm in here. I don't feel dressed without my tie, but..."

Rand Clemmons was already there, at the foot of the oval, brushed steel table, frowning over papers, occasionally glancing at a laptop. He was a heavyset man, with a wide mouth, weak chin, big eyes—a froggish face. He sat hunched over the paperwork, shirtsleeves rolled up. Eli could smell the man's sweat. There was a rancid undertone to it, like a dead thing.

Rand tapped the laptop. "Damn thing..." His voice was always surprisingly high pitched, to Eli's ear. He had a pretty sharp New Orleans accent. "...just does not want to work..."

"Can't get a laptop to work?" Eli said, trying to kid him. He sat down to Rand's left. "You were the technical whizkid Al snatched up right outta MIT...and you can't get a laptop to work!"

"I'm a chemical engineer, Eli," Rand said, his voice whiny, as he jabbed at the keyboard. "Not an *IT* engineer goddammit..."

Clarke, who was more computer comfortable than the other ones, came and glanced over Rand's shoulder. He seemed taken aback by whatever he saw on the laptop. "What the hell. What kind of a screensaver is that? Boy, what a picture. Looks like that'd hurt, all right."

"It's not a screensaver," Rand responded, in his irritated whine. "Must be something off the wi-fi. Might be from a computer virus."

"You try rebooting it?"

"Yeah!" Rand snapped. "Of course! But...I can't even seem to get it turned off. Never mind." Rand slapped the laptop shut. "I've got everything here in these papers. Lord it sure is *hot* along here..."

He opened the second button on his shirt, showing part of his tee.

"Don't you open that shirt anymore," Eli said. "We're likely to faint if you do."

Rand shot him a savage look. "You think you're funny. You always think you're so..."

Abashed, Eli looked at Al, sitting at the head of the table, his turned back to the window. The blurred cityscape behind him seemed to quiver and dance, as if the buildings were gelatinous. Must be the heat...

"Why can't we get the air conditioning fixed?" Rand persisted. "Al? I don't ask for a big bonus every year. But some air conditioning don't seem unreasonable."

"Hell, you get a bonus anyway," Clarke muttered, sitting down across from Eli.

"I get a *moderate* bonus! And all I ask is working air conditioning..."

"And you get stock options," Al growled. "Now just...shut up. We have to get with the routine."

Eli looked at him in puzzlement. The routine? That wasn't something he'd usually say at a meeting. The thought prodded Eli with a nagging feeling that there was something important he'd forgotten. Something he couldn't quite remember; as if that steaming haze outside was fogging up his memory.

Al took a deep breath, put his elbows on the table, clasped his hands—almost as if he were going to pray—and then said, "Let us..." His lips twisted. "Let us...review the material. In preparation for the deposition..."

Clarke opened his briefcase, handed a sheaf of papers to each man, as Eli looked around. "Where's Louise? And Grace?"

Clarke glanced around in confusion. "Aren't they supposed to be here?"

"She resigned," Al murmured, to himself. "Resigned...I'm resigned...she resigned..."

"She resigned?" Eli shook his head. "I don't remember...Why did she..."

Then it was as if something unseen gripped Eli by the throat. A voice whispered in his ear, *"Follow the protocol. Do as usual. Stop fighting. Play nice."*

Eli gasped for breath. "Yes..."

The pressure on his throat eased. He looked at the papers dazedly. The fog curled in his memory... It seemed to him the edges of the papers on the table were curling up, like wet leaves drying out in the heat...

"We...We could cancel this meeting," Rand said suddenly, in a strained voice. Eli glanced up at him—saw rank desperation in the froggish face. Rand licked his thick lips and went on, "No air conditioning. Not healthy. Eli's having trouble breathing. Might be asthma. We could...postpone it."

"Asthma!" Al said, his lips buckling. He laughed bitterly. "Or emphysema. Or...lung cancer. That what you mean? Lung cancer?"

"No, I..."

Then both Rand and Al began to wheeze. Eli thought he could see hand-marks appearing on their necks.

"Okay..." Al gasped. "Okay!"

They breathed more easily and looked hastily down at their paperwork.

Play nice...

Al looked at the papers Clarke had given him and scowled. "*Hexavalent Chromium's association with cancer is undoubted.* What the hell's this?"

Eli, as head of marketing, knew what he was supposed to say to that. "Who *says* it's undoubted? We could challenge the basis of the science on that alone—there're always doubts..."

Clarke shrugged. "It's thought...the *firm* thinks...we need to make as small a settlement as possible, and insist that just because we manufactured the stuff we didn't expect people to have real exposure. They're supposed to be cautious around it. Of course some of them didn't know they were exposed to it...that's..." He wiped sweat from his eyes. "...what *their* lawyers say. But we can argue that they should have known..."

"But the point is," Eli said, "that *we* didn't know, and that's what I'll...what I'll imply. Without really getting into the...the research..." He had just seen the paperwork that showed that ChemiTex had in fact known that the chemical used in so many industrial settings did in fact cause lung cancer. And that employees exposed to it were not informed as to how dangerous it was. "What about this other part of the suit—this propylene glycol business...I mean, how can they sue us for more than one chemical at a time?"

"In some cases," Clarke said, peering at the paperwork, "the same people were exposed to two cancer-causing—"

Where The Market's Hottest

"*Allegedly* cancer-causing," Eli corrected him. "Or anyway, in small enough amounts...I mean, you know, there's some disagreement about how much is safe but as far as we knew..."

"Page seven, Eli," Clarke said, sighing. "God, we really need the air conditioning back on, this is crazy. Multibillion dollar company and we can't even...Can't we get a swamp cooler, for god's sake, or...how about a fan?"

"We don't have time for that," Al said. "We need to get this resolved. We have a deposition to do."

"How about some water?" Rand said, his voice ever whinier. "We could call *down* for it. I checked the fridge in the conference kitchen—*empty*. Fridge wasn't even *running*. Couldn't even find a working *water* fountain..."

"I tried calling down to secretarial for water, right before the meeting," Clarke said. "Someone I didn't know answered. They said sure, sure—and then they just laughed. Need to get their asses fired..."

"We could meet somewhere else," Eli suggested. "Somewhere cooler."

Al shook his head. "Stick to the routine," he growled. "Pretend you don't notice the heat."

Jeering laughter came from the window behind Al. That's how it seemed, anyway—that someone, or something, on the other side of the big window behind Al was laughing.

It really was getting hotter in the conference room. Just hotter and hotter. The air was wavering in front of his eyes. There was a strange smell in the air—as if someone were cooking vomit.

Got to get out of here.

He glanced toward the door. Why not just get up, and walk out? What was keeping him here?

A titter of laughter from the window...

"...and that's not all," Clarke said. "There's a new lawsuit—about the PCBs at that school."

"We didn't tell 'em to build a school there," Al said, mopping his forehead with a kerchief. "The idiots."

"We sold 'em the property, Chief," Clarke sighed. He took off his jacket, laid it sloppily on the table beside him. Steam rose from it. "And when we signed, we said it was safe..."

"I thought we did some kind of...abatement there," Al said, clenching his fists.

"Just the first few inches of soil. The PCBs went down way deeper than that."

That déjà vu struck Eli again. *Just the first few inches of soil. The PCBs went down way deeper than that.* He remembered those exact statements from Clarke. From the last time they'd had this meeting...

No, not this meeting. One like it. Similar. Not the same meeting. Not possible.

"You know," Eli said. "Kids get cancer without the help of PCBs. They didn't manufacture those chemicals in, what, the 15th century, but people got cancer then." His words seem to bounce around in the room, as if it were an echo chamber. It *was* an echo, really. Reverberating over and over...

"Right," Clarke said. "But the risk factors..." He shrugged. "Their lawyers—and their scientists—will argue that we increase the risk of the cancers with some of our industrial chemicals. And now this new EPA—they're harping about how most of our new chemicals aren't even tested. They're planning to require full testing..."

"Let's focus on the problem at hand," Al said, wringing out his handkerchief. Sweat glossed his face. The table was slick with sweat, around each man. Steam rose from the metal in wavering columns.

On impulse, Eli reached out and touched the steel table—and snatched his burnt fingers back.

Laughter warbled from the windows. Or was that from the broken air vents?

Clarke seemed to take a deep breath. He closed his eyes a moment, then opened them and said with more determination, "Look—in the long run we could lose out. That's my take as company counsel. If we keep suppressing...uh, spinning, whatever you want to call it...the data on carcinogenic chemicals, it could just lead to prosecutions and bigger fines..."

"Fines!" Rand snorted. "They fine us a hundred thousand bucks, so what, we make *billions* keeping these chemicals in the marketplace."

Clarke nodded, wiped sweat from his upper lip with the back of his hand. "But still—we could lose billions in lawsuits. I mean there are millions of chemicals—we could do a lot more research, find out what the safer ones are, for those applications."

"Research costs money," Al said. "Maybe later."

Research costs money. Maybe later. Eli had heard that exact phrase before. He had heard it in this very room...

"See," Clark went on, with a note of desperation. "If we could say, in court, that we're looking for safer ones..."

"So go on and say it!" Al said. "Maybe we'll *find* some. Sometime. Right now we got to ask ourselves, what market's *hot?* We've still got a very hot market for BPA, for plastic liners. Now, they claim that way down the line it'll cause breast cancer, lot of other problems—Hell, we'll be retired by then."

That last remark actually shocked Eli a bit. He almost spoke up. But he didn't.

Eli never did speak up, never challenged Al...

"But look," Clarke persisted. "They've got that whistleblower—he showed them our research on BPA, our *own research* showed it can lead to breast cancer. So that means we *knew*...and if we knew and kept making the stuff. When lots of people die from it—and they claim it's a lot of people—it's going to hurt us in court, and hurt us bad..."

"We'll *pay* the price," Rand said, shrugging. "Damn it's hot in here. We'll pay whatever fine, whatever settlement—still won't cost us as much as we'll make on sales to South America. They don't have a clue about the stuff down there. We're still selling them DDT for...for God's..."

He wants to say For God's Sake, Eli thought. *And for some reason he can't.*

Laughter pealed from the window behind Al again. Eli glanced toward the window—and stared.

The city was hidden—the whole skyline was concealed by a writhing wall of smoke.

"Oh my God," he said, standing. "I think the building's on fire!"

Al nodded with dreary resignation. Sweat dripped from his forehead, onto the table. The sweat sizzled when it hit the table. The room rippled with heat.

When he spoke, his voice was hoarse. "Almost over, for this one. Gotta try not to forget. If I could just pray. But they won't let me..."

Now the smoke outside the window was split by flame, attenuated flames of red and blue, licking past the blackening glass.

The window glass darkened—and began to melt. The papers on the table burst into flame.

Clarke screamed and pointed at the back wall. Eli turned to see the wall darkening. In the middle of the dark patch a glowing red spot was expanding. Yellow flame flicked up from the glowing red spot, eating away at the wall. The flames grew, consumed the wall, lapped at the ceiling.

Eli stood, knocking over his chair. He wanted to run but his feet felt so heavy. He managed to turn with great difficulty toward the door—he stalked toward it, lifting his heavy feet up with an enormous effort at each step, as if they were encased in blocks of concrete. *So hot.* Smoke spread, choking the room. He was afraid his clothing might ignite from the heat. The soles of his shoes were melting, sticking to the floor, he had to struggle to pull them free.

He stopped a pace from the door—and saw that it was only a painting of a door. There was no actual knob—just an image of a knob. The door was just a two dimensional image printed on the wall, undulating in the heated air. He reached out to it, brushed his fingers on it...flat. Just the blackening wall...

That laughter again—he was afraid to look toward its source. But he did. He saw the roaring oven that the window had become, and the striated lines of sooty flames had formed faces, bodies, leering and laughing...

The demons.

They were reaching for Al, who was sitting on his chair, sobbing. And Al waited for them to enclose him in their blazing embrace, as they had so many times before. Their fiery arms enfolded him, and he arched his back with agony, and began to burn. A soul doesn't burn quite like a body—it's never quite consumed completely. Al became a living coal, shaped like Eli's boss—and then became Al again, and then a coal again...over and over, writhing, screaming, imploring, his pleadings blotted out by the ever increasing volume of demonic laughter.

How many years ago? How long ago had the original meeting been? The meeting they were forced to relive, over and over...

It didn't matter. There was no time here, really. There were sequences of events, when the demons willed it so. Like film loops, a loop that started again the moment it ended...

Rand screamed, as the demons embraced him, and Clarke, looking at the ceiling, shouted in a cracked voice, "I'm sorry! I *tried* to talk them out of it—I tried to change their minds!"

But you never left the company, Eli thought. *None of us did. We didn't work to change the policy. We didn't blow the whistle, we just kept playing along. Ironically, Clarke died of cancer fourteen years after that meeting. Al died of a heart attack a year after that. Rand was killed by some thug in a boy-prostitution bar during a vacation in the Dominican Republic. And me, I shot myself—I remember it now—when my fourth wife left me...*

What a relief it had been, to pull the trigger. Boom! And blessed silence.

But the silence didn't last. *Footsteps in that hallway, walking along with Clarke. And then...*

The oven that the conference room had become was dark with smoke, red with fire, the flames everywhere, each one sprouting a gleeful face, snapping jaws, the jaws reaching for Eli's head...

Eli didn't bother to scream. There was no use in screaming. He opened his mouth and no scream came out as he undulated with agony. The burning went on and on...

Walking along in that hallway...and the air conditioner had been broken that day, the day they'd sold the last feeble flicker of their souls...

*

"Air conditioner's broken again," Clarke observed, quite unnecessarily.

"Chalk up another deduction for Sherlock Holmes..." Eli Henderson was well aware that the air conditioning in the ChemiTex skyscraper was broken. His shirt was clinging to his back; his hair was pasted to his forehead as he walked beside Clarke Devreau down to the conference room. Sweat burned Eli's eyes, and so did the glare from the big panel window they passed. The picture window overlooked the city below. No movement of traffic down there. Just a kind of vague writhing through the haze, the murk...

PAGES OF PROMISES
BY STEPHEN JAMES PRICE

"I'm sorry Mr. Sutton, but that's not an option." The elderly doctor leaned back in his chair. "Your pancreatic cancer is in its late stage and is inoperable. It's already metastasized. Our only options now are therapies aimed at improving the quality of your life."

"How long of a life are we talking about improving?" Tony Sutton asked.

"Six months at best."

"Then I guess I should go home and put my affairs in order." But Tony had other plans. His wife Myrtle died of ovarian cancer and he swore he would never go out like that. He walked to the phone booth in the lobby and looked up the address for the nearest gun shop. Their Loss Pawn and Gun was at 125 Summit Avenue, less than ten minutes away.

Tony drove the six blocks deep in thought.

Should I get a handgun or a shotgun?
Should I put it in my mouth or to my temple?

There was an empty parking space directly in front of the store. He got out of his car and started to search for some change for the parking meter when he noticed that there was still a little more than an hour left on it, a gift from the space's previous occupant.

Pages of Promises

"My lucky day," he said aloud, with more than just a hint of sarcasm. This day had been anything but lucky.

All of the lights were still on, but the front door was locked, and it had a pair of those sliding security bars chained together with a lock big enough to secure Fort Knox. There was a sign on the door.

BE BACK IN 20 MINUTES.

Tony turned back towards his car when he noticed The Writer's Block bookstore directly across the street. He thought he could kill some time while he waited for the owner of the gun shop to get back.

Maybe I can find that Suicide for Dummies *book*, he half joked to himself as he crossed the street.

He walked around the store for a few minutes, while an old man with a nametag that said "DONALD" helped a young couple pick out several overpriced baby books.

This couple is a perfect pair, Tony thought. *She doesn't look* too *pregnant, and he doesn't look* too *happy.*

Tony walked toward the back of the store and froze as soon as he saw it. The book he was staring at had a shiny black cover with brilliant gold lettering. It had a picture of itself on its cover. The book was beautiful, and Tony had to have it. It was titled *Pages of Promises*, but it could have been called *Twenty-Seven Ways To Cook Dog Droppings* or *Collecting Dust Bunnies For Fun and Profit* for all that it mattered. It was the *having* that was important.

Stephen James Price

His fascination with the book did not go unnoticed by Donald Severance, the owner of the shop. He hurriedly rang up the purchases of the young parents-to-be, shoved their books into one of those semi-fancy canvas book bags with the name of the shop printed on one side, and rushed over to where Tony was standing.

"Help you?" he said without looking at Tony. Donald was now staring at the book in the center of the table, too.

"I want to buy this book," Tony answered but didn't look away from the book, either.

"Certainly, sir. We have several of them behind the front counter. I can ring you up over there."

"No, you don't understand," Tony said. "I want to buy *this* book."

"I'm sorry sir, but this one is not for sale. It's my personal copy and I only use it for display. Like I said, we have several of them in stock right now. I'd be happy to show you the others. They are all identical."

Tony looked at the stack of books Donald was pointing to, but dismissed them with a wave of his hand.

"They're not as shiny and they don't look as thick," he said. "I want *this* one."

"I assure you that they are all identical, sir. This copy is special. The author wrote his initials on the back of it. It's one of only two copies he did that to and no one knows where the other one ended up."

"I'll give you a hundred bucks for it."

"I'm sorry sir but—"

"Two hundred."

Pages of Promises

"The book is very special to me."

"Five hundred ... in cash."

"I'm sorry sir, but this copy is simply not for sale. Not at *any* price. Now I am getting ready to close in a few minutes. Are you sure you don't want one of the other copies?" Donald asked.

"Quite sure," Tony said harshly, as he turned around and headed for the front door. He stopped just as he got there and turned back for one more look at the book. He would have stayed there all night long if Donald hadn't turned out the lights.

Tony reluctantly left the store and walked across the street to his car. He didn't notice that the gun store was closed and wouldn't have cared even if he did. All thoughts of suicide had disappeared from his mind. He saw that the parking meter had expired as he pulled away from the curb. *Was I really in there for more than an hour?*

He started to circle the block. Donald Severance came out of the store on Tony's third trip around. The book was tucked tightly under his arm as he crossed the street.

Tony closed his eyes and stomped down on the gas pedal. He hit the old man at about sixty miles an hour. Donald's body flew over the hood of the car and landed in the center of the street. Blood splattered on the windshield and there was an awful crunching sound. Tony skid the car to a stop about a hundred feet down the street.

Tony opened the door, got out, and ran back toward the body. Donald was clutching the book to his chest, even in death not wanting to relinquish it. Tony snatched it out of his hands, looked around quickly and then ran back to his car when he was sure that no one had seen him

*

He sped away with the blood-covered book lying in the passenger seat next to him.

He looked back and forth between the book and the road as he drove, paying a little too much attention to the book and nearly sideswiping several parked cars before realizing he was driving on the wrong side of the road. He heard sirens somewhere in the distance. The sirens and the near miss made him a little nervous, so he turned down the first side street he came to and started looking for an empty parking lot.

Once he was parked, he focused all of his attention on his new treasure. The blood that was covering it slowly started to disappear. Even the blood on the seat seemed to be absorbed by the book. When the blood was gone, the book began to throb, growing and shrinking in thickness with each pulse. After it pulsated a few times, it seemed to find a rhythm. It reminded Tony of a heartbeat.

He touched the book and it stopped throbbing, but he could still hear the sounds of its heartbeat in his head. He picked it up, opened it, and touched the pages with his fingertips. They were crisp and bright. There was no blood anywhere to be seen. The words seemed to jump off the page at him. He thumbed through it for a couple of minutes, reading passages from several of the stories. They all seemed to be about horrible happenings: murders, cannibals, ghosts, werewolves and all kinds of unspeakable things.

"How can something so beautiful be filled with such ugliness?" Tony asked.

Remembering what the owner of the bookstore had told him, he turned the book over and looked at the author's initials on the back cover. They were dark red and looked a lot like fresh blood. He touched the signature to make sure it wasn't still wet. As soon as he did, he could feel the book's life force pulsing through his body. After a long time, he turned it over and stared at the cover. He ran his fingers over it, stroking the book as if it were a lover.

He noticed the blood on his windshield out of the corner of his eye. *Had it been there all along?* He had been too caught up with the book to notice. He got out of the car, walked around the front, and surveyed the damage. The front bumper was dented a little, but the car had fared surprisingly well considering the amount of blood that covered the hood and windshield. Tony reached out with his left hand and gingerly touched some of the blood that was running down the side of the fender. As soon as he touched it, the book that he was still holding began to pulsate again. The image of it absorbing the blood from the front seat was still fresh in his mind as he laid it down on the hood. Once again, all of the blood began to rush toward the book as it throbbed and pulsed, all the while the sounds of its heartbeat echoed steadily in his head.

Tony got back into his car and started driving home. About four blocks from his house, he looked at the book a little too long, and didn't see the traffic light change. Luckily there wasn't anything coming in the other lanes, but a cop who had just turned into the lane behind him saw his car shoot through the red light. The siren and flashing lights brought Tony back to reality, and also filled his stomach with a sense of dread.

Do they know I ran over the old man?
Am I going to be arrested?
Will they take my book away?

He slowly rolled down his window as the officer approached the car.

"What's the hurry tonight?" the officer asked.

Tell him your wife is having a baby and you are on your way to the hospital, a voice echoed in his head.

Tony could not hear the police officer. The voice in his head was too loud.

"What did you say?" Tony asked the voice.

"I asked what your hurry was tonight. Now can I see your license and registration?"

Tell him your wife is having a baby, the voice repeated.

"I'm sorry officer. My wife is having a baby, and I'm just trying to get to the hospital," Tony said.

"A baby? Well congratulations, sir. My wife and I just had a baby girl last week. Just keep the speed down and watch those red lights. You don't need to get there in an ambulance." The officer tapped twice on the side of the door as he walked back to his patrol car.

Tony was dumbfounded, but he tried hard not to look at the book as he drove away.

Pages of Promises

Drive a few more blocks toward the hospital and then backtrack to your house ... just in case he's following you.

Tony finally looked over at the book. "Are you *talking* to me?" he asked.

I can do so much more if you let me.

Suddenly, a conversation with a book didn't seem that incredulous, even a conversation where the book's voice was only audible inside of his head. "What do you mean?"

I can keep you alive and keep your pain away.

"How? How can you do that?"

I can do many things, but first you must do something for me.

"Anything, just name it. I'll do anything to stay alive."

I too must stay alive. I must feed. I must feed everyday.

"Feed? I don't understand," Tony said, remembering the blood and fearing that he really did know exactly what the book was asking of him.

I must feed on human blood.

"I don't think I can do it again," Tony said as he pulled his car to the curb.

The once-shiny book now looked very dull. The lettering had turned almost gray and was becoming increasingly difficult to read.

We'll both die without it. The voice in his head was weaker and sounded far away.

"Oh, my God, what have I done?" Tony cried out as he grabbed the book. It suddenly brightened to its original luster. "I'll do it."

He drove home with the book in his lap. He put it on the nightstand next to his bed and only woke up seven or eight times during the night to look at it.

Tony reluctantly followed the book's instructions the following evening. He saw a bag lady pushing her cart along the seedy part of University Avenue and followed her in his car. She eventually went under the bridge that crossed Old Black Creek. He pulled into the place where she disappeared over the embankment, got out, and followed the path she had taken. Her back was to him and he didn't see anyone else around. He snuck up behind her, picked up a large rock, and hit her over the head with it. She was dead before she hit the ground.

Tony hadn't thought any of this out; after all, planning was for rational people. He realized that he didn't have any way to get the blood back home. He searched through her shopping cart looking for something that he could use. Realizing that the more time he spent there, the more apt he was to get caught, he used a piece of broken glass to cut away a large chunk of her upper thigh. He fought back the urge to vomit as he worked. When he was done, he put it in a black plastic garbage bag that the woman had used to carry her aluminum cans. He put the bag in his trunk and drove home.

He could hear the heartbeat from the garage. The whole room seemed to vibrate with each beat. He took the plastic bag out of the trunk of his car and walked through the door leading into the kitchen. The heartbeat seemed to get faster. Tony turned his head in disgust as he emptied the contents of the bloody bag into the sink, momentarily forgetting to put in the stopper, and losing a fair amount of the blood down the drain. He could hear the book calling to him in his head.

He hurried to the antique roll top desk and fished around in his pants pocket for the large-headed brass key. He unlocked the top drawer and took the book out. By now, it was screaming in his head.

"I'm here. I've done what you asked. Please be quiet," he said as he lovingly cradled it to his chest.

He carried it into the kitchen and laid it in the sink. Its heartbeat was getting faster and faster. The thought of what it was doing repulsed him, so he had to turn his back on it. When the book's heartbeat slowed to its normal rhythm, Tony sensed it had finished feeding. He turned back around and took it out of the sink, which was cleaner than it had been in years. The book had absorbed everything in there. It seemed thicker and heavier as he walked with it.

He sat down on the couch and put the book on the coffee table in front of him. Opening it to the very front, he once again looked at the page that the editor had autographed. That page looked different from the others now. He touched it and his hand instinctively recoiled. The page felt like skin—human skin. He stared at it for a moment to be sure. He could see the tiny hair follicles on it. It was skin. He then touched it again. This time it felt good.

Flesh and blood will make me human. One page per feeding. Then we can live together forever, the voice in his head said.

"Forever? We'll be together forever?" he asked.
We need each other. We need each other to live.

"We need each other," Tony repeated, still stroking the cover of the book.

When Tony retired for the night, he put the book on the nightstand next to the bed again. A few minutes after turning off the light, he switched it back on and picked up the book. Kissing the shiny, black cover, he placed it on the pillow on the other side of the bed. It felt good not to sleep alone, a feeling he hadn't known in the three years since his wife died.

Not wanting a repeat of the previous day's problems, Tony packed the trunk of his car with his homemade tool kit. He made several trips to various hardware stores so that he wouldn't attract any suspicion if the cops eventually found a connection between the murders. He had several rolls of plastic sheeting, a hacksaw with six extra blades, two pairs of thick, yellow rubber gloves, two three-gallon buckets with the tops that sealed tightly, an aluminum baseball bat, and a long, black flashlight that held six D-cell batteries.

Just as it was getting dark, he put the book in the top drawer of the desk and locked it again. He didn't dare take it with him—its voice echoing in his head made it hard to concentrate—but feared some unknowing burglar would steal it if it was left out in the open while he was gone. He opened the trunk and studied his recent purchases, looking for anything missing. He couldn't think of anything else he would need, so he closed it and drove down to the railroad station.

Pages of Promises

He parked behind one of the antique train engines that they had on display, took several items out of the trunk, and crept around to the back of the terminal. There were a handful of homeless people standing around a fire that someone had started in one of the trash barrels that had spent the initial part of its life as a fifty-five gallon drum. Tony watched them for about a half hour. Every once in a while, one of the men would stumble behind a small building, which looked like some sort of storage shed, to relieve himself. Two of them started to fight over a cigarette butt that they both claimed, and the others gathered around to watch.

Tony snuck behind the building and waited in the shadows. It didn't take long before an old man stumbled back there and walked within ten feet of him. Tony hit him over the head with the baseball bat as the old man was reaching for his zipper.

He used the hacksaw to cut off both of the man's arms, wrapped them in one of the plastic sheets, and stole back to his car. He put everything in the trunk and drove home.

Just like the night before, he could hear its heartbeat as he drove into the garage. He took the package out of the trunk and laid it on the floor next to the car. He carefully unwrapped it and went inside to release the book from the desk drawer. The book was screaming in a language that Tony didn't understand, but that didn't hinder his understanding of what it was asking for. He went into the garage and gently placed it on one of the severed arms. He turned around and closed his eyes tightly as it fed.

It took about twenty minutes, but when the heartbeat slowed back to normal, he turned back around. The book lay on the clean sheet of plastic. There was no evidence of what had been there before, not even the bones or the man's shirt sleeves. Once again, the book had absorbed it all.

Tony took the book into the house and went directly into his bedroom. He laid it on the bed and took a quick shower to wash off the events of the night. Once he was back in the bedroom, he picked up the book and held it closely to his chest.

"I love you," he said, not expecting a reply.

I love you, too.

Tony was so excited. He needed to feel the jolt of energy that he got when he touched the autograph, so he opened the book and thumbed to the front. As he expected, the second page was now made out of human skin. What he didn't expect was the old, faded tattoo of an anchor with the words US NAVY printed under it. This horrified him for a brief second, but the words in his head soon made him forget everything else.

I love you, Tony.

"I love you, too. I'll do anything to keep us together."

I need more. Tomorrow, bring me the whole body.

Tony nodded his head as he traced the autographed signature that still looked like it was written in fresh blood. He traced it more than a hundred times before he finally closed the book and put it on the pillow next to his own. He reached over to turn off the light on the nightstand when the gleam from his wedding band caught his eye. He hadn't taken the ring off in over twenty-seven years. His wife had been dead for almost three years, but he had still thought of himself as married. He got out of bed, took off the ring, and put in it the bottom of his wife's jewelry box. Wearing it just didn't seem right anymore.

The following night, Tony cruised around the north side of the park for a little while. There were several couples in the park, but Tony needed to find somebody alone. On his third trip around, he saw a police car slowly driving into the park entrance. Not wanting to attract any attention, he left and drove about five miles out of town before making a U-turn. He turned a little wide and the rear passenger-side tire went off the road and bounced over something. Tony immediately felt the tire go flat. He got out to assess the damage and discovered a large piece of mangled metal sticking out of the tire. He cursed himself for taking the spare tire and the jack out of the trunk, but he knew it had been necessary. There was barely enough room for his tools and a body now as it was.

He was out in the middle of nowhere and only had one option, so he walked back to town. It took him nearly two and a half hours to get to a payphone and call a tow truck. He finally had a new tire installed and got back on the road, but he had lost over four hours in the process. When he drove back to the park, it was deserted. He drove down along the street that the locals called "Tail Trail" looking for a prostitute, but it was after three o'clock in the morning and it appeared that they had to sleep, too. Tony drove home empty-handed. The book was screaming when he drove into the garage.

"I'm sorry," he said. "I couldn't get one tonight. I had a flat tire. I had to walk—"

I must feed every night! The words reverberated in his skull.

Tony's stomach cramped. He fell to the floor in agony, curled himself into a tight ball, and prayed for the pain to subside.

Your cancer is back. Your time is nearing.

"Please stop. I'll get you one tomorrow night. I promise. I won't come back here without one again," Tony screamed.

His pain stopped as suddenly as it started.

We need each other, the voice in his head said. *We need each other to live.*

Repeating a task over and over again—even something as morally reprehensible as taking a human life—usually enables the task to be performed with little or no conscious thought. Tony thanked God for this fact as he continued to feed the book over the course of the next month. It took a little practice, but he had it down to a science now. He would cruise the back streets near the river or the railroad tracks looking for a lone wino or a hooker. Once he found one, he would pull over and offer them a bottle of cheap wine if they would get into his car. Most times, he got one on his first try.

That night was no exception. She was sitting on a bus- stop bench smoking a cigarette, but her choice of clothing suggested that she wasn't waiting for the bus. She was wearing a bright red mini-skirt and a black halter-top that was barely able to keep her breasts contained. She could have been anywhere between forty and sixty, it was hard to tell. Tony pulled up to the curb directly across from her and held up the wine bottle.

"That and twenty bucks'll get you what you want," she said in a voice that might have been sexy twenty years and five thousand packs of cigarettes ago.

He nodded his head so she got up and slowly shuffled over to the car.

"Show me the money first." She eyed him suspiciously. He took a twenty-dollar bill out of his wallet and held it out the window. As she reached for it, he opened his fingers and let it fall to the ground. As she bent over to pick it up, he hit her over the head with the blood-caked brick he kept between the front seats. He was out of the car almost as soon as she hit the ground. After hitting her two more times, just to make sure, he put her body in the trunk and drove home.

He pulled the plastic sheet around her body as he lifted her from the trunk. Aware of the urgency of the guttural screams in his head, he quickly situated the package on the floor and went inside. He unlocked the desk drawer and took the book to the garage like he had done every day for the past month. Still not comfortable with watching it feed, Tony turned his back and tried to think about how good it felt to touch the book and how shiny it looked after each feeding.

Suddenly, his head filled with the book's screams of agony. He spun around and rushed to it. The only thing left on the plastic sheet was a long gold chain with a cross on it.

You said you loved me. If you really loved me you would have thrown that *away!*

"I'm so sorry. I didn't think... I didn't know!" Tony picked up the book and saw the image of the cross burned into its cover. He touched it and the book screamed in pain. "I'll remember next time."

The book did not answer. It remained silent for the rest of the night and Tony cried himself to sleep.

The next night, Tony locked the book in the drawer again and started cruising the residential neighborhoods. He had several opportunities but turned them all down. He was looking for something special, a way to appease the book's anger for the mishap the night before. It was almost midnight and he was just about to give up and head back to the railroad tracks when he finally spotted the perfect one. The man was huge, probably weighing close to four hundred pounds. Tony knew the book could feed for hours on this peace offering, and he hoped that this would make it forgive him. The man was walking a small dog along the sidewalk as Tony passed him the first time.

Tony drove about a block farther down the street before pulling over. He got out of the car, opened the trunk, got his baseball bat, and then crouched down behind the car to wait. It seemed to take forever for the fat man and the little dog to get close enough for him to strike. Tony hit him across the bridge of the nose with a swing that would have made Babe Ruth proud. The fat man's nose was crushed and the entire front of his face seemed to move backwards about two inches. He fell forward, crushing the barking dog as he landed on top of it. Tony opened the trunk and realized that the man would not fit inside without the help of a small crane and a chainsaw, and even then it would be a tight squeeze. After a little deliberation, he decided to put him in the back seat. It was either that or strap him to the hood of his car like some trophy ten-point buck during deer season.

It took another fifteen minutes, but he finally got the body in far enough to shut the door. He grabbed the body of the dead dog and threw it in on top of the huge pile of flesh that now took up the entire back seat. The book had said it needed *human* blood, but Tony thought it might appreciate the gesture. *After all, some cultures think of dog as a delicacy.*

He sped home, eager to make good with the book. He noticed that the book was not screaming when he drove into the garage. This alone was cause for concern, but he felt panic when he walked inside and heard the steady beep-beep-beep noise in the distance.

"It's the phone. It's off the hook," he said aloud. As he walked into the den, he saw the book lying on the counter next to the telephone. As he had guessed, the receiver was off the hook. He rushed to the book and grabbed it up, hugging it tightly to his chest. He looked around in a panic. His mind was filled with questions.

Who was in here?
Who moved the book?
Who was on the phone?

The loud knock on the front door brought him back to reality. He put the book down on the counter and walked tentatively to the door. A caller at one o'clock in the morning always meant bad news. Tony opened the door and stood face to face with a man holding up a badge. There were several uniformed police officers standing behind him. Tony recognized one of them as the cop whose wife had a baby a week or so before he met the book.

"Are you Mr. Sutton?" the plain-clothes officer asked.

"Yes, I'm Tony Sutton. What's this about? It's very late, and I was just going to bed."

"Mr. Sutton, my name is Detective Hillman. I'm with the Trinity Police Department. We've received an anonymous tip that you are the man responsible for the series of murders that we've been investigating. The caller also said that you have a body here right now. Is it okay if we come in and look around?"

Tony panicked and pushed the detective down the steps and started to run for the garage. One of the uniformed officers tackled him just before he got to the door.

They placed him in handcuffs, read him his rights and sat him down on the couch while they searched the house. Detective Hillman went into the den and still hadn't come out after fifteen minutes.

"Detective, I think you ought to see this," the officer who had recently become a father called to him. "We found the body. It's in the back seat of his car in the garage."

The detective had to tear his gaze away from the book that he had been staring at since he entered the den. "I'm coming," he answered.

Pages of Promises

He picked up the book and stuffed it down the front of his pants, straightened his shirt over it, and started to walk to the garage. The heat the book was giving off felt good against his skin and the beating of its heart was almost in tune with his own.

The cop who was guarding Tony said, "You're going to spend the rest of your life in prison for this."

Tony ignored him though. He was too busy digesting the book's words that were booming in his head.

And you're going to live forever.

Anna Taborska

UNDERBELLY BY ANNA TABORSKA

It had taken weeks to get a doctor's appointment, then months to persuade her GP to refer her to a specialist, more months to get the hospital appointment with the specialist, more weeks for the results of the undignified and painful tests to which she was subjected to be analysed, another week for the test results to get back to her GP, and a few more days for Anna's GP to call her in and say that there was nothing they could do—perhaps if they'd caught it a couple of months sooner it wouldn't have spread from her cervix to the rest of her abdomen, from where it was already happily on its way through her lymph system to her entire body.

Anna struggled to find a position in which she could survive the night, survive the next five minutes, survive the next few seconds. She tried curling up into a ball, she tried lying on her back with her knees bent. She started thrashing about on the bed in pain and fell onto the floor, where she started to crawl towards the front door. Sweat poured down her face, her entire body fired up by the pain in her underbelly.

Anna reached the door and grabbed hold of the handle, pulling herself up. She left her bedsit and stumbled blindly along the corridors of the horrible old building. It had once been a Victorian school or lunatic asylum—Anna didn't know which and at this point in time she didn't care. She reached the fire-door leading out onto the staircase and, clutching the handrail, she stumbled downstairs, not knowing what she was doing or where she was going. She kept going down as far as she could. She reached the ground floor, but kept going down, ever downwards until she could go no further. She stopped for a moment and looked around, surprised to find herself in the basement. Then a particularly violent wave of pain hit her and she fell to her knees, retching.

After a couple of minutes Anna got up shakily, and walked ahead—into the dark winding corridors of the building. She needed to keep moving forward, moving into the darkness. Maybe if she disappeared into the darkness, the pain would disappear too. Anna had never been adventurous by nature, but, delirious with pain, she stumbled on into a place she would not have had the slightest urge to go near had she been in her right mind. Finally she found herself in the farthest corner of the basement—there really was nowhere else to go. Anna clawed at the brick wall desperately and a fresh wave of tears stained her face as she cried out loud into the night. After a long while she turned to go and her foot caught on something. She fell heavily, and for the briefest second it appeared that the sharp pain in her hands and knees would silence the pain in her belly, but no—it seemed that nothing could do that. And there it was—once throbbing, once sharp as glass.

Anna felt around in the darkness for what had tripped her up. It was a large metal ring. She tried to pick it up, but found that it was attached—to what turned out to be a trapdoor in the basement floor. Anna worked out the perimeter of the trapdoor, and moved to one side of it. Then, using all her strength, she pulled at the ring. Eventually the door shifted and came loose from the opening it covered. There was just enough light for Anna to be able to see wooden steps going down into the darkness, and her thoughts started to race in a bid to work out what might be down there - if the muddled images and disconnected flashes that fired in her pain-addled brain could be described as thoughts. Not knowing why or how, Anna descended the wooden steps into what appeared to be a cellar. She had almost made it down when the pain increased again to an unbearable pitch, causing her to cry out and fall from the final step to the damp ground beneath, where she crawled a metre or so, then curled up into a ball and lay clutching her abdomen.

When Anna finally stopped crying, she listened to the beating of her own heart. But then she thought she heard something else—far too close for comfort—the sound of something moving in the dark. Anna lay as still as she could and willed her heart to stop beating so loudly. The sound came again. "Rats," she thought. But then she heard what sounded like a cross between a growl and a squeal—two-toned—low and guttural, yet at the same time high and penetrating. It was like no sound she had ever heard, and, even though she had wished for death a thousand times in the past weeks, Anna suddenly feared for her life.

The chilling feral sound came again. Before the cancer took over her life, Anna had enjoyed watching nature programmes, and she was familiar with the sounds made by even the strangest animals living in the remotest places on earth. But that mewling, growling sound didn't come from any animal on earth that Anna could think of. The movement and the growl came again, and Anna started backing towards the steps leading out of the cellar. She had almost reached the bottom one when a guttural shriek froze the blood in her veins, causing every hair on her body to stand on end. She felt a rush of air as something hurled itself at her at unnatural speed, and then something hit her full force in the side, spinning her round. She found herself being hurled by the force of the thing across the cellar, and screamed as something sharp pierced her belly. Then she was lying against the cellar wall, paralysed with fear, the creature that had attacked her sitting on her, what she assumed to be its fangs buried in her abdomen.

Anna's eyes had grown accustomed to the dark and she could see the thing that was on top of her, almost crushing the breath out of her. It had short, black, course fur, rather like that of a tarantula, it was muscular like a Rottweiler, and almost round in shape. Its appearance reminded Anna of the vile creatures in the Hieronymus Bosch paintings she had seen in the Louvre as an art student.

As Anna prepared for death, the strangest thing happened. The creature evidently still had its fangs—rather like those of a giant spider—embedded in her abdomen, but Anna realised that not only did she no longer feel the sharp pain from the fangs, but for the first time in weeks the pain in her belly was bearable. In fact, the pain in her belly was slowly draining away—fading away to nothing. Anna stared down her body at the thing that she assumed was feeding on her, wondering whether it had injected her with some kind of anaesthetising substance—like a mosquito or a vampire bat—so that it could drain all the life out of her without her even being aware. If that was the case, then so be it; her only regret being that her corpse would rot down here, in the dark, with no-one knowing what had happened to her, and no trace of her left—not even a tombstone to state that she, Anna Weedon, had ever lived at all. It would be as though she never even existed, never walked the earth for thirty-nine years. But she could live with that—or die with that - as long as there was no more pain.

As Anna gave herself up completely to the creature, it suddenly withdrew its fangs from her abdomen and looked at her. Its slanted red eyes glowed with an unfathomable malevolence. Those eyes were more human than animal, and yet they were neither. They bored into Anna's mind, seeing every dark thought she'd ever had, every sin she'd ever committed, every crime she'd ever contemplated. Those eyes spoke of places darker and more horrifying than anything Anna could imagine—anything, that is, except her pain.

"Thank you," Anna managed to utter as the creature shifted slightly, allowing her to breathe more easily. It bared its massive, bone-coloured, long, slightly curved fangs at Anna in what could have been a grin. "Are you going to eat me now?" Anna asked, calm and strangely clear-headed now that the pain was gone.

"Not you."

Despite her resignation to whatever fate the

creature had in store for her, Anna jolted in fear as the unspoken voice rang in her ears. She had never heard a voice like that before—loud and jarring, while at the same time sounding like it came from a million miles away—from the bottom of hell itself. She stared at the creature, but its hideous grinning mouth hadn't uttered those words. "I don't want *you*," the voice in Anna's mind continued. "You're already being eaten—from the inside out. Why would I want to eat *you*?"

"Then why did you inject the venom into me... the anaesthetic... whatever it was?" asked Anna.

"I didn't inject anything into you. I just took the pain away."

"Thank you... but why?" Anna gazed into the red all-knowing, all-seeing eyes. She knew from those eyes that the creature must be very old, very wise, and very malevolent.

"You woke me. I was asleep for a long time and you woke me. I knew I couldn't eat you—I could smell your disease a mile away. But I'm very hungry and you have to feed me. I took the pain away so you can bring me others,"

"Others...? You mean people?"

"Yes."

"I can't bring you people."

"You have to." The creature hissed at Anna through its fangs and increased the pressure on her abdomen, making it hard for her to breathe.

"I can't."

"You will."

"I'm very grateful that you made the pain go away," gasped Anna, "but I can't bring you people to eat. I wouldn't even know how to, even if I wanted to."

"You'll work it out, once the pain is back."

Just then, that familiar twinge in her abdomen and Anna cried out as the pain came flooding back into her body.

"No, please!"

"Very well," said the voice in Anna's head, and she breathed a sigh of relief as the pain dissipated. "But I need to eat. You will bring me someone tomorrow night or the pain will be back and it will be worse than ever."

"Okay," promised Anna.

Then, as quickly as it had assaulted her, the creature leapt off her and merged with the shadows in the cellar. In the instant before it disappeared from sight, Anna noticed that it had two powerful muscular hind legs, two long ungainly arms that it used to walk on some of the time, leaning on its knuckles—rather like an ape—and two membranous wings that were folded along its sides, which it also occasionally used for support while walking—rather like a bat. Anna got up slowly and headed up the steps out of the cellar, eventually making her way back to her bedsit. The first light of dawn was breaking over the horizon and the dawn chorus was raising hell outside Anna's tiny window.

Anna sat on her bed for a long time, wondering if she had imagined the whole thing, but the glorious lack of pain in her belly reminded her that—no—there *had* been a foul-smelling hideous demon in the cellar which had bitten her and taken her pain away, and told her to bring it people to eat. Yeah, right... Wasn't it more likely that the whole thing had been a nightmare - the creature, the pain, the hospital visits, the cancer. Wasn't it more likely that she'd fallen asleep and dreamt the last few unbearable months in a couple of minutes of cruel REM sleep, her lonely brain summing up her greatest fears and conjuring them up in the flesh to torment her? If only that were true...

Anna looked around the room and noticed how dusty it was, how dirty. She looked into a mirror and winced, as a hundred-year-old woman with a sickly complexion, dark rings beneath her eyes and long strands of greasy hair looked back at her. "Christ."

Anna spent the rest of the morning cleaning the bedsit, having a bath, washing her hair and putting on make-up. She was surprised at how good she felt despite having had no sleep whatsoever. She looked in the mirror again and, satisfied that she looked thirty-nine once more, she got dressed and went out in search of food. She felt hungry without simultaneously feeling sick for the first time in months, and, as she walked to her local Morrison's for lunch and supplies, she smiled as men eyed up her in the street—admiring her ample breasts and long legs.

Anna spent the afternoon wandering around the local park, soaking up the sunshine, delighting in life and lack of pain. For a moment she even thought about phoning Frank - the love of her life, the man she had spent seven wonderful months with until the growing pain and the constant hospital visits and waiting—waiting for referrals, waiting for appointments, waiting for results—had dampened her sunny disposition, making her moody, grumpy and needy, and her inability to get work during the recession had shrunk her bank account to nothing, and Frank had evaporated like the last breath of a dying man. His departure had left Anna heartbroken and with no desire to live, the cancer seizing this great opportunity to attack her grief-weakened body with extra strength and speed. But it would take a lot more than Anna's undying love, and desire to see him, to bring Frank back.

As night fell, Anna remembered the creature's words and started to fear that the pain would come back. She watched television for a while, but couldn't concentrate on anything, and decided to go to bed as normal. She was tired after a full day of cleaning, shopping, walking, and the previous night's lack of sleep started to take its toll. She dozed off at around eleven pm, thinking that perhaps she would be okay.

At midnight, Anna awoke screaming. The pain in her abdomen was like being stabbed over and over, as if a medieval executioner were thrusting a blunt saw into her underbelly and twisting it slowly, only to pull it out again, and stab her a few more times. Anna grabbed the bottle of painkillers by her bed and thrust a couple of pills into her mouth, gagging as she tried to swallow them without water. She staggered to the kitchen and turned on the cold water tap, not waiting for it to run for a while, but drinking the water lukewarm and cloudy—the liquid splashing over her face and chest.

It would take time for the pills to start working.

Underbelly

Anna knew from experience that lying down wouldn't help, that sitting wouldn't help, so she staggered around the bedsit, bumping into the walls, knocking things over, hoping that the movement would accelerate her heartbeat and speed the drugs through her bloodstream, making them work quicker. After five minutes she couldn't wait any longer—she would take more pills, even if it killed her, which might, in any case, be for the best. She got a handful more pills out of the bottle and swallowed those down with water, this time with the aid of a glass, but her body started to spasm violently and she retched, bringing up the whole lot—drugs, water and all.

The pain in her abdomen was like a spiky metal ball thumping her over and over, doubling her up and making her curse God, curse herself, the world and everyone in it. Suddenly she was urinating all over herself—the pain such that all control over her pelvic muscles was gone. Howling and humiliated, Anna ran for the door, for the stairs, for the basement, for the cellar, for the abomination that she prayed to the Devil was waiting for her in the darkness.

Anna slid down the cellar steps on her arse and crawled blindly forward into the darkness. Fear mixed with relief as she heard a growl-squeal ahead of her, and the familiar gust of displaced air hit her a split second before she was thrown backwards, the creature crushing the breath out of her with its heavy, compact body.

"Where's my food?"
"Please," Anna begged, "make it go away."
"Where's my food?"
"I hurt."

"How do you think I feel? I haven't eaten for eighty years."

"Make it go away."

"Will you bring me food?"

"Yes. I swear," Anna gasped under the weight of the creature on top of her. "I swear on my mother's grave. Just make it go away." The familiar short sharp stabbing pain as the fangs sank into her abdomen, and then the sweet gentle relief as the pain subsided and disappeared. "Thank you."

The creature's red eyes glared at Anna furiously. "You have one hour to bring me food or it will be back and it will stay until you die screaming."

"Two hours," bargained Anna, her brain suddenly crystal clear and computing ways of bringing it food. She remembered the way men had looked at her in the street on her way to the supermarket. In the anonymity of darkness men like that would be even more willing to act upon their sordid impulses with a complete stranger.

"Two hours," agreed the creature, reading every thought and emotion in Anna's mind, and grinning at the woman with its bone-coloured fangs. The cancer may take her body, but the creature would have her soul—and that was far more satisfying.

*

"Blondie!" The man was drunk and horny. He'd been drinking in the pub all evening with his mates, but had popped out for a quick smoke. When he saw the big-titted blonde in the short skirt walking past, he thought that Christmas had come early. Any woman with legs like that was obviously gagging for it, and he wasn't going to take no for an answer. He looked around the street—it was empty apart from him and the girl. He looked back into the pub—no-one was paying any attention to him, the Chelsea-Manchester United match keeping all eyes glued firmly to the television screen on the wall. "Hey, blondie!"

Anna instinctively ignored the man and was about to walk past, when he grabbed her arm.

"Hey darling," the man slurred in Anna's ear, "I been waiting for you."

"Have you?" asked Anna, her heart pounding with fear. All her damaged insides needed now was to get raped by this large brute.

"We're gonna have some fun, baby," the man told Anna, pulling her away from the pub. "I know this great alley just round the corner—very romantic."

"I know somewhere even better," Anna mustered all her courage to steady her voice.

"Oh yeah? Where's that?"

"My place," Anna told him. The man paused for a moment, looking doubtful.

"Yeah?"

"Yeah. It's just round the corner."

"You're having me on."

"No, I'm not." The man still had a strong grip on Anna's right arm, so she used her left hand to fondle his genitals.

"Let's do it right here." Anna winced as the man thrust his hand between her legs.

"I thought you were a romantic," she said, trying to pull his hand away from her.

"Oh I am. A right romantic—that's me."

"Well, let's go back to my place then, and make a night of it." Anna tried to move off in the direction of her street. The man threw a glance over his shoulder toward the pub, then shrugged and let himself be led back to Anna's house.

*

"Where we going?" The man asked, making another attempt to pull Anna's top off as they walked through the basement.

"Be patient. We're nearly there." Anna tried to keep the man's rough hands off her as she led him towards the cellar.

"Right, that's far enough, I'm having you right here."

"Wait! It's just there." Anna pointed to the corner of the basement.

"What is?"

"The entrance to the cellar."

"I'm not going in any cellar, you stupid bitch." The man threw Anna on the floor.

"Wait. It's really cosy down there. Really nice, you'll see." Anna backed away from the man on her backside, scraping herself on the basement floor. "It's just there—look!"

"I don't see nothing."

"There on the floor. You see the ring?" The man peered into the shadows. "You just need to pull it up and there are steps leading down. It's really cosy down there. It's like a secret love den. There's a mattress down there, and beer, and everything,"

"You're talking shit."

Underbelly

"Just look!"

The man's curiosity got the better of him. He pulled up the trap door and peered down into the darkness.

"I don't see anything,"

"Once we get down, I'll switch on the light."

"You want to lock me in down there!"

"No, I don't." The man was getting angry and Anna was getting very frightened. "I'll go down first, okay? Look, I'm going down first."

Anna bolted down the steps and the man followed cautiously. She was going to pay for bringing him down here. He had planned to treat her nice, but now he was going to do her hard and rough for dragging him all the way down into this stinking damp place.

The man descended the steps slowly, backwards, like a ladder.

"So where's the light switch?" he demanded, and the next thing he knew—there was a snarling, howling sound and something struck him in the chest. He was thrown backwards, his chest, neck, stomach, face exploding in blood and chunks of flesh as fangs and claws moved over him and inside him at lightning speed. He was dead before he hit the cellar floor.

Anna screamed as blood splattered all around her. She hid behind the cellar steps and whimpered as the snarling, tearing sounds continued. As her eyes grew accustomed to the dark, she could see the creature devouring the man—chunk by chunk. Anna threw up, then wiped her mouth and cried. The man had been a sleaze, but he hadn't deserved this: he was being eaten like a piece of barbecued steak, and Anna was directly responsible. She cried for the man, she cried for any family he might have left behind and she cried for her immortal soul. But after a while, she stopped crying and was a little disturbed to find herself wondering how the creature was able to eat the entire man in one sitting. It hadn't just been eating the man's flesh; it had been crunching up his bones with logic-defying ease and swallowing those as well. There was almost nothing left of the man, except the tattered remains of his clothes, and Anna wondered why the creature's stomach didn't burst. Her repulsion and guilt turned to a morbid curiosity, and she peered out from behind the steps, watching the black furry winged thing eat. It was quite impressive really—the thing was one efficient eating machine. Anna wondered whether it had an extending stomach, her mind conjuring up images from the *The Little Prince,* which her grandmother had read to her when she was little, and in which she remembered seeing a picture of what looked like a hat, but was actually meant to be a snake that had swallowed an elephant.

As Anna's mind wandered back to her childhood, the creature finished its feast and looked through the cellar steps at the woman. Anna noticed its blazing red eyes and cowered back in fear, but then remembered that the creature wasn't going to eat her. The creature looked into Anna for a long while, then turned around and moved off languidly into the shadows.

"By midnight tomorrow," the distant, deafening voice reverberated through Anna's mind, and then the creature was gone. Anna took a last look at the blood-stained rags lying on the cellar floor and hurried back to her bedsit.

*

Anna woke up late after the previous night's horrors, and lay in bed thinking about Frank. She had given every single atom of her being over to loving him. Her tutor at university had told her—after she had been dumped by her first love—that she shouldn't give all of herself away to a man; that she should always hold a little bit back for herself, so as not to give another human being the power to destroy her completely if things went wrong. She'd listened to her tutor all her life after that—throughout all her relationships—but she stopped listening when she met Frank. She was so convinced that he was her soul mate and that they would stay together forever, that she had stopped listening, or perhaps she had forgotten her tutor's words. She had let herself go for the first time since she was eighteen, and she had allowed herself to fall in love completely—catering to Frank's every whim, giving him love, sex, money and everything he asked for. Then when she had asked for more than the one night a week he was willing to give her, he had turned on her, comparing her to his ex and telling her that he didn't need 'any of that emotional stuff.' The final straw had come when Anna didn't have any more money to 'lend' him. The loans, which added up to a couple of thousand pounds over seven months—were ones that Anna never expected to get back, and Frank had no complaints about that. Anna realised how ridiculously one-sided their relationship had been, how the 'love' that Frank professed was based entirely on what she could give him and not on what they could give each other, but she didn't care.

Now that the pain was no longer filling her entire world, she felt a large gap in her life—a gap that only Frank could fill. And she was absolutely desperate to be with him again.

"Hello?" Anna's blood pressure shot up as she heard Frank's voice on the other end of the phone. Her heart was pounding, and she could feel herself getting light-headed.

"Frank, it's Anna." There was a long pause at the other end, then Frank said, "I thought you told me you were dying."

"I am," said Anna, fighting back the tears that were welling up in her eyes—tears not about her imminent death, but about the cold tone in Frank's voice that she had come to dread in their last weeks together. "But I'm feeling better at the moment and I was hoping you could come over."

"I'm working,"

"After work, then."

"Look, it's over, Anna. We're not together anymore."

"I know, it's just that I..."

"It's just that you what?"

"I..." Anna felt herself drowning. Like that time when Frank said he couldn't handle how needy and emotional she was, and that he couldn't be with her anymore. She looked around for a straw to grasp before the water closed over her head. "I've won the lottery," she blurted out, sickened at her own desperation.

Underbelly

"You what?" She could tell he wasn't buying it—he could see right through her desperation. Why had she said she'd won the lottery? How was she going to get out of that one?

"Not millions or anything. Just three hundred and eighty thousand. You know, five balls and the bonus ball."

Silence at the other end. Then, "You're kidding!"

"No, I'm not. I really won it. Ironic, isn't it—winning the lottery when I'm about to die."

"I can't believe it!" Frank couldn't believe he hadn't stayed with the needy, whining bitch. It would have been worth it. Three hundred and eighty thousand. He could have left his crappy dead-end job and become a fulltime writer. Maybe there was still time... "That's fantastic, baby!" he told Anna.

"It's true." Anna had always loved it when he called her 'baby'. "That's why I'm calling, actually."

"I'm so happy for you, baby!"

"Yeah, well. You know, I'm not going to spend all of it and I've been thinking that, well, if I let you have some of it—most of it—you could give up your job like you wanted and become a fulltime writer."

"I couldn't take your money, baby."

"I've got no-one else to leave it to. It's not like I've got any children, or any brothers and sisters. My parents are dead, and I never liked my cousins, so I just thought..."

"Baby, I can't believe you thought of me. I don't know what to say. I mean... I couldn't take your money, but maybe if I could borrow some—just until I sell my first novel..."

"Yeah, well, maybe you could come over tonight?"

"Sure, I can come over. What time were you thinking?"

"As soon as you can after work. I can cook some dinner?"

"Sure. That'll be great." The bitch couldn't cook for shit, but he'd eat dog turd if it meant he could get his hands on three hundred and eighty thousand. "I'll get to yours for about half six."

"Great," said Anna. "I've missed you," she added tentatively.

"I've missed you too," echoed Frank, without much conviction. Anna had a strong urge to say, "Well, you could have called me anytime", but she refrained. She hung up the phone and felt happy for a few moments, but then the reality of the situation hit her and she started to panic. She would put on some really sexy, feminine clothes and cook a nice dinner, she would be cheerful and she wouldn't talk about her illness. Perhaps when Frank spent some time with her, perhaps when they made love and he saw that things could be back to how they used to be, he would forget about the money and forgive her for making it all up—he would understand that she'd done it because she loved him and wanted to see him. Perhaps... But who was she really kidding?

*

Frank arrived, looking every bit as sexy as when Anna first laid eyes on him. He froze when Anna went to hug him, shattering any hope she might have had about them getting back together. Dinner was awkward: Anna waiting on Frank, nervous about her cooking, Frank forcing himself to be polite and not to be the first to mention the lottery money. When they had finished dessert, Anna leaned over and tried to kiss him, but Frank pulled away.

"Cancer isn't contagious, you know," Anna told him.

"Look, Anna, I really appreciate you helping me out with the money..."

"Frank, there's something I have to tell you..."

"What is it?" There was a long silence as Anna thought frantically whether to tell him or not. "Well?"

"There is no money."

"What?"

"I really wanted to see you..."

"What do you mean there is no money?"

"I'm sorry. I really wanted to see you..."

"So you pretended to win the lottery?"

"I'm sorry."

"You stupid fucking bitch! You made me leave Monica and come all the way over here..."

"What do you mean, leave Monica?" Anna suddenly felt sick.

"We were supposed to go out to dinner tonight..."

"You're back with your ex?"

"I'm not *back* with her, Anna. I've always been with her."

The room spun and Anna had to hold onto the table.

"But when we met, you said you'd split up with her six months earlier."

"Yeah well, I didn't think you'd sleep with me if I told you the truth."

"So all the time we were together you were living with Monica?"

"Oh, come on, Anna, don't try to tell me you didn't know."

"How could I possibly have known?"

"I never had you over at my place, I hardly ever stayed the night at yours." The pathetic look on Anna's face was really winding Frank up. "For God's sake, Anna, don't tell me you're that fucking naive?"

"So our whole relationship was a lie?" Anna could hear her voice cracking up, but there was absolutely no way she was going to cry in front of Frank again.

"Look, I'm not here to discuss our non-existent relationship. It was over ages ago. If there's no money, then I'm going." Frank got up to leave.

"Wait." The abrupt change in Anna's tone stopped Frank in his tracks. "There is money. You can have it. But you have to help me get it out. It's in the basement."

"What?" Frank looked at Anna and she searched his eyes for the slightest hint of the man she thought had loved her. She saw only a mixture of incredulity, contempt and greed.

"It's not safe in here. There's all sorts of people going up and down the corridor, and my flat isn't very secure. One kick and they're through the door. So I hid it in the basement."

"You hid three hundred and eighty thousand pounds in the basement?"

"It's only three hundred thousand. I'm using the rest to get proper healthcare."

"Whatever... Are you having me on?"

"Frank, it's okay that you're still with Monica. Maybe we could still..."

"For God's sake, Anna!" Anna raised her hand to stem Frank's anger.

"Okay. Let's go get the money."

"Can't you just bring it up and I'll wait here?" If anyone was dumb enough to keep three hundred thousand pounds in a damp rodent-infested basement—if the money even existed - it was Anna, but he didn't fancy creeping around in the dark, looking for it.

"It's heavy—there's quite a lot of it. It's best if we go together."

"Okay," sighed Frank. "Let's go."

*

As he watched Anna descending the stairs into the cellar, Frank was not happy. He wondered whether there was in fact any money, he wondered whether Anna even had cancer; he had often wondered whether she had made the cancer up just to pressure him into spending more time with her. He was tempted to turn around and walk away, but even the slimmest chance of three hundred thousand pounds was something you didn't just walk away from.

Anna paused at the top of the steps and looked back at Frank, searching his face in the darkness one last time. Nothing there - only impatience, wariness and annoyance. Anna continued down the steps, the tears she'd been holding back finally breaking out and trickling down her face.

Anna Taborska

*

Anna lay whimpering in the corner, her eyes closed until the creature finished feeding. Frank hadn't even had time to cry out, but Anna heard the tearing, slurping, crunching sounds despite clamping her hands over her ears. When the sounds ceased and Anna opened her eyes, the creature was gone. Anna threw up her dinner, returned to her bedsit and cried herself to sleep.

*

Anna was still grieving over Frank when the time came to provide the creature's next meal. She found that most of her former friends—friends who had suddenly become very busy when Anna's money ran out and even busier when she got sick—were more than willing to visit her at short notice when she told them about her lottery win. On nights when nobody wanted to come over, she went out and brought back men.

One night she was watching the thing feed on a married stockbroker called George, when she found herself admiring the creature's thick black fur and the way the scant light falling into the cellar penetrated its extraordinary membranous wings. She wondered if it could actually fly. As it finished feeding and turned to go, Anna called out to it.

"Wait!"

The bloated fiend turned back and gazed at Anna, mild interest in its slanted red eyes, its fangs bared in what looked to Anna like a grin.

Underbelly

"You feed so fast," Anna said to it. "I mean, you kill so fast... I'll bring you someone tomorrow night. I was wondering if you could... kill that person... slowly?"

The creature contemplated the woman before him for a few moments. A hollow, sinister laugh reverberated in Anna's ears.

"Very well," the thing said finally, its mouth never moving as it spoke. "I'll eat your doctor slowly."

"How did you know...?"

"I can see inside you."

*

Anna's GP refused to speak to her and, after many phone calls and much pestering of the receptionist, when he did finally talk to her, he refused to come.

"I don't make house calls," he told her.

"But I'm in pain, Doctor," pleaded Anna, "I'm scared. Please, I'm too sick to leave the house today, and my painkillers have run out."

"If you feel so bad, you should call an ambulance."

"Please, Doctor. You've been my doctor for fifteen years. Please, I need you... I can make it worth your while."

"Don't be stupid, Ms Weedon. The NHS pays my wages, and I don't make house calls."

"I didn't mean to offend you, Doctor. It's just that I won the lottery recently, and I don't have anyone to leave the money to. And you've been my doctor for fifteen years. I thought you could do with the money—perhaps you could expand your private practice. And I really need you to come over tonight. Please."

"You won the lottery?"

"Yes, Doctor, and I would really like to leave you the money when I die—which, as you know, won't be long now."

"Well, I guess I could make an exception. After all, you *are* an exceptional patient, and I *have* been your doctor for fifteen years..."

*

It had been hard getting her GP to come down to the basement, but it had been worth it. The creature was true to its word and killed the doctor slowly, holding him down while it ate him piece by piece, making sure the man could see and hear his own flesh being chewed and swallowed.

Anna's doctor screamed to her to save him.

"Help me! Get it off!"

"*You* should have helped *me*, the first time I came to you with bleeding and abdominal pain," Anna screamed back at him.

"Please, help me!"

"No!"

Underbelly

The doctor continued to scream and struggle, but the creature held him firm, and his movements weakened as exhaustion, blood loss and excruciating pain sapped his strength. Through the darkness and the tears that were streaming down his face, he thought he could see Anna smiling.

"Why?" he gurgled at her, blood spewing from his mouth.

"Because it takes away my pain, which is more than you ever bothered to do!"

Despite the creature's best efforts to keep him alive as long as possible, after half an hour of being eaten, the doctor's heart finally gave out and stopped. Five minutes later, there was no trace of him left, apart from some bloody, tattered rags. The creature turned to go, but Anna called it back.

"Wait!"

The creature turned back and the two of them eyed each other for a long while.

"May I touch you?" Anna finally asked.

"Why do you want to touch me?"

"You're my only friend."

The creature laughed—that distant, hollow, grating laugh that scared Anna, even as the creature itself no longer scared her—well, not as much as it used to.

"You fed me all your other friends," the creature grinned with its bony, bloody fangs.

"They weren't my friends. Not really. They never did anything for me. Not like you."

"Touch me then". The creature was amused by the woman. It was always amusing to watch how fast humans gave away their immortal souls - and all their nearest and dearest - to get what they wanted: money, success, sex, longer life, an end to pain. It was enough to look inside them, see what they wanted the most, and once you offered it to them, they just rolled over for you.

Anna crawled uncertainly over to the creature and reached out a trembling hand. When she found that the creature didn't bite it off, she gently touched its black fur. Anna was amazed to find that its fur was quite soft—not hard and bristly as she had thought. As she stroked the monster's fur, it narrowed its red eyes—rather like a cat—and after a while it started to purr-mewl. Under its fur, the creature's muscular body was round and firm. Exhaustion overcame Anna; she leant her head against the creature and fell asleep.

In the early hours of the morning, the cold woke Anna up. She was lying on the damp floor of the cellar alone; the creature was gone.

*

The next day, a policeman and policewoman came round to Anna's flat and asked whether she had seen her doctor the previous day—he had not returned home last night and had not turned up to work in the morning. His last appointment had been Anna's house call.

Anna said that he had been with her for about ten minutes, and then left.

"What was the exact purpose of his visit?" The policeman tried to make himself comfortable on the small sofa.

"He prescribed me some painkillers."

"Can we see the prescription, please."

Anna's heart started to pound, and she had to think fast.

"I don't have the prescription anymore," she said, "I already bought the medicine,"

"Can we see the medicine, please," said the policeman.

"Of course." Anna went to the bathroom and started looking for an old bottle of pills. The GP had been so keen to discuss the money that the two of them had forgotten all about the painkillers that Anna had said she needed. She finally found a bottle half filled with pills and brought it in.

"That's only half full," The policeman took the bottle from Anna, and studied it closely. "And it was issued a month ago."

"Oh," Anna was starting to panic. "I didn't notice, I'm sorry—I'm not very well. I have cancer, you know. Perhaps you can help me find the right bottle."

"That won't be necessary," the policeman smiled sympathetically. The policewoman also smiled, but her smile didn't reach her eyes.

*

Barely a few days had passed, and the police were back, questioning Anna about her friend Teresa.

"We understand from her husband that she came to see you last week."

"No, she didn't." Anna was feeling sick again. "I mean, she was meant to come and see me, but she never showed up."

"So what did you do when she didn't show up?" asked the policewoman, "Did you call her house?"

Anna had the distinct feeling that both the policewoman and the policeman knew the answer to that already.

"No, I didn't," Anna told them. "I didn't do anything. I mean, Teresa often told me that she would be coming round, and then I wouldn't hear from her for six months. I didn't think anything had happened to her."

"Her husband said that you'd won the lottery and that you wanted to give her some of your money. Is this true?"

"No, it's not true."

"No, you didn't win the lottery, or no, you didn't tell Mrs Trent that you'd won the lottery."

"Neither."

"Then why would Mr Trent say such a thing?"

"I don't know."

"I think you told Mrs Trent that you'd won the lottery and that you'd give her the money, and when she came here and found that there was no money, the two of you had an argument and something happened."

"Like what?"

"Like maybe you killed her."

"What! How can you say that? I wouldn't kill anyone. I've got cancer, you know."

Underbelly

"Yes, we know."

"I told you, Teresa wasn't even here."

"Well, two of your neighbours told us they saw a woman matching Mrs Trent's description entering the building."

"Well, she wasn't here."

The policewoman sat back, finished for the moment. Her colleague took over.

"Do you mind if we have a look around?" he asked. Anna shook her head. They found nothing, of course, and left.

"We'll be back," they told Anna. And they were—a few days later.

*

This time the two police officers were armed with a list of missing people—all linked by the fact that they knew Anna—and more eye witness testimony: concerning men entering the building with a woman who matched Anna's description. Anna co-operated and gave them a full statement, under threat of having to do so in the police station. A further search of her bedsit revealed nothing, but Anna was sure that they were watching the entrance to her building.

That evening she went down to see the creature, empty-handed.

"I can't feed you for a while," she tried to explain. "The police are watching the building. I can't bring anyone here."

"I need to eat," the creature's voice resounded in Anna's ears, and the fiend's eyes blazed at Anna angrily.

"I can't bring anyone."

"If you don't feed me, the pain will return."

Anna felt that familiar twinge in her abdomen. She hadn't felt it for weeks now, and she doubled over, clutching her underbelly and crying out.

"Stop! Please stop! I thought you were my friend." It would be a lie to say that the fiend's betrayal of their 'friendship' hurt almost as much as Anna's abdomen, but it hurt nonetheless.

"I *am* your friend," the creature told Anna. The pain subsided, but Anna was left reeling and scared. "You will bring me someone tonight and we will continue to be friends."

*

Anna found the young Polish man sitting on a bench in the local park, drinking a can of beer. By the look of the grass around the bench, he had drunk more than one already. His English was poor, he had obviously not been in London long, and was homesick and lonely. Anna told him that her boyfriend had dumped her and she needed someone to walk her home, as she didn't like walking home on her own when it was dark. She didn't know if the young man understood what she was saying, but he certainly seemed keen enough to follow her home, and drunk enough to follow her to the cellar.

As Anna led the man down the steps, she had a change of heart. He had done nothing wrong: he hadn't betrayed her, he hadn't tried to grope her, judging by the lack of ring on his ring finger he wasn't hoping to cheat on his wife with her. All he

Underbelly

had done was walk her home and smile at her in a tipsy, perplexed kind of way. Anna stopped abruptly on the steps and was about to tell the man to go back up, that this had all been a mistake, but just then bright lights appeared behind them, followed by running footsteps and shouting.

"Police! Freeze!"

Anna screamed and tried to run down the remaining steps, but slipped and fell. Her head hit something hard and the world went grey, then black.

*

Anna dreamt about stroking the creature's fur and listening to its strange purring as she fell asleep. She woke up cold and alone, and started to get up, intending to go back up to her bedsit, but instead found herself in a small cell with bars in the window. And that's when the pain hit her.

As Anna screamed in vain to God and the Devil to take the pain away, the thing in the underbelly of her building scuttled back through its gateway into the hell from which it had come, and settled down to sleep. By the time it would wake up, Anna's suffering would long be over.

HEAL THYSELF BY SCOTT NICHOLSON

Jeffrey Jackson peeked over the top of the magazine. His eyes went to the clock on the wall. Had it really been only four minutes since he'd last looked?

His hands shook, so he put the magazine aside before the pages started flapping. Every session with Dr. Edelhart left him calm for a day or two, fists unclenched, the red behind his eyelids dulled to brown. But always the raging night crawled out on its belly, fingers tickled his brain, his cabbies got radio messages from Mars, and sweaty, dark figures flitted along the perimeter of his dreams. And in the mirror he saw the man he had once been. Those last days leading up to the next session were a cold turkey of the soul.

Jackson wondered if what he'd read were true, that patients became more addicted to therapy than they ever could to drugs. He gripped the arms of the waiting room chair, palms slick on the vinyl. He tried one of the relaxation techniques that Dr. Edelhart had taught him. That wallpaper pattern, reproduced a thousand times in the expanse of the room. If Jackson crossed his eyes slightly....

No good. He settled on watching the receptionist, who pretended to be busy with paperwork. She was white and almost pretty, but Jackson no longer had much interest in the opposite sex. Or any sex, for that matter.

He started from his chair when the buzzer rang. The receptionist gave him a two o'clock smile and said, "Dr. Edelhart will see you now."

Why did the doctor never have an appointment before Jackson's? If only Jackson could see another patient walk out of Dr. Edelhart's office, face rosy with beatitude. Perhaps that would give Jackson hope of being healed. He crossed the room and, as always, reached the door just as it swung open.

Dr. Edelhart smiled broadly, teeth bright against his wide, dark face. He extended his hand. Jackson wiped his own hand on his pants leg and shook Edelhart's.

Prelude to The Ritual.

"How are you, Jeffrey?" The same question as always.

You know damned good and well how I am, Doc. You've shrunk my brain and cracked open my past and put every little memory under your magnifying glass. Walked me back to my childhood. Into the womb, even. And beyond.

Way beyond.

Jackson blinked, barely able to meet the taller man's eyes. "I...I'm doing fine."

He brushed past the doctor, headed for the security of the familiar stuffed chair. Edelhart didn't believe in the couch. He was too post-Freudian for that. Edelhart was of the New High Church, a dash of Jung, a pinch of Skinner, and equal portions of new age-right action-spirit releasement-astral projection-veda dharmic-divine starpath to inner beingness.

Add water and stir.

Edelhart's mental porridge cost $150 an hour, and Jackson considered it a bargain. He settled in the chair as Edelhart closed the door and adjusted the window shades. Since the office was on the seventh floor, the traffic sounds below were muted. Jackson was almost able to forget his fear of cars. And windows. And the faces on either side of them.

Jackson closed his eyes. Edelhart's chair squeaked behind his polished mahogany desk. The room had an aroma of carpet cleaner and sweat. Or maybe Jackson was smelling his own panic. He tried to breathe deeply and evenly, but he was too aware of his racing heartbeat. And the past, where he would soon be headed.

"So, where were we, Jeffrey?" The doctor's voice was deep, resonant, a soul-singer's pipes. Even this familiar question took on a musical quality, a sonorous bass. Or maybe he was stereotyping. After all, not every black had the rid'dem.

"We were..." Jackson swallowed. "Going back."

Jackson didn't have to look to visualize the doctor's head gravely nodding. "Ah, yes," said Dr. Edelhart. The shuffling of papers, a quick perusal of notes, Jackson's round peg of a head being fitted into this square hole and that triangular niche. "So you've accepted that present life conflicts and traumas can have their roots in past lifetimes?"

"Of course, Doctor." Jackson was too eager to please and too afraid to do otherwise. "Especially that *one* past life."

Heal Thyself

"We each have at least one bad former life, Jeffrey. Otherwise, there would be no reason to live again. Nothing to resolve."

Jackson wanted to ask which of the doctor's past lives were the most haunting. But of course that was wrong. Dr. Edelhart was the one behind the desk, the one with the pencil. He was the *doctor*, for Christ's sake. The answer man. The black dude delivering The Word to the square honky.

Sheesh, no wonder you're on the teeter brink of bumblefuck crazy. Starting to shrink the SHRINK. And this guy's the only thing standing between you and a rubber room. Good thing dear Dr. Edelhart doesn't believe in medication, or you'd be on a brain salad of Prozac, Thorazine, lithium, Xanax, Xanadu, whatever.

No, the only drug that Edelhart believed in was plain and simple holism. Jackson's soul fragments were all over the place, in both space and time. Edelhart was the shaman, the quest leader, the spirit guide. His job was to take Jackson to those far corners of the universe where the fragments were buried or broken. Once the fragments were recovered, then all it took was a little psychic superglue and Jackson would *Become Authentic*.

Jackson just wished Edelhart would hurry the hell up. Seven months of regression therapy and they were just now getting to the good stuff. The tongue in the sore tooth. The fly in the ointment. The nail in the karmic wheel. The past life that pain built.

"I'm ready to go all the way," Jackson said, surer now. After all, what was a century-and-a-half of forgotten existence compared to thirty-plus years of real, remembered anxiety?

"Okay, Jeffrey. Breathe, count down from ten, your eyes are closed and looking through the ceiling, past the sky, past the long night above..."

Jackson could handle this. He fell into the meditation with practiced ease, and by the time the doctor reached "Seven, a gate awakens," Jackson was swaddled in the tender arms of a hypnotic trance. He scarcely heard Dr. Edelhart's feet approaching across the soft carpet. The doctor's breath was like a sea breeze on his cheek, the deep voice quieter now.

"You're on the plantation, Jeffrey. The wheat is golden, the cotton fields rolling out like a blanket of snow. The oaks are in bloom, the air sweet with the ripeness of the earth. Somebody's frying chicken in the main house. The sun is Carolina hot but it will go down soon."

Jackson smiled, distantly, drowsily. The Doc was good. It was almost like the man was there himself, simultaneously living Jackson's past life. But Jackson had described this scene so well, it was seared so deeply into his subconsciousness, that it was no wonder Dr. Edelhart could almost watch it like a movie.

Part of Jackson knew he was half-dreaming, that he was actually sitting in a chair in a Charlotte highrise. But the image was vivid, the farm spread out around him, the boots heavy on his feet, the smell of horses drifting from the barn, a cool draft on his neck from the creek. This wasn't real, but it *was*. He *was*

Heal Thyself

this farmer, edging along the fence line, poking along the rim of the cornfield.

Past visits to this life had made it familiar.

He *was* Dell Bedford, Southern gentleman, landowner, a colonel in the Tryon militia. Because they all knew Lincoln and them Federalist hogwashers were going to try to muscle the South back into the Union. But what Lincoln and his boot-licker McLellan didn't figure on was that the Confederate States of America might have other plans.

The nerve of that Lincoln, telling them what to do with their niggers.

Jackson swallowed hard, back in the modern padded chair, sweat ringing his scalpline. This part bothered him. He wasn't a racist, not anymore, not *now*. He'd voted against Jesse Helms, he supported illegal immigrants. He even saw a black therapist. He was cool with it all, brotherhood of man, harmony of one people.

But he had no proof that he hadn't once been Dell Bedford, slavemaster and arrogant white swine. How could he deny the word "nigger" that sat on his tongue, ready to be spat over and over again, a sick well of hate that never ran dry? He *was* Dell, or had been, or...

"Are you there, Jeffrey?" came Dr. Edelhart's voice. Decades away, yet right on the plantation with him, like a bee hovering around his ear.

"Yep," Jackson/Bedford said. "Corn's come in, gone to yeller on top. If I can round me up some niggers, might get an ear or two in before first frost."

"Those slaves. Always causing you problems, aren't they? Building up stress, making your chest burn with rage." Dr. Edelhart's voice was nigger-rich with sympathy.

"Damned right." Jackson/Bedford felt the muscles in his neck go rigid. He thrashed at the corn, then hollered. "Claybo!"

The shout scurried across the stalks of corn, rattled the corners of Dr. Edelhart's office. "Never can find that Claybo when you need him, can you?" said the doctor.

Bedford left Jackson, had no use for him, just as well let him sit in a chair and talk to a dandified free boy. Bedford had chores to get done. And there was only one way to get them done. Work the niggers.

"Claybo," he shouted again.

Sweat ran down the back of his neck, the brim of his hat serving hell for shade. Bedford hurried into the field, leather coiled in his taut right hand. His oldest son was on horseback in a far meadow, galloping toward the Johnson place to scramble hay with one of Johnson's bucolic daughters. Bedford gritted his teeth and waded into the corn.

"Claybo, if I ever get my hands on you..."

"Then what, Dell?"

It was the dandy nigger. Dell shook his head. A damned voice from nowhere. The nerve of an invisible nigger to mess in a white man's business. A white man's dreams.

"Then I'll kick his uppity ass. What else can you do with a sorry nigger?"

"He's not in the cornfield, Dell. You know that, don't you? We've already been through this."

Heal Thyself

"Shut up, nigger." Bedford tore through the corn, knocking over stalks, heading toward the thin stand of pines where the slaves were quartered. "Bet that damned good-for-nothing Claybo is taking himself a little snooze. And the sun ain't even barely touched the trees yet."

"That Claybo. He's nothing but trouble. Probably even learning to read. Bet he's got a spelling book under his strawtick," the invisible nigger said.

"Niggers. Don't let 'em read. The first word they teach each other is 'no.' Well, I know how to drive the book-learning out of them." Bedford let the whip play out as he ran, jerked his wrist so that the length of leather undulated like a snake.

"That's it, Bedford," came the easy voice. "Feel the anger. Embrace it. *Breathe* it."

Bedford scratched at his ear and ran on. He burst from the cornrows and crossed the bare patch of dirt that served as nigger-town square. Six cabins of rough logs and mud squatted under the spindly pines. A little pickaninnie sat in front of one of them, playing with a rag doll. She'd be able to walk soon, and finally be able to work for her keep.

Bedford went to the last cabin and kicked at the door. It fell open, and Bedford shouted into the dark. Then he saw them, three pairs of white eyes. There was nothing quite like a nigger in the dark. Hell, he didn't even mind when his neighbors had runaways, because they were so much fun to hunt.

"Tell me what you see," said the distant voice. Smooth-talking nigger, like one of them Yankee preachers that come down once in a while to rub in their faces that, up North, niggers were free. How

Northern niggers owned all kinds of land, while Bedford had only thirty hardscrabble acres of Carolina clay.

"What the hell you *think* I see? You were here with me *last* time I done this." Bedford was nearly as mad at the invisible nigger as he was at Claybo. He hurried into the cramped dark.

"Don't hurt me, Mar's Bedford," Claybo pleaded. Like a little sissy girl who was going to get a hickory switch across the bloomers. "My baby's took sick. I swear, I was going to go back and work. I just had to come look in—"

"Shut up, nigger." Bedford's eyes had adjusted now, and he could make their outlines. The woman on the bed, holding the infant, both of them slick with sweat. Claybo kneeling beside the bed, hands lifted up like Bedford was Jesus Christ the Holy Savior, but Claybo should know that Jesus never helped niggers, only good, holy whites.

The woman wailed, then the baby started crying. Bedford's blood coursed hot through his veins, his pulse was a hammer against the anvil of his temples, his head was a powder keg with a beeswax fuse.

"You're right to feel anger," whispered the educated nigger, the one that was so far away. "You've been wounded. This is where your soul bleeds, Jeffrey."

Bedford wondered who the hell Jeffrey was, but that didn't matter, that was another world and another worry. He grabbed Claybo by the shirt and tugged him toward the door. As much as he would have loved to stripe the nigger in front of his woman, the cabin didn't allow for good elbow room. Claybo only

Heal Thyself

half resisted, dead weight. He didn't dare struggle too much. Because the nigger knew if he did, his woman would be next.

Bedford's anger settled lower, took a turn, became something warm and light in his stomach.

Joy.

He *loved* beating a nigger.

He pushed Claybo to the ground, tore at the big man's shirt. He gave the nigger a kick in the ribs to get the juices flowing. The whip handle almost throbbed in his hand, as if it had a turgid life of its own.

"Seize the fragment," came that confounded, invisible nigger, the one in his head. "Look at yourself, Jeffrey. You're splintered, apart from the world. Outside the circle of your own soul."

"My fragment." Bedford grunted through clenched teeth.

"These are the traumatic emotions and body sensations that have tracked you through the years. This is where your pain comes from. This is your unfinished business. This is your *wound.*"

Bedford tried to ignore the nigger-talk. He stepped back, hefted the whip, sensed the graceful leather unfurling, rolled his arm in an easy motion, sent the knotted tip into Claybo's broad back. The ebony flesh split like a dropped melon.

A sweet pleasure surged through Bedford, a fever that was better than what he found between his wife's legs, even between the nigger cook's, a honey-hot heaven. He whisked the whip back to deliver another blow—

"This is your discarnate self, Jeffrey. Doesn't it

sicken you? Don't you see why your soul is so far from release?"

Bedford paused, the leather dripping red, hungry for a second taste.

"Restore balance, Jeffrey."

Bedford/Jackson looked down at the huddled, quivering Claybo.

Dr. Edelhart spoke again, gentle, encouraging. "Resolve the conflict and heal the emotional vulnerability. Seek your spiritual reattachment."

Jackson felt dizzy. The whip wilted in his hand. He wanted to vomit. He couldn't believe he had ever been so brutal. Not in any of his lives. "I didn't..."

"Denial is not the path to wholeness, Jeffrey. Empower yourself."

Tears trickled down Jackson's face. He could feel the eyes watching Bedford from the cabin door. A witness to his spiritual fracture. How could he possibly make this right? How could he become a soul-mind healed?

Sobbing, he turned to the only one he could trust. "What do I do now, Dr. Edelhart?"

"You know the answer. I can only lead you to the door. The final steps are yours."

Jackson bent to his victim. Claybo looked at him, wide-eyed, wary. Jackson placed the whip at Claybo's feet. Then he slowly unbuttoned his shirt, his skin pale in the sunset.

Jackson knelt on the ground. He put his face against the dirt, pine needles scratching his cheek, dust clinging to his tears. "Free me," he said to the man he had whipped.

"Mar's?" Claybo's voice was wracked with

Heal Thyself

hidden hurt.

"Do it."

"Yes, suh." Claybo slowly lifted himself, his shirt hanging in rags from his dark muscles. Both men were on their knees, equal.

"Whip me," Jackson commanded. Then, begging, "Please."

Claybo stood, six-three, a man, black anger. He fumbled with the whip, making an awkward arc in the air with its length. He snapped his wrist and the leather slapped against Jackson's bare back.

Not a strong blow, yet the pain sluiced along Jackson's spinal cord.

Jackson swallowed a scream, his lungs feeling stuffed with embers. He gasped, then panted, "Harder."

The agony was soul-searing, but Jackson knew the blow wasn't nearly hard enough to drive the transpersonal residue from his soiled psyche.

The whip descended again, more controlled this time, scattering sparks across Jackson's fragmented but hopeful spirit-flesh. Claybo was intelligent for a darkie. A fast learner. The whip fell a third time, inflicting a deeper, more meaningful misery. Flogging Jackson closer to whole.

"Your hour's up," Dr. Edelhart interrupted.

Jackson came around, brought back by the words that he'd been trained to recognize as the trigger that would pull him from hypnosis. He blinked as he looked around the office. He was soaked with sweat, his muscles aching, his throat dry. Dr. Edelhart stood over him.

"How do you feel?" said the doctor, eyes half-closed as if studying a rare insect.

Jackson tried the air, found that it came into his lungs, then out, though it tasted of tannin. He was alive, back in the reality he knew. Years away from the scarred night of his soul. A strange peace descended, though he was tired, drained.

"I...I feel..." He searched through Dr. Edelhart's catalog of catch phrases, then found one that seemed to fit. "I feel a little more *integrated*."

Dr. Edelhart smiled. "I feel that we've made true progress today, Jeffrey."

Jackson sat up in the chair, energy returning. "Wow. I haven't felt this good in years."

"A hundred and forty, give or take a few."

"How...how did you know?"

Dr. Edelhart waved at the diplomas and framed certificates on the wall behind his desk. "I'm the doctor. I'm *supposed* to know."

Jackson stood, walked the soreness from his legs. "I could run through a crowd right now, and not even *notice* all the eyes watching me. I don't feel angry at all. Nobody to hate."

"Progress through regression. But. . . " Dr. Edelhart's word hung suspended in the air, like a tiny sliver of discarnate spirit.

"But what?" Jackson said.

"Let's not forget. This is only the beginning. A giant step, to be sure. But only a step."

Jackson looked at the carpet. "I should have guessed it wouldn't be that easy. Not after spending months just to get to this point."

"Now we know where your spiritual bondage is. Next time, we can go a little farther."

Heal Thyself

Jackson gave a smile, enjoying this moment of enlightenment. He was on the road to recovery. Sure, it might take months, maybe years. But he'd be whole. Even if it killed him.

Or rather, killed Dell Bedford.

"Funny, isn't it?" Jackson said. He always felt a little more informal at the end of a session. He'd be on top of the world for the next few days, no worries, the spiders at bay, the clowns snoozing in circus shadows. He'd even be able to take the elevator to the street.

Dr. Edelhart seemed to be in a good mood as well. "What's funny?"

"My fragmented past life. That my psychic wound would be racism. Well, racism, sadism, masochism, the whole laundry list we've already been through."

"What's so funny about that?"

"Well, you being black and all. Or should I say African-American?"

"Black's fine. Maybe it's not a coincidence at all, Jeffrey. Spiritual paths do have a way of intersecting here and there along the way. Sometimes more than once."

Jackson looked into the doctor's eyes. For just a second. Then the brightness was gone, the doctor shielded behind his clinical expression, lost behind the other end of the magnifying glass.

But for just that one second, Jackson had seen Claybo in there, hunted, haunted, vengeful. Wet with his own psychic scars.

No. Jackson shook the image from his head. He wasn't here to drive himself crazy. He was here to be healed.

"See you next week, same time?" Jackson said.

Dr. Edelhart smiled.

"I'm looking forward to it."

HARBINGER BY STEPHEN LAWS

It begins with a dawn raid by Tottenham's Police Drug Squad on a squalid house on a council estate.

There are twelve police officers present; all briefed at headquarters on the previous evening about the family who live in that property, their drug-dealing activities, their day-to-day movements and expectations at what will be found. That briefing continues into the early hours of the following day, after all those officers have rested and prepared.

There have been no developments in the past twelve hours that would negate the raid taking place; indeed, everything that has been forecast appears to be following its course. Two non-family residents will have visited in the evening between police briefings, as predicted, with a supply of Class A drugs, which all involved will have separated and shared in preparation for dissemination and sale in the surrounding area. The police have been waiting for this moment—and everything appears to be proceeding according to plan. Adrenalin is surging, since several of the family members involved have lengthy criminal records, involving convictions for assault and grievous bodily harm. The younger, less experienced officers are reminded of the importance of procedure and not allowing that adrenalin rush to result in an over-stepping of response that might hinder the operation as it proceeds and the aftermath.

Yeah, right, thinks the team.

The team are kitted up and ready to move at 3.50am. No one questions why it should not be 4.00am. Nice round figures appear to suggest a lack of planning.

The streets are deserted at that time of morning. The council housing estate looks deserted—as if everyone has simply decided to pack up and leave. The remains of a mattress smoulders on a building site. Curious birds circle the smoke, movement suggesting the presence of food. No one yawns in the police van. Adrenalin is up.

The targeted council house is a mid-terrace property, with four other dwellings either side; the total comprising a solid, featureless cinder block of three-up, two-down rooms to each property. That block looks to have been built to survive a rocket attack.

The police van glides to a halt behind the property; newly maintained so that the brakes make no sound when the vehicle halts. Team A exits from freshly-oiled sliding doors, splits into two pre-arranged sections of three officers each and, clad in combat gear, run quickly left and right around the building on either side; converging at the front of the property, entering the front. The gate giving access to the front has long since been removed for sale at a scrap metal merchant, so there is no telltale squeal of hinges when the officers arrive at the front door, battering ram prepared. In the meantime, similarly garbed officers of Team B have arrived at the back door at the rear of the property.

At the front, timings are confirmed between teams by radio contact—and the required knock on the front door is quickly given with the shouted request of: 'Open up! Police!' The peculiar formality, required by regulation, is followed instantly by the application of battering ram to the top left and bottom left hinges of the door. The second blow results in the door splintering and collapsing into a littered hallway. Team A charges into the premises with ruthless efficiency, cries of 'Police!' and only one expletive when an officer briefly tangles with a bicycle left in the hallway. At the same moment, Team B has applied a battering ram to the rear door—and follow inside with the same brutal precision.

There are no sounds from the residents; no cries of alarm, or sleep-blurred, startled expletives.

Eight minutes later, when no response or contact is made to police headquarters by Team A or Team B despite instruction to make radio contact on first arrest, the first of multiple radio enquiries are made to the team leader's individual radio communication.

Similarly, there is no response from the police van, which should have one officer on standby throughout.

Four minutes after that, an emergency alert is given—and three police panda cars are despatched with six officers to the target address.

The officers attempt radio communication throughout, but have no response—relaying lack of communication back to headquarters at every stage of the journey. Upon arrival, the police van is discovered empty, no officer present. The rear door of the property is open, and officers rush in. It is difficult to assess whether the internal state of the property is a result of the squalid living conditions of the residents, or whether there has been resistance and 'aggravation' resultant from the police invasion. The front door lies shattered on the hallway floor.

There is no sign of residents, and no sign of Team A or Team B.

The property is deserted.

Continued calls on the missing officers' communication equipment appear to suggest that signals are being received; but the officers and their radios have disappeared. Hurried confirmation by radio suggests that there should be three males and two females on the premises. But they too, are nowhere to be found. Now, with the bustle of police activity, the other residents of this concrete block have become alerted to the fact that 'something' is happening around them. Alarm and anxiety at the clearly troubled police presence soon gives way to outright aggression in some cases—and further police reinforcements are called in, not only to undertake interview and questioning of the neighbours, but also to quell what threatens to become a small riot—particularly when residents' mobile phones are used to contact friends and other neighbours. In less than an hour, the local media have picked up on the fact that 'something' is happening—and news teams begin to arrive. It is clear that the situation is spiralling out of control.

The area is cordoned off by the police.

Higher authorities are made aware of the situation, and plans are made for a D notice, whereby legal enforcement of restrictive reporting abilities is put into operation while the police and authorities determine the best course of action to continue investigation.

The residents of the block are evacuated on the false premise that there may be a gas leak, and that they must be moved for their own safety while investigations continue. Residents are decamped against their will to a local community centre. The ousted news reporters descend upon the community centre, are instantly threatened with legal action; but this does not prevent certain renegade factions broadcasting locally about the 'strange turn of events'. Three reporters are arrested under emergency powers, and the remainder clam up in the knowledge that their own liberty is most definitely under threat. Internet and mobile phone activity, however, continue to fan the flames that a major incident is taking place and that 'someone is missing'.

I see some of the news reports before the media blackout takes place. But this is not something that concerns me. With an imminent divorce, and the possibility that my children will be taken away from me, I have more important and personal matters to occupy my attention. I turn a local news report on the radio off angrily, and spend the remainder of that morning in my kitchen, with my head in my hands and worrying what my next step will be to recover my hopeless personal situation.

It is not yet time for my involvement.

It has not yet been made known to me that I am a harbinger.

That will come later.

Harbinger

In the hours that follow before noon, I remain unaware of other events taking place in the United Kingdom.

A party of school children, returning by coach from a holiday in Norway, has disappeared on a stretch of motorway between the ferry at North Shields and Newcastle upon Tyne. There have been no reports of accidents, or road delays. There have been no mobile phone calls homes from children or their teachers on the bus. The coach driver's radio is still operating, but he is not returning the increasingly frantic calls from the tour operator, the police and the education authority. A search by police will reveal in due course that the bus is parked on a hard-shoulder of the motorway, but there is no sign of the occupants.

Distressed flight officials are unable to find any of the 45 holidaymakers intending to fly from Glasgow to Majorca on the 11.25 am flight. Tannoy requests to attend the departure lounge are ignored. Not one person arrives at that flight lounge, and the aeroplane remains grounded, much to the bewilderment of all.

A swimming pool attendant in Leeds leaves his colleague to supervise the indoor pool at a leisure centre while he goes for coffee. Halfway through his cup, he realises that something has changed, but at first is unable to work out what is wrong. At last he realises that there is no sound coming from the pool. He returns, to discover that his colleague and thirty-seven swimmers have disappeared. Their clothes and bags remain in the changing rooms.

Stephen Laws

*

I awake from a night full of strange dreams in a bedroom that is devoid of sound. There is no traffic noise from the street outside, no birds sing and the neighbours are not playing their music at high decibels as usual. In that moment, I know that I have changed.

I shower, dress and eat a light breakfast.

I pack an overnight bag with everything that I will need for a journey. I have no idea how long that journey will be, or my ultimate destination. I only know that I will be walking south, for as long as it takes to get where I'm going. There is a purpose to my task, but it has not been revealed to me. When I arrive, I will know. Instinctively, I know that I won't be told—that I will just *know*. I am different—I know this in every fibre. But I do not know how or what I have become overnight. There is only one certainty— one word that is imprinted in the back of my mind, as if written there on my psyche. I do not have time to check a dictionary to remind myself of what that word truly means, because I have to leave. I say that word aloud as I close my house door behind me for the last time, sling the overnight bag over my shoulder and walk down the deserted main street to the highway heading south.

"Harbinger," I say.

For that is what I am.

The street remains deserted. No traffic passes. Behind the windows of every house I pass, I see only empty rooms.

Harbinger

When I reach the highway I come across the first abandoned cars. Some have stopped in the middle of the traffic lanes; some have slewed onto the hard shoulder. A lorry has stopped in the middle lane, its driver and passenger doors open.

They are all empty.

I continue to walk south—and as I walk, I lose sense of time. There is only an unknown, withheld, but definite purpose. I will be guided on this long straight walk, and will know where to go at the appropriate time.

*

I have no idea how long I walk.

Time has no meaning. There is no purpose other than arriving at my destination - a singular sense of purpose that is overwhelming, manifesting within me solely as 'direction'. Knowledge of my journey is not so much withheld from me; more a blankness or empty space within, which I know will be filled with the necessary knowledge at the appropriate time.

It is useless to try and contact that thing inside me which gives me such direction. The blank space remains empty, waiting to be filled.

South.

That, for now, is all that I need to know.

I stop occasionally to forage for food and drink in the empty vehicles left abandoned on the motorway or slewed off onto the hard shoulder. There is no sign of struggle, or violence or despair. A fruit and vegetable lorry, canted at 45 degrees across two lanes, provides a rich bounty; its back doors wide open and inviting.

A small, 'independent' part of me, deep inside, suggests that I should find a car, a van or a truck—see if the key is still in the ignition. Wouldn't it make more sense to drive, than to walk—wherever it is that I'm heading? But the thought is stillborn, and I don't know whether this is because none of these abandoned vehicles will work—or whether that it is an important part of my journey that I should simply walk.

So walk I must—and as the sun goes down, I keep walking—my shadow gigantic across the deserted motorway and eastern fields. Just before it dips below the tree-lined western horizon, I find a station wagon and caravan. The caravan door is also open and inviting. The interior sofa folds down and becomes a bed. There is a mattress and quilt. I prepare for my sleep in complete darkness, by touch rather than sight. There is no one to set timers for the motorway lights, no one to maintain the power of correct mechanical or electrical failure.

I fall instantly to sleep.

There are no dreams.

When the sun rises, so do I.

There is tinned food in the caravan, but no way to heat it. I eat it cold—and resume my journey.

Always south

Harbinger

*

Time continues to have no meaning as I follow the main motorway, passing hundreds—perhaps thousands—of abandoned vehicles of all descriptions. For the first time, I realise that there are no aircraft vapour trails in the sky; no smoke from factory chimneys. The sky has never looked so blue.

Although I observe and note - my mind is devoid of reasoned thinking and I am in a strange kind of limbo. My body is a machine, my legs keep moving—but I pay no heed to any of the motorway signs because I am being directed and my body knows where to go. Although I feel no hunger or thirst now, it is as if my body has a mechanical instinct of its own, knowing when to take water or scraps of food from empty cars or service stations. When I enter the latter, it reminds me in a curious but detached way of the sailing ship Mary Celeste; with plates of half-eaten food on the tables and unfinished drinks. I am at one with the silence and emptiness—and I continue on.

Days, weeks, months—perhaps even years pass as I walk. If this is some kind of sleep walking, there are no dreams. I walk during the day until the sun goes down. I sleep in whatever shelter is available—it is dreamless. At dawn, I rise and carry on.

Drinking, eating, defecating, urinating—I suppose that I continue to do these things, since I am still alive and walking; but I remain mentally in this strange limbo, even though this engine of a body of mine keeps performing its mechanical function -

heading south.

I know that I have arrived on the outskirts of London without having seen a motorway sign and now, at last, I know that I am being directed to a specific location within the metropolis. That is the limit of my awareness. As ever with this inner guidance, it lets me know what I need to know when I need to know it.

I continue on.

Has it been centuries since I embarked upon this unknown trek?

As ever, there is no sign of a single living human being or a corpse. No remains, no shreds of clothing being pecked at by birds.

The streets of London are deserted—an empty maze.

I walk on, avoiding abandoned vehicles on all sides; some parked neatly at pavements, others slewed, some in the middle of the road with their doors open. I have been seeing this scenario on television and films about the 'end of the world' ever since I was a boy. But now here it is for real.

Is it the end of the world?

There are no fires, no smoke rising from burning buildings. There are no signs of crashed or burning vehicles—they have merely been abandoned. There are no sirens. There is no rubble or debris; no signs of looting. And, of course, still no sign of human beings, either living or dead.

My head is down as I walk, but I am still guided - and when I do look up and see the Houses of Parliament, I know now that this is where I am headed—the seat of this country's government and power.

To my left, the clock face of Big Ben remains stuck at 11.59.

Nothing within me suggests that this is significant.

As if acknowledging my arrival, it gives one last and shivering spasm: a single, sonorous knell that leaves an empty echo that is rejected by an empty city. A flat and empty silence remains.

I look up—but the minute hand remains at 11.59

I move away from the clock, towards Palace Green—a grassy square that I recall from television interviews where press and media once interviewed politicians and political pundits. There are large black bollards like tank traps which prevent vehicles from making any kind of military or terrorist charge at Westminster—something that is now never going to happen.

I continue on down a ramp which takes me through to what appears to be a security building—now, of course, no longer secure. Passing through this empty building takes me into a courtyard. From there, my 'inner direction' takes me straight into a deserted Westminster Hall—mediaeval, large, plain, cold and imposing. On my right, I pass a deserted cafe—noting the familiar sight of unfinished food on tables and empty chairs. I pass through the hall and up a flight of stone stairs. As I move down a silent corridor, I become aware of more stately 'decoration' around me. There are more stairs, more corridors—and my body knows where to go, even though my mind does not. A further, increasingly decorative corridor takes me through to what seems to be a central, octagonal lobby.

How do I know that this is the 'crossroads' where all parts of the building meet?

From here, I know I must enter the House of Commons.

There are brass statues at the entrance, including Margaret Thatcher, David Lloyd George and Winston Churchill. Churchill is directly by the door as I enter the chamber (with Lloyd George opposite), and he has a shiny foot which I know that Tory Members of Parliament traditionally 'rub' for luck. The chamber itself is much smaller than I recall from television viewings.

I look across the chamber. This too, is a place that I recall from watching Prime Minster's Question Time on the television, what now seems to me to be a lifetime ago. It seems so small, somehow strangely intimate for a place that could be so adversarial; with its ranks of green-leathered seats facing each other—those of the Party in power on one side, and the Opposition on the other—now abandoned and empty, not even the ghosts of argument whispering in my mind as I see my ultimate destination across the chamber.

This at last, is the place I have come to be.

Now, I know.

I stride purposefully across the chamber, between the despatch boxes of the Prime Minster and the Leader of the Opposition—in the space where their arguments have traversed over the years, footsteps ringing in the emptiness. My footsteps sound like something else to my ears—like a sharp and determined, solitary handclap.

Harbinger

When I reach the chair, I brace my hands on its armrests—then turn, and sit slowly.

I am in the Speaker's Chair.

The Speaker of the House of Commons—the moderator of political discussion.

I look up at the public galleries above, now screened by reinforced plexi-glass since an onlooker threw bags of flour at a previous Prime Minster years ago. Then I look back at the empty seating areas for the absent Members of Parliament, hands again braced on the arm rests—and wait.

The chamber is deserted.

But they are here.

And they are somehow aware that I have arrived. Perhaps the sounds of my footsteps, echoing through the empty corridors. Perhaps it is something else that has made them aware.

Fearful, they have remained in the shadows—hiding in the alcoves and in the shadowed places. I hear them whispering, but I do not call out or respond. I remain where I am, waiting in the enshrouding gloom.

Do I sleep?

Perhaps. But there are no dreams.

I am only aware that there has been another great passing of time—and suddenly I am now aware that a bottle of mineral water has been placed on the floor before me while I slept. I consume it in one draft.

There are shadows here in the Chamber now.

Ragged and barely discernible shapes are sprawled or crouched in the seats. I can sense who they are. Most are wearing what used to be business suits. Even in the dark it is possible to see that they are ragged and frayed.

These are the former leaders, the politicians, the spokespersons, the rulers—and although I can barely make out their faces in this gloom, I can see that they are still occupying the seats formally allocated to their political parties in this debating chamber, despite the fact that such representation is now redundant in a land where those who were once governed are—it would seem—no longer resident.

Has it really been so long since I embarked on this journey?

Can all this have happened in such a short space of time—or has it taken me decades to arrive here?

Someone is emerging from the greater darkness in the centre of the Chamber, in the place between the despatch boxes.

That figure stops fearfully about thirty feet from where I sit. I can not see its face, but I recognise this person as a once significant and powerful political figure. He stands for a long time, trying to compose himself—looking from right to left, left to right—at the shadowed and ragged sprawl of those who remain. Perhaps he is waiting for me to speak first. Finally, he rallies to find that now fragile composure—and speaks.

He has been chosen by those who remain to speak on their behalf—chosen by all sides once divided, but now able at this moment to find those differences irrelevant.

He asks me what has happened.

He asks me where everyone has gone.

When I do not answer—because the time is not yet right to do so—he tells me that those who were elected to political power and those in political opposition are all that is left.

"Why?"

I do not respond.

Those who were present in the Houses of Parliament were unaffected—they remained. Others, scattered throughout the country, were also unaffected. Alone, bewildered, afraid—many of them have done what I, apparently, have done. They have made their way here.

"Why?"

Is it the same throughout the country? Is it like this in the rest of the world? Will they be able to leave—or must they stay?

The silence that follows is longer.

And then, he asks—who am I?

They all know, they all 'feel' that I am 'different'—that I have been sent.

But sent for what?

And by whom?

Please—will I tell them who I am, and what has happened?

Can't I see what they've resorted to?

Scrambling through the deserted streets and empty buildings, hunting for a slowly diminishing food supply in a country—perhaps a world—without power, without electricity, without communication and any means to sustain themselves.

Good God, man! Don't I know what some of them have even resorted to...? But he cannot bring himself to say that forbidden word.

What must they do?

He is afraid, but he is not happy with my silence.

Even in the shadows, I can see anger and fear moving over his features—and even in these new and extreme circumstances, old habits of preserving power die hard. Struggling to regain composure, he turns to look back at the others in their own shadowed places. When there is no response from any of them, he again turns back to look at me.

What can they do—to make things better?

You're alone, I say at last.

He waits for me to continue—and when I do not, I seem him struggling to understand, trying to interpret the hidden meaning in these simple words.

He asks—is it always going to be like this?

Somewhere behind him, someone on the benches asks in a tremulous voice: "Must we stay?" There is real fear in his voice.

You will always be alone, I say.

Their leader says that he—that they—don't understand.

I say—*I know*.

For God's sake, man! Is that all you have to say? Just *tell* us what has happened—just *tell* us what is going on!

You have lost them, I reply.

His anger boils over. He rages at me, shaking his fists—demanding to know who the hell I am, who the hell I *think* I am.

No one, I say. *And everyone.*

Why you, he demands? Why you of all people—and who the hell has sent you?

I am the harbinger, I say. *This is the coming of the new way.*

Harbinger

He steps forward, shaking with anger—and opens his mouth to make another demand.
I say - *Now you only have yourselves.*
And then I am gone away.

William Meikle

THE UNFINISHED BASEMENT
BY WILLIAM MEIKLE

Dave Collins stood at the kerb and gave the house the once-over. From the outside it didn't look like much, but that was sometimes a good thing in this business. A quick flip, both interior and exterior, could polish the unlikeliest derelict. It wouldn't be the first time that Dave managed to turn a hundred grand profit on something that no one else had seen money in.

I've got a nose for it.

He'd heard about this one on the grapevine - a Fifties mock-Tudor on a corner lot that had gone to seed. It wasn't even on the market yet - Dave had a day's head start on the competition, and he intended to make the most of it.

First he made a quick survey of the outside. To his trained eye the structure looked sound. There would be some work needed on the guttering, and one of the rear windows needed replacing, but there was nothing to frighten him off. As he stood on the back lawn he felt a vibration run through him, like the *thrum* of a giant guitar string, but it passed as quickly as it had come. He made a mental note to check on any possible sewer work in the area, then went inside.

The ground floor looked like it hadn't been decorated since the house was built. Flock wallpaper

The Unfinished Basement

had peeled in places, exposing patches of damp beneath, but again it was nothing that had him worried.

She's an aging beauty. All she needs is some fresh make-up and new clothes.

The main living area surprised him. Where the rest of the house felt empty and neglected, he had the feeling that someone had left this room just seconds before. The second surprise was the large piano sitting dead centre on the polished hardwood floor. It looked to be a full sized grand in good repair, and Dave was at a loss to understand why the previous occupants had left it. But he knew from experience that pianos were a notoriously difficult sell in the trade.

Maybe it was just too big to be worth the trouble? Or warped and out of tune?

He ran a hand over the keyboard. The instrument rang and chimed. Somewhere below him the ground vibrated again.

There's definitely something going on down there that needs looking at.

Dave didn't have a musical bone in his body so there was no way he was going to be able to tell if the piano was salvageable. But he knew a man who might. And maybe the instrument would help squeeze even more profit out of the deal. As he left his footsteps on the hardwood floor set up a sympathetic vibration and the piano *droned.* He felt it rise through the soles of his feet.

It's as if the house is singing for me.

It wasn't an unpleasant sensation.

*

He signed the papers that same morning, and early the next day was back at the property with his contractors, knocking on walls and assessing the scale of the work that needed doing. They were just about to move down to the cellar when Dave's piano man arrived.

He'd used John Thorpe's experience before, and knew him as a quiet, steady man not prone to emotion, so Dave was surprised at the man's reaction to the instrument.

Thorpe whistled in appreciation as soon as he set eyes on the piano.

"This is a real find Mr Collins," he said, running a hand along the instrument's flanks as if it was a lover. "There's no maker's mark, but a craftsman put many weeks of love into this, no mistake."

"Just tell me it won't cost more to take away than it's worth," Collins replied.

Thorpe smiled.

"Mr Collins... it might just be worth more than you'll make on the house. Leave me with it for a bit and I'll let you know."

Collins joined Thorpe in smiling, and he still had the grin on his face as he led the contractors down to the cellar. But his good humor was to be short lived. Where the upstairs of the house held an air of faded grandeur, down here it was as dark and dank as a cave. The single lightbulb flickered, sending a spluttering strobe effect through the cellar. There was no plasterboard on the walls, or flooring on the ground. Instead it looked like the area had been hewn

The Unfinished Basement

straight out of the bedrock; the appliances and old furnace looking strangely out of place in a space that could easily have been made to contain something *older*.

The three contractors he had brought with him stood at the foot of the wooden stairs, looking to Dave for guidance. He saw the look in their eyes, and felt the same concern himself. What had been an opportunity to make quick easy cash had suddenly turned into a potential money pit, for no-one in their right minds would buy a house with a cellar in *this* state.

"Let's just get on and assess the damage," Dave said. "Maybe it's not as bad as it looks."

It was worse.

A dark, almost black, pool lay still and stagnant across the whole far end of the basement, an acrid odour rising from it that made all four men step back, hands to mouths. Over to their left, where the cellar stretched beyond the limits of the house above, white pallid plant roots hung from the ceiling, wafting in the air almost as if alive.

Collins stepped over and kicked at what passed for a furnace. His feet hit the casing... and kept going, knocking a large hole in the rusted metal.

One of the contractors poked with the tip of a knife at a timber column supporting the floor above. It went into the wood as if cutting into soft butter.

This is a disaster.

Thorpe chose that moment to start playing the piano in the room above.

Dave felt it first in the pit of his stomach, but soon his whole frame shook, vibrating in time with the rhythm. His head swam, and it seemed as if the walls of the cellar melted and ran. The lightbulb receded into a great distance until it was little more than a pinpoint in a blanket of darkness, and Dave was alone, in a vast cathedral of emptiness where nothing existed save the dark and the pounding beat.

Shapes moved in the dark, wispy shadows with no substance, shadows that capered and whirled as their dance grew ever more frenetic. He tasted salt water in his mouth, and was buffeted, as if by a strong, surging tide. He gave himself to it, lost in the dance, lost in the dark. He had no conception how long he wandered, there in the space between. He forgot himself, forgot where he was, in a blackness where only rhythm mattered.

He only came to his senses when Thorpe stopped at the end of the piece. Something roiled in the pit of his stomach. Collins headed for the stairs at a run, and made it as far as the kitchen sink before he lost his breakfast in a steaming bundle. He slowly became aware that the contractors were in a similar state, and when he went back to the main room he found Thorpe slumped over the piano in a stupor.

He had to shake the man twice before he stirred, coming up as if out of a deep sleep.

He looks worse than I feel, Dave thought.

The contractors had already fled by the time Dave dragged Thorpe to the front door and sucked in welcome fresh air.

"What did you do?" Dave whispered. "What the hell did you do?"

Thorpe didn't answer. Dave noticed the man staring intently at a sheaf of papers in his hand. At first he thought it was a musical score, but a quick glance showed that it was what looked like random scrawls, strange groups of lines and dots.

Thorpe shuffled the papers, folded them, and put them in an inside pocket.

"I found them inside the piano," was all he would say. "I'll do some research on the instrument and get back to you. Just don't move it anywhere. It's precious."

Dave had no intention of going *near* the piano. He turned to tell Thorpe that, but the man was already scurrying away down the driveway.

Dave closed the door behind him and turned his back on the house. As he went down the path he thought he felt a vibration under his feet, and his stomach rolled over. He went home and fell into a fitful sleep. He dreamed of dark pools and ringing chords.

When he woke the next morning it was amid a tangled mess of sweat-damp sheets and he was more tired than ever. He dragged himself to the office only to be told that his contractors had, to a man, resigned rather than return to the old house.

I know just how they feel.

He spent the day finding any excuse he could to stay away from the building, but the sound of the piano continued to reverberate in his head whenever he found a moment of quiet. He had just about determined to head for a bar and attempt to drink it away when he got a phone call from one of his competitors.

"Dave? Phil Johnson. I thought I'd check out the Fifties Tudor, but it seems you got there first. Did you know there's someone still living there? I took a look at a new one on the market across the road, and they said there was someone in the Tudor last night, and the piano playing kept them awake for hours."

The bar seemed like a good idea again, but the call of money was stronger. Dave couldn't afford to take a big hit on the Tudor house. Piano or no piano, the renovations were going to have to start.

He drove straight over.

He wasn't surprised to find Thorpe sitting on the stool by the keyboard. The piano-man looked like he hadn't slept since the day before. He looked up from the keyboard and waved the sheaf of papers towards Dave.

"I know what you've got here," Thorpe said. "You have to demolish this place. Raze it to the ground and concrete over the ashes."

Dave didn't get time to ask why. Thorpe tried to stand but his legs gave way and he tumbled, insensate, to the floor. The thud as his head hit the boards caused the piano to ring and thrum in sympathy.

*

Dave spent the whole evening in the E.R. while doctors fussed and fiddled over a still-unconscious Thorpe. As the night passed an air of deepening worry grew, and by the time Dave came back from a fruitless search for coffee at eleven-thirty the worry had turned to sad resignation.

The Unfinished Basement

"There's nothing we can do for him," a tired doctor said. "He's lapsed into a coma, and the cancer might take him at any time."

"Cancer?"

The doctor nodded.

"End stage... very near the end. I'm surprised he was mobile long enough to get here. How long has he been bedridden?" It came from so far out of left field that Dave didn't understand the question, let alone be able to answer it.

The rest of the night was reduced to a jumble of snatches of sleep stolen in waiting rooms and bad food in the hospital canteen. Thorpe was *stable* according to the doctors, but they gave little hope of him waking. Dave was near ready to head for home and his own bed when he was called into Thorpe's room.

"He's asking for you," the doctor said. "He says it's important. But he may not live long enough to tell you."

Dave could not stop the shock showing as he walked into the room and looked at the shell of a man on the bed. If he hadn't known better he'd have thought he was in the wrong room... the *thing* on the bed looked soft and pulpy and somehow *decayed*. But it was Thorpe's striking blue eyes that looked out of the sweat-drenched face, and the piano man's voice that spoke.

He had the sheaf of papers clutched to his chest.

"I know what you have there," he whispered. Flecks of blood showed at his lips. "It's all in these papers."

"Shush man," Dave said, moving to stand at the side of the bed. "Save your strength."

"It's too late for me," Thorpe said. "But not for you. I told you. Raze it to the ground Mr Collins. Burn it, then make sure nothing else is ever built on the spot."

Dave didn't get time to respond. Thorpe's eyes rolled up in their sockets and he fell back, unconscious once again. The doctors ushered Dave back out into the corridor, but on his way he lifted the sheaf of papers and stuffed them into his jacket pocket.

"I'd go home sir," the attending nurse said. "It's doubtful that your friend will wake up again. We have your number. We'll ring if there's any change."

Dave took his weary body home and fell, fully clothed into bed.

Sleep wouldn't come. His mind filled with images, of dark pools and pale roots, of Thorpe's greasy skin and the blood, too red, bubbling at his lips. He rose, unrested, in the early hours and made a pot of coffee.

It was then he remembered the papers. He took them from his jacket and smoothed them out on the table. The top page had been ripped from a diary and was dated March 29th, 1959.

I had visited several Neolithic tombs, in Carnac, in Orkney and on Salisbury Plain. This gave the same sense of age, of a time long past. What I hadn't expected, what was completely different, was the overwhelming feeling that this place was in use. The walls ran damp and there was a stale taste in the air

The Unfinished Basement

but there was no sign of moss or lichen on the walls - only softly wafting roots, milk-white and smooth like mouse-tails.

Roger moved over to one wall and held the flashlight closer.

"Here," he said. "Here's why I called for you."

The wall was covered in small, tightly packed carvings. At first I thought it might be a language, but it was none that I recognised from my studies, indeed, it bore no resemblance to anything I had ever seen before.

""I can't make head or tail of them," Roger said. "But I believe they hold the secret."

The remainder of the papers seemed to be a transcription of the afore-mentioned symbols, page after page of dots and lines that looked like gibberish to Collins. But whoever had written the diary entry had done better. Tagged on at the end after the notation were two more lined pages, dated March 30th 1959

Roger drummed his fingers on his piano, a martial beat, only a few seconds long. The piano rang in sympathy... and the answer came to me, all at once.

"It's not a language... it's a musical notation."

Roger merely looked at me in astonishment as I jumped out of my chair and headed for the piano. I spread the transcribed papers over the top.

"Look. These lines, separated into groups corresponding to quavers, minims and crotchets… but it's not music as such… there is no sense of a scale."

Roger drummed his fingers once more, and again the piano resonated in sympathy.

I moved him off the stool and sat down at the instrument.

"So if it's not music… it must be rhythm," I said. "Rhythm and vibration."

I shuffled the papers and placed them on the music stand in front of me.

"How do you know where to start?" Roger said.

"I don't. Let us just see if I am right first."

I picked a solid minor chord, and began striking the keyboard in time with the rhythm transposed on the pages. Almost immediately I felt the sympathetic resonance rise from the chamber beneath.

"It's working," Roger shouted. But I was already lost in a world of pounding chords.

Something was far wrong. I knew it at an intellectual level. But the music controlled me deeper than that, in the hindbrain where the evolutionary equivalent of a gibbering monkey hit a log with a stick and enjoyed the noise. My hands pounded the keyboard, hands clenched into fists. The beat sped up a notch and the walls shook, loose mortar falling from the ceiling.

Just as I felt I could go no further, the beat slowed, mellowed.

The Unfinished Basement

My head swam, and the walls melted and ran. The fireplace receded into a great distance until it was little more than a pinpoint of light in a blanket of darkness, and I was alone, in a vast cathedral of emptiness. A tide took me, a swell that lifted and transported me, faster than thought, to the green twilight of ocean depths far distant.

I realised I was not alone. We floated, mere shadows now, scores... no, tens of scores of us, in that cold silent sea. I was aware that Roger was near, but I had no thought for aught but the rhythm, the dance. Far below us, cyclopean ruins shone dimly in a luminescent haze. Columns and rock faces tumbled in a non-Euclidean geometry that confused the eye and brooked no close inspection. And something deep in those ruins knew we were there.

We dreamed, of vast empty spaces, of giant clouds of gas that engulfed the stars, of blackness where there was nothing but endless dark, endless quiet. And while our slumbering god dreamed, we danced for him, there in the twilight, danced to the rhythm.

We were at peace.

I came to lying on the floor beside the piano. The first thing I was aware of was the pain in my hands; my knuckles bloodied and torn. At some point I had vomited, and the sweet sickly odor drove me away and up to my feet. The door to the cellar creaked and I heard stumbling footsteps headed downstairs. I called after Roger, but there was no reply.

I followed as quickly as I was able, stumbling down into the dark room.

But there was no sign of my friend, just a white sticky trail leading straight to that dark pool in the corner.

I fled back upstairs.

That was an hour ago. I have fortified myself with whisky, and on completion of this memoir I shall once more venture downstairs. It knows I am here... I have felt its vibrations. But if my friend is still there somewhere, I must go to his aid.

Collins turned the last page over, but it was blank. His gaze kept turning back to the scrawls and scratches on the papers.

Rhythm and vibration?

It made no sense at all to him, and he was too tired to think. He drained his coffee just as his phone rang, causing him to jump and spill the dregs over the papers on the table.

It was the hospital.

"He's gone?" Dave asked.

There was no answer at the other end for some time.

"Not exactly sir." He recognized the voice of the nurse he had spoken to earlier. "He's gone all right... his bed is empty, and we can't find him anywhere."

A sudden chill hit the back of Dave's neck, bringing with it a whiff of damp and mold that he recognised all too well. He turned, just in time to see a pale bloated arm raised above him. It smacked into the side of his head and Dave fell sideways. His temple hit the table and darkness took him down and away. He went thankfully.

The Unfinished Basement

*

When he woke it was to thin morning sunshine washing across the kitchen floor. He stumbled to his feet, having to climb up the table-leg to keep balance. He had to stand still and quiet for long seconds before the dizziness abated.

The transcribed papers were gone from the table, only a rectangular clear patch in a drying coffee stain showing where they had been. And there was something else—a white viscous fluid, disturbingly seminal, that was tacky to the touch. A trail of it led to and from his apartment door.

Thorpe. And he's heading for the house. Raze it to the ground? Over my dead body.

He was hampered by nausea and dizziness, but the thought of the house burning, and his investment money along with it, got him on the move. He drove through the early morning, hoping he wasn't too late, his mind full of the thought of burning.

It was a momentary relief to find the house still standing, but as soon as he turned off the car engine he heard the thumping martial rhythm of the piano. Even out here on the lawn he felt his head spin and threaten to send him back to the rushing tide of oblivion.

He stuck fingers in his ears and made for the door. Even then he felt the beat through his feet. He pushed through the open door.

At the same instant the music stopped and the house fell deathly quiet. He ran into the piano room just in time to see the cellar door swing shut. There was a moist *slumping* sound from the stairs on the other side. He walked across the floor, kicking aside coffee stained papers, and listened.

What if he's taken gasoline down there? He could burn the place down around me.

Despite his better judgement he opened the door and moved to the top of the stairs. The smell hit him immediately... the same dank odour he'd been smelling since he first went down into the basement.

"Thorpe. Come back up here. Let's talk about this."

There was no answer. He went down three steps. The single light-bulb sputtered and flickered, revealing only a trail of white mucus stretching down the stairs and off out of sight across the cellar floor.

"Thorpe?"

There was still no answer, but *someone* was down there... he could sense it. He stepped down to the cellar floor. The only noise was a soft *hiss* from the lightbulb overhead.

"Thorpe?" he called.

In answer there was a *splash* from the pool at the far end of the cellar.

There's no way I'm going over there.

But his legs thought otherwise. He stepped slowly forward, taking care not to step in any of the pale slime that showed him Thorpe's path. It led straight to the dark pool of water.

There was another splash, and something white moved in the darkness.

The Unfinished Basement

"Thorpe? Is that you?"

Two more steps took him to the edge of the pool.

He looked down into the water.

What he saw there sent him screaming for the stairs, out into the world in search of as much gasoline as he could get his hands on.

Later, as he watched the house burn, he knew he would never forget the sight of the white bloated mass that sank slowly into the pool, receding into some far depths where shadows surged in the tide... and all the way down as it descended, Thorpe's startling blue eyes staring back up.

ALIEN LOVE BY NANCY KILPATRICK

My lover is an alien. Not a person from another culture, but a being from another planet.

Many women feel that way about men, of course, and vice versa; it's a statement of how disparate the genders often seem to one another. But that's not what I'm talking about. I'm talking about a real alien. A being unlike any other that walks this planet.

I'm not a patient in a mental hospital, writing this on scraps of toilet paper, and I'm not some SoHo performance artist who wants to shock and enlighten. I'm just a woman, an ordinary human being. And because of destiny, I managed to hook up with Thomas, or at least that's the name I call him, since the sounds he makes are enough like that name that I find it comforting.From the start I'll admit that I've always had a fascination with extraterrestrial life. That may taint some of what I'm about to say. Even though the majority of North Americans if not citizens of this planet believe that intelligent life exists in space, admitting to that seems tantamount to implying eccentricity at best and lunacy at worst. I will also acknowledge that I went through a period of time—about a year actually—when my marriage was breaking down where I'd drive around Philadelphia at night in my little silver Toyota, searching the skies.

Alien Love

Of course, as Fox Mulder would have been the first to tell us, a city is the last place where a space ship would land. The fact that I, like most people, know that didn't stop me from looking. But then I was close to a breakdown. Whenever I traveled on business or for pleasure, I'd rent a car and drive around—in Atlanta, in Phoenix, in Stanford, Connecticut. I did not see any ships or any aliens. I was not a passenger on one of the commercial aircraft where the pilots saw alien vessels trailing their Boeings. I did not visit that town in the Yukon where the entire population saw lights that were not the aurora borealis streak across the sky for several nights in a row. I have never been aboard an alien craft, either voluntarily or as a kidnap victim. At least not that I remember.

That year of searching the skies was an anomaly in my life. And when the divorce was finalized and I began to heal, I read Carl Jung and something he said, about space ships and extraterrestrial life being symbolic of a search for the divine and a latent desire for wholeness, well, that made sense to me.

Besides Jung, I read a lot of science fiction. There seems to be several theories of why these beings come to Earth. Foremost is to make contact. Another reason is to keep tabs on us, the techno-idiots of the universe. To take us over is a third, and to intermingle and create a new species is last but not least. But there's another reason they come here, at least with Thomas there seems to be. We met in Toronto. I was there on business, staying at one of the big hotels on Lake Ontario where the computer conference was being held. It was summer, a pleasant evening, and I decided to take a walk along the harbor of this notoriously safe city.

The sun had just set, but the sky was still light. Sail boats dotted the water, and to my left I watched one of the ferry boats carrying people from the mainland to a five mile strip of terra firma called Toronto Island. I walked slowly along the flagstoned harbor path and stopped to rest against the ropes that acted as a barrier between land and water.

We've all had that feeling, of someone staring at our back. In the twilight, I sensed him. And turned to my right. Coming along the path was a man with white hair in a light-colored suit. He was not old, but in his late thirties, my age, or so it seemed to me then, although then as now I cannot clearly recall his face, and he does possess a timeless quality. His body emitted some type of invisible energy that drew my attention. I know that sounds very New Age, but believe me, other than that year of living dangerously close to the border of breakdown, I normally have my feet firmly planted on the ground.

When he reached me he just stopped and turned, so that he, too, stood facing the water. It was as though we were old friends who didn't need words to communicate with one another. We simply stood there, inches apart, shoulders almost the same height. Now, I do not normally talk with strangers, except in a crowded place, like a bank, or a restaurant lineup, and then it's cursory and polite. I'm not paranoid, simply cautious. Being in a strange city usually inspires extra caution. And since there were no other people along the waterfront, at any other time I would have walked away.

Alien Love

Why did I stay there? I've thought about it a lot. There's the obvious—I was lonely. But loneliness has never been enough reason to cause my good sense to abandon me before, other than my search for space ships, and I think I've explained that. With all the pondering I've done, though, I still can't honestly say what kept me there, other than that I felt something happening that I liked. It was as if the level of iron in my body had been seriously depleted and I hadn't been aware of it. Then, suddenly, my receptors were open and reaching out towards this being to be replenished. I know that sounds vampiric of me, and I suppose that our relationship is like that in a way. But there's more to this relationship. Much more.

But that first evening, we stood at the water's edge until the sky darkened and the new moon rose. I was keenly aware of him, the intensity of the life that pulsated from him. That intensity left me afraid to actually look at him. But when I did turn, he turned also, mirroring me, as if he were a mime. I stared into pale almond eyes that seemed to darken then lighten as I watched them. They enlarged and emitted a warmth that cocooned me from head to toe. Had he touched me physically the sensations could not have been stronger. I found myself gasping, overwhelmed by a kind of passion I had not envisioned existed. It was like orgasming on the sidewalk, and I was both afraid and excited. Suddenly, he turned. Whatever energy connected us connected us still. As he walked away, I was pulled along, behind him, by invisible bonds.

Nancy Kilpatrick

We walked and walked, as far as the harbor path would take us, then through a park, then to a marina. At the far end finally he boarded what I can only describe as a black metallic vessel that blended with the night, so well, it seemed to be invisible. I trailed behind him up the midnight gangplank, my heels clacking against the metal, still engulfed by these silky yet invisible threads of passion kneading me. Once down below deck, he shut the door and we were plunged into complete darkness.

It was at this point that I became aware of being very afraid. I've never felt comfortable in the dark, and there I was, in a peculiar, isolated place, with a stranger, in a strange city. I tried to speak but found I couldn't form words. I imagine this is what aphasia feels like: you know the concept you are trying to get across, but can't quite remember how to say the word. Although I was not physically bound, I might as well have been, because I was unable to move.

My eyes became accustomed to the metallic blackness. I couldn't actually see anything identifiable, but I had vague impressions, one of which was this man—for a few moments more I still thought of him as just a man—standing there, facing me, silently. I realized my heart was beating hard, and my lungs filling and expanding rapidly. Chilly sweat coated my body, and my limbs trembled. I wanted to ask him what he was doing to me that left me immobile. I wanted to know why he had brought me here and what he had planned. I wanted to know who, no what—because by then I began to realize that he was not quite human—he was. I wanted to ask him why he had no scent. Of all the other questions, that was the one that startled me most when I became aware of it. I simply could not smell him. Stainless steel has a smell. Even plastic has an odor. And certainly anything organic. But he did not. And although my own sense of smell has never been outstanding, it isn't bad and I recognized that scent was the one sense missing.

Finally, when I thought my heart might not be able to take the tension any longer, a sudden wave of calm rolled over me. I realized he was flowing closer—that I could sense.Oddly enough, the closer he got—as he had at the harbor—the more my anxiety turned to pleasure, and the pleasure to passion. When he reached me physically, I gasped. He lit up—that's the only way I can put it—phosphor in a metallic night sky. The light took the shape of his body, but more than his body, as if what the psychics call an 'aura' was visible and his solid molecules actually mingled with the air molecules and I could see that there was no clear division between them. There were colors I recognized, but many I did not, as though he used a different spectrum and my eyes could finally see what they normally were unable to distinguish. Colors that had the intensity of red and yet were more like combinations of blackened silver and yellow and peach, although that does nothing to describe them or do them justice. I found the visuals fascinating. So much so that I did not at first realize that his body was enfolding mine. The colors that he vibrated encased me and then I felt them enter every pore in my flesh. But they entered me as a scent, like thousands of tiny vapors working their way into every pore. The scent was new to me, more pungent than sweet or tart, greater than anything I had encountered before. It was a penetration I could not have envisioned and one that kept me on the edge of something akin to climaxing in a delicious, delirious state of almost being sated. A state where time and space became meaningless and all that mattered was this essence that filled my body through my pores as, by way of a poor analogy, the smell of a rose would have filled my nasal cavities and lifted my spirits. And through it all I heard him. And yes, it is likely that in my fragile humanity I reached out and used the sounds to form a name, to find something familiar...

In the morning—and I must skip to morning because I cannot honestly remember details—I found myself lying on the path, at the harbor, where I'd first seen him. There was no sign of him. No sign that he had even been there. And, of course, my sanity returned. With it, anxiety resurged. It wasn't long before I was at a police station, filing a complaint with them, trying to describe a man I could not remember visually with a crime that seemed like rape but which I could not articulate.I scanned hundreds of photos. The dark metallic ship was gone, of course. The police dusted the harbor ropes for fingerprints and found only mine. And the worst part of it all was that a physical examination revealed no signs of intercourse. I couldn't bring myself to tell them that the entry had been through my pores as well as every orifice of my body, but I did ask for a skin analysis. Nothing unusual showed up. And by the time the DNA results of blood and vaginal secretions finally

Alien Love

came through, I was back home. Only my own DNA was present.

That encounter occurred a year ago. I went through much trauma and soul-searching. I even saw a psychiatrist for a few sessions. Until the next new moon.

Every month, at the new moon, Thomas shows up, no matter where I am. I could be home alone in my living room. At a movie with friends. Working overtime. Traveling again. Each time it is the same. I am drawn to him, as if my body needs to recharge. He takes me somewhere where we can be alone. And I go willingly. And then he is recharging as well, with what he gets from me, through my pores. Whatever that is. I still don't know.

I have been afraid. Utterly terrified to be precise. Never with him, but between the times when I see him. And what terrifies me most is how much I long for him.

It took me three months to realize it was the moon that determined when he would appear, which leads me to feel that the moon plays on him as it plays on our tides. Perhaps his home is a moon, black and metallic. It took time to see the symbolism of that beginning the new moon represents. It took time for me to realize exactly how I have changed.

Needless to say, I am different. Whereas once I was outgoing, now I live only for those hours when I am with Thomas. I am obsessed, yet to my family, friends and colleagues I am the same woman I have always been. I go about my business and interact in familiar patterns. But my life is like an orange with the juice extracted from it. When we are together

Thomas gives to me, but he also takes from me and leaves an ever-hollowing shell behind. Oddly enough, I do not hold this against him. Somehow, it makes me love him more.

Physically, I am constantly dehydrated. That, of course, leaves me exhausted, but then, as the new psychiatrist says, I'm depressed; Prozac doesn't help. I have many of the symptoms of HIV and yet the tests are negative and no virus can be isolated. The doctors are stymied by that, and more so by what they have labeled a noxious odor my body emits. These colors with their wondrous fragrance that Thomas leaves inside me seem to transform into something not so pleasant to others. To hear people talk, you would think I was rotting inside, and one day I will wake up and be nothing but decay. But the decay smells sweet to my nostrils, because it reminds me of him.

And Thomas? Each time I see him I know he is stronger. His colors smell brighter, more vivid, and the range has expanded. He lives while I die. It seems unfair, and yet what he gives me is all that has meaning in my life. All that keeps me going. All that matters. And I would gladly give him every drop of my existence for one more breath of that alien scent.

It amazes me now that I spent an entire year searching the heavens for aliens, when one was walking this planet. Is that why he found me, because I searched for him? What he shows me I realize is his home planet, which must be so far away, perhaps in another time or dimension. I do not know exactly why he has left there and come here, but I feel he is the only one of his kind and that he has found a way to survive. I feel, too, his loneliness. Except for me

Alien Love

he has no contact, although I could be wrong. It's possible that every night he absorbs the essence of another who acts like a battery providing him energy, until the battery is dead and is either recharged, or a replacement is found. But I don't think so. I think that it is my essence he wants and needs, and my greatest worry is what he will do when I'm gone. Because I know in my heart that he does not understand death. On his planet, wherever he comes from, life continues in a dark, ever-changing form. It is simply a matter of revitalizing. He cannot know that we poor mortals who strive for wholeness do so in order that we might blend with the whole, with the divine, with what is larger than us and absorbs us when our frail bodies can no longer contain who we are.

What I have come to understand is that as he takes me in, I take him in, and it's possible that internally he is changing as I am. Why do I think that? Because I can now smell him. And he smells sweet. Very very sweet. The sweet essence of all life itself, the life of this planet Earth. It makes sense to me; that's why he has come here.

To take us in.

David A. Riley

A GIRL, A TOAD AND A CASK
BY DAVID A. RILEY

The girl stretched a finger towards the toad, her head cocked to one side.

"Come on, little swee-ty," she cajoled, meeting its expressionless eyes with innocence - pale blue, glistening innocence as pure as the cloudless sky. Cool shadows hemmed them in on the edge of the pool where Salwayn knelt on a stepping stone edged with moss, the toad half sunk in the dark water only feet away from her, unmoved by its discovery.

"Come on." Salwayn felt the joints of her knees strain beneath her leggings as she bent even further, steadying her balance on the uneven stone. Aunt Lussa told her again and again to watch out for toads like this. Prime toads, she called them. Rich with juices. Fattened by flies, by dragonflies. Bigger than both her fists put together, its warty skin looked thick, impervious, toughened like well-tanned leather moist with wax, Batrachian and strange. She stretched out, breath held tight as she inched her fingers nearer, hardly daring to think she'd caught it yet.

Not yet. Not yet. Not just quite yet, she thought to herself as she tensed her calves.

Cold water sucked at her legs as she plunged, thigh-deep, into the pool, mud clinging to her feet. Its tiny heart beat with the disquieting speed of a faster

A Girl, A Toad And A Cask

time scale as Salwayn grasped the toad in her strong fingers, gripping it firmly, but carefully, mindful of the fragile bones beneath its flesh.

"Now, now," she soothed. She straightened and brought the toad's face nearer her own. "No one will hurt you."

Yet, she thought, her imagination tinkling with a secret laughter, her face and voice subdued. "No one will hurt you, sweety."

She headed home, earlier thoughts of collecting herbs and the poisonous spore of Heartwrench, Spleen and Deathbed weeds forgotten now. Aunt Lussa would be pleased with this, she knew. At twelve winters old she was mature enough to appreciate the uses to which her adoptive mother, teacher and guardian would put the creature in the kitchen of their home.

She climbed till she left the woods behind. The sun beat hot on her back and arms as she shielded the toad in the shadow of her chest. She was too pleased to feel the ache in her legs as she hurried up the slopes.

*

"Duncan, ease your speed. We'll rest a spell. The day's too hot. It'll kill the horses if we press on." Frowning through dust caked on his scarred face, Captain Gordon eased himself out of his saddle. The tawdry remnants of his mercenary troop, all ten of them, followed him onto the sun-baked roadside, weapons clanking as they discarded swords, crossbows and spears to stretch their limbs. His sergeant, Duncan, went to check what remained of their rations.

"We've not much left," Duncan reported a short while later. "We'll need more soon. Two days, no more, and we'll be forced to eat the leather of our saddles."

"Two days from now we'll have found somewhere to plunder, don't worry. We'll have food enough then." Gordon's eyes narrowed. He nodded his head. "Perhaps we'll have no need to wait so long."

Duncan turned, his eyes following those of his captain to sweep the hillsides ahead of them till he, too, caught a glimmer of motion. Small. Hurrying. A single figure, racing uphill. "A girl?" His sharp eyes caught enough at this distance to hazard the guess.

"Perhaps." Less keen of sight, Gordon was non-committal. "Leastways there's sign of life. And where there's that there's almost sure to be a dwellin'. Or dwellin's."

"A village would do me fine. Filled with lumbering peasants, pigs and hens, a cow or two. That'd do me fine just now." The man grinned through the grime on his face, his calloused thumb aslant the pommel of the sword at his side. "After what we've been through even a large one would seem easy meat to me now." In leaner times, before he joined the mercenary trade, Duncan had been a brigand. He and the band he'd been a member of had plundered many a hapless village. Yokels were no match for a well-led band of armed men, used to handling swords and spears. Even an out of the way laird, with a part-time muster, would be a less than serious threat to hard-bitten mercenaries. Easy meat, as the Captain had said.

"Bran, mount your horse and run that bugger down," Gordon ordered. With the swiftest horse in their troop, Bran was in his saddle and away in seconds, a broad grin on his pockmarked face. The mercenaries watched him gallop off, the hoofs of his horse thundering as it tore down the winding track, then veered away across the hill towards the tiny figure in the distance.

Even as Bran hurried towards it, though, the figure passed beyond a copse of trees. Moments later Bran disappeared too.

"Should've run her down by now," Duncan muttered as moments lengthened and still no sign of their comrade, bearing his captive, reappeared over the hillside. "That bastard's prob'ly got her stretched beneath him."

Gordon grunted. He didn't doubt this was exactly what Bran was doing. No less would he have expected. It would help, at least, to make her talk when he brought her back for questioning. Besides, she was as good as dead. Still hunted by their enemies, they couldn't afford to let her live to give their pursuers information about them. Nor could they afford to drag her along with them. She'd only slow them down.

Duncan glanced at his captain, eyes slitted. "D'you ken he might've met with something he couldn't cope with?"

"Maybe. We don't know what's beyond that hill, do we?"

"If there's anything he can't cope with he'd've turned tail and ridden back to warn us. He's no fool to risk himself for no reason."

"Maybe." Gordon signaled for his men to mount. Doing likewise, he led them at a swift canter towards the hilltop. "We'll see for ourselves."

The sun, slanting low against the sky, sent shadows across the grassy hills. In a few hours they would be bedding down for the night. Maybe in a well stocked farmstead. And maybe not. Gordon had grown too disillusioned since the battle to hope for much. Even so, for all the gloom that soured his expectations, what they saw when they passed the copse and found the remains of their comrade, shook him.

Flies buzzed about the gaping hole where the mercenary's crotch had been. His eyes stared up in a sightless look of utter horror, frozen on a face from which all color had been drained. His hands were clenched in claw-like tangles, distorted beyond their normal shape by the agony of his death.

Duncan muttered an oath. His sword hissed from the well-worn scabbard at his side. "Search for her - search for her. And hack the bitch that did this down," he growled to the stunned mercenaries. They glanced at Gordon.

Dismounting, their captain trudged towards Bran's corpse. Flies blew up into his face as he knelt beside the body. Close to, the wound looked huge, as if a taloned paw had gouged deep into the man's groin and scooped the flesh from him, though nowhere could Gordon see where they had gone.

"She's taken his horse," Duncan bellowed.

Downhill more woods obscured their view. On horseback she could have got beyond the nearest of them long before they arrived. Standing up, Gordon said: "There's more to Bran's death than a girl's desperation. No girl could've caused the wound he has. No *normal* girl."

"Then what?" Duncan returned to Bran's corpse. "What else could have done it?"

"A beast, maybe?"

Slowly, the mercenary shook his head. His brows dripping beads of sweat he measured the span of Bran's wound against his own broad-fingered hands. "No beast," he muttered. "No beast could have done it. Not one around here." He straightened up and glanced down the hillside. "But a devil could. A devil could have caused that wound."

*

"Aunt Lussa! Aunt Lussa!"

Sprite-like, Salwayn leapt from the horse and raced towards the mound-shaped cottage that lay hidden between the trees that surrounded it. Long and low, dark windows looked out from its matted walls, slit-like and grim. She hugged the toad to her chest as she rushed through the narrow doorway and raced across the bare earth floor of the first two rooms, till she reached the kitchen at the back. Covered in straw, the ground was grimy with grease and scraps of food. Smoke filled the air. In the center, built upon ancient bricks, long cracked and blackened like lumps of coal, was a small wood-fire, over which, hung from chains suspended from a beam across the ceiling, iron cooking pots steamed and bubbled. Around the room were solid wooden tables, cupboards and chests. Earthen pots, crucibles, jugs, jars, bottles and bowls of glass were heaped on shelves. Most were filled with herbs, dried flowers and seeds. Others were filled with stranger and less wholesome things: preserved eyes, parts of skeletons, brains, lungs, hearts and intestines from various mammals, reptiles and birds.

"Aunt Lussa! I've got one! A huge prime toad."

"*And* what else, snippet?"

The voice, emanating from a large cask of dark wood in a corner of the room, was a querulous whisper, muffled by the lid pressed tight on top and sealed by wax.

"I threw it away," the girl exclaimed indignantly, as if she was shocked to think of keeping *that*. Her right hand still dripped blood, though it was beginning to thicken on her fingers into dark scabs. She glanced at them. "I had no choice. If I hadn't done what I did I could no longer have served you the way I do. What I took from him would have robbed me of the powers you have given me. You know that. You warned me what would happen if a man had his way with me. No man ever has. No man ever will. I treasure your gifts, Aunt Lussa, too much."

She flexed her fingers, so small, so frail, so weak. And yet...

*

A Girl, A Toad And A Cask

"Hell's venom!" Duncan slid from his horse and crouched above the fly-ridden object on the grass, his hands clenched tight. "This is where the bitch discarded Bran's..." His lips writhed, unable to voice the word. "She came this way, at least," he struggled finally, rising and turning to face the rest of the mercenaries, seated on their horses behind him, their weapons gripped uneasily as they scanned the woods at the bottom of the hill. There was a mixture of hatred and fear in their grim faces as they settled in an unsteady circle about the torn remains on the ground.

Steeling himself with an effort of will, Gordon said: "Remount, sergeant. We'll ride on till we find the bitch and string her up." His voice was hard, incisive, as he met the eyes of each of his men in turn. "The hand that mutilated Bran's body will be hacked from her arm and burnt before her eyes before we let her die." His eyes settled on Duncan's. "That I swear."

*

"Snippet!"

Placing the toad in a large bell-jar, Salwayn turned with a curious smile. "Snippet, wash the blood from your hands. There's work to be done. We have company. I sense them coming, moments away. They're friends of the man you killed."

For a moment Salwayn glanced at her hands. She flexed her fingers as if they were claws.

"Nay, child, forget it. What worked with one would fail with many. They'd hack you down before you killed a third of them. You have been taught too much for me to waste like that."

A small tremor of fear for the first time rippled across her face. Salwayn ceased the movements of her hands. Her eyes grew wide.

"If they find me, though, they will attack me, Aunt Lussa. Like the other one."

"Of course they will, my snippet, of course," Aunt Lussa's muffled voice went on. "That's why I want to use that toad you found. The first I've seen in years. 'Twas luck - or fate - or both, but now I'll teach you a trick for which that warty lump can be used." Aunt Lussa chuckled moistly, as if the diversion humored her, despite the danger. Oils seeped from the bottom of the cask as movements from within forced gaps between its wooden slats.

*

Weary though he was, Gordon refused to let this show as he led his men towards the cottage beneath the trees. Bran's horse could already be seen, chewing grass beside the elm-filled glade with an animal's disdain for the fate of its master. Whoever killed Bran and had ridden away on his steed had obviously done nothing to unsettle the beast. But what could have done what it did to Bran and still be human enough to leave his horse so calm it could placidly stand eating grass? Gordon narrowed his eyes suspiciously. The innocence of the scene worried him.

"Dismount," he ordered. "Jack, Robbie, look after the horses. The rest, move in on the cottage on foot. Spread yourselves out. Whoever's in there can't break out and get past us."

A scream rang from inside the cottage, loud and shrill. A young girl's scream. High-pitched, with a nerve-splitting terror that made the mercenaries' flesh turn cold.

"Hold still," Gordon warned them. "It may be a trap."

A young girl ran from the cottage, clutching the tatters of her clothes to her half naked body. Blood dripped from her hands.

"Help me! Please help me!" she pleaded, running towards the mercenaries.

"Halt!" Gordon shouted. But one of his men had already run forward. Reaching her as she stumbled on a tussock of grass, the sudden scream that burst from the mercenary's lips ended in an inarticulate gasp. He rolled away from her, his chest torn open. Ribs jutted from his flesh. In her hands the girl held his lungs in front of her.

Horror-stricken, Gordon shouted: "Kill her!"

Charging forwards, Gordon raised his sword for a stroke that would split the girl's head in two. But, before he was even a few strides from her, she flung the offal at his face and darted sideways, catching one of the other mercenaries with an upwards cut of her open hand, fingers like talons. They ran like knife blades through his flesh, cleaving bones and cartilage, flesh and veins bared to the air.

Gordon spun on the ball of his foot, the momentum of his sword stroke helping him turn. But again, with a speed that left him lumbering like a clod-footed oaf, the girl leapt with a curious, bowlegged gait past the nearest of the mercenaries, as they raised their weapons against her. She sprang as if by instinct for the least hot-blooded of the men. His scream was drowned in the blood that surged in a crimson flood from the opened artery torn from his throat.

Growling with anger, Duncan stabbed with a satisfyingly chunk into the base of her spine. He drew the sword from her, grunting at the effort, then stabbed her again. She had started to turn towards him by the time his second blow forced the blade in her chest. Blood bubbled from her lips.

"Die, bitch, *die!*" Duncan snarled. Triumph flooded his swarthy, overheated face.

But his blade stuck between her ribs. As she turned, its hilt was tugged from his hand. She leapt for him even as blood gushed from her. There was murder in her eyes, a murderous blood lust that temporarily overwhelmed the growing weakness her wounds spread through her. For a moment more she could act.

And attack.

Her hands snatched at the sergeant's face. They clamped about his temples till blood ran from them. Duncan reached for her arms to wrestle her from him and finish her off, confident that his own greater strength would be more than enough. Even as he gripped her his hands froze and he watched with growing horror as her thumbs began to arch towards his eyes. They quivered, bloody nails poised like spring-loaded hooks.

A Girl, A Toad And A Cask

"NO!" Duncan bellowed as he realized their purpose. They sprang, stabbing deep into his eyes, bursting through the tough outer membranes and cornea and jarring against bone, till they broke even that, penetrating and crushing the walls of his sockets. With a sickening, drawn-out crack, her hands parted the splintered bones of his skull.

Gagging with nausea as he charged, Gordon swung his sword in a sideways blow that struck the girl's neck and sent her head spinning on a crimson trail high into the air.

"Die! Die! *Die!*" The next blow cut both arms off at the wrists as the corpse of his sergeant collapsed in a heap on the grass. Again and again he hacked at her, chopping her down into a shapeless jumble of raw flesh.

One of his men moved to him as his arms, growing weary at last with the effort, began to slow.

"Cap'n, she's dead. You can stop now. I tell you, she's dead."

Hesitating, Gordon blinked his eyes, in a daze, realizing just how completely the bloodlust had gripped him.

He looked round at the remaining mercenaries. There were only six of them now. Incredibly, four of the ten who had got this far had been killed by a slip of a girl. He glared at her body, unable to believe that someone so frail could have accounted for so many seasoned fighters. "Let's see if there's owt worth eatin' in this place," he said at last. He turned with an effort towards the cottage, his limbs heavy.

"Captain!" A bearded, hook-nosed man with a past even murkier than most of Gordon's mercenaries, was stood by the dead girl. "What was it you killed?"

"What was it? Are you blind, man?" Gordon growled, too tired for senseless chatter. "You saw what it was."

"I saw what I thought it was," the man retorted gruffly. He jabbed his sword at the stew of blood-soaked flesh on the ground. "What's this, though, now? A girl or some kind o' toad?"

Gordon felt as if reality was wavering, distorting itself even as he looked. It *had* been a girl. Vicious, unbelievably strong, yet still a girl. Yet this thing, this tattered green abomination on the ground, wasn't her. He glanced at the man. "There's more to this than we understand."

"There's more to this than I want to understand, Captain. Give me a straight fight, man to man, and I know where I stand. But this thing - this thing stinks of something else."

"Witchcraft," one of the others muttered. "That's what it stinks of."

Gordon backed from the remains on the ground, what appetite he'd felt for whatever they might find in the cottage gone.

*

"Well done, snippet. You did well," the voice of Aunt Lussa whispered in the dark kitchen.

The girl crept back from the narrow window through which she'd watched the mercenaries.

A Girl, A Toad And A Cask

"They've killed it, though. What else can we do? They'll soon be here. "."

"Don't worry my pet. I can help you much more yet."

*

Gordon studied the cottage intently. Its thatched roof overhung its walls till it all but touched the ground, hooding its windows. There was no sign of life inside, though the building was so gloomy within that this meant nothing. The whole of Gordon's remaining company could have hidden inside and not been seen.

His men spread out on either side of him as Gordon cautiously walked towards it. If the place were empty it would at least provide them with shelter for the night and probably provisions. That alone was worth the risks that might remain.

Gordon strained his eyes, staring hard through the narrow doorway.

"Jock, you and Jamie rush inside. The rest of us will follow. Daggers only. The place is too cramped for anythin' else."

The two mercenaries sheathed their larger weapons and drew their dirks. Half crouching, they advanced. Without a sound, they rushed the final feet and flung themselves inside.

Moments later Gordon led the rest of his men in, daggers at the ready. For a second sheer horror checked their steps. Then Gordon lunged at the leering, maggot-ridden head of the creature that barred his way, splitting its face like a pus-filled turnip. Momentum carried him past the stricken *thing* as the rest of his men piled into the room. Another corpse, rotting and shrieking like a fiend from hell, crossed knives with one of Gordon's men, their blades clashing with a ring of steel. They parried once more, then the mercenary was gutted with an upward sweep that sliced open the mans tunic, burying itself in the base of his chest after spilling his bowels.

For a second Gordon stared at the bloodied knife as the creature backed away from the oncoming mercenaries. One of the men made a lunge at it, missed, and was felled by a blow to the crown of his head that bared his scalp. Then Gordon shouted: "Stop! All of you! Stop!" He recognized Jamie's bronze-hilted dagger in the creature's hand. He knew the creature could not have had time to kill and disarm Jamie before they burst in. He knew, though his eyes denied him the fact, that the creature had to *be* Jamie, his features distorted in some sorcerous way. "Stop fightin'! We're bein' deceived!"

His words went unheeded. First one, then another of the mercenaries stabbed at the rotting creature they saw before them, and twice Jamie drew back, evading their blows, before delivering a fatal stroke of his own.

As the last of them fell, his chest pouring blood from a well-aimed cut, Gordon and Jamie stared at each other. Gordon strove to see the reality beyond. Jamie, his features too hideous for anything to be read in them, uneasily returned the gaze of his Captain.

"For God's sake, Jamie, listen to me before you act. We've been deceived," Gordon said. "What I see,

A Girl, A Toad And A Cask

what all of us saw, it wasn't you and Jock, but fiends. *Dead* fiends. I don't know what you see, if you're bein' deceived as well, but it's me, Gordon. Your captain."

Slowly, uncertainly at first, Jamie lowered the dagger he'd raised before his face in defense.

"I see maggots, a death's head dripping decay," he whispered. "But I recognize your voice, Cap'n Gordon."

"Ignore what you see. Listen to what I say. We must keep together and press on, killin' anythin' that moves in this place. There's little more that can be done to deceive us."

Nodding his agreement, Jamie turned. He kicked the door into the next room open with so much force it almost shattered. Together they rushed forwards, weapons ready. Inside, a straw-filled mattress on a crudely constructed wooden bed stood by one wall. Elsewhere there was a bare table and a bookcase filled with fat, leather-bound volumes, almost shapeless with age as they bulged from their spines. A burnt-out candle stub stood on a stool by the bed. The dimly lit room's Spartan simplicity gave no hint as to who used it.

Gordon nodded at a door leading from it.

Again Jamie kicked it open.

Framed against the far end of the room stood a girl, one arm raised.

"Duck!" Gordon pushed hard against Jamie's back as he saw the bow in the girl's hand, an arrow aimed towards them. Too late. The shaft shot through the air, thudding hard into Jamie's chest. The mercenary fell with a groan.

"Damnation and blood!" Gordon raced, sword raised, across the smoke-filled kitchen, jostling pots on the ends of chains out of his way as he chased the girl. Discarding the bow, she fled from the doorway. He followed as she ran from the cottage, back towards the open ground at the front. For all her speed and lightness of foot, he was sure he had stamina enough to run her down, however long it took. Sooner or later she would tire.

A grim smile, psychotic in its tightness, drew back his lips as his feet thudded in pursuit. He saw the distance between them shorten as she darted up the hillside, too panic-stricken to leap onto one of the mercenaries' horses. Gordon knew then that he had her. She wouldn't make it to the brow before he ran her down.

His breath rasping in his throat, Gordon put on an agonizing spurt of speed which would shorten the distance quickly between them. Already she was stumbling, her legs losing their strength on the slope.

Half way up the hill things suddenly changed.

A line of cavalry appeared across the brow of the hill. His stomach became leaden with despair, as Gordon recognized their shields.

Gasping for breath, Gordon stopped in his tracks, his fist clenched with a feeling of despair about the hilt of his sword. He was doomed, and he knew it. He glared at the girl. She, too, had stopped, only yards away from him. Too far for his sword to reach her now. He let his weapon fall to the ground. For the next few seconds he knew his surrender would hold the cavalrymen back. Which might, he thought, reconciled to his fate, be long enough to do what he

A Girl, A Toad And A Cask

wanted to do before things changed. With quick movements he reached for the dagger at his side. He clenched its blade between his fingers even before the girl had time to realize his intentions. The knife spun twice as it sped through the air. On its second spin it struck, point first, deep in her chest.

As if this was a signal, the cavalrymen urged their horses forward. By the time they had passed on their way downhill only dark red, churned-up rucks of mud marked where the mercenary captain had stood. Onwards, down into the valley they surged in a ragged line, seeking any more of the mercenaries hiding there.

Surprised though they were at the carnage they found as some of the cavalrymen dismounted to search the cottage, it was explained away easily enough as a squabble amongst the mercenaries, probably over whose turn it was to rape the girl. This, at least, was what their captain had decided by the time he reached the kitchen at the back of the cottage.

"Ah!" His dark eyes spotted the large barrel in a corner of the room. Settling himself on a bench at the table, he ordered two of his men to drag the barrel nearer.

"Perhaps we'll find some wine to refresh ourselves with before getting on our way," he joked, relieved how easily they had accomplished their mission. "Crack it open for me and we'll see what's stored inside it."

Somewhere, as the cavalryman he'd spoken to drew a knife, they seemed to hear a scream. A strange, discordant, distant scream. Like an echo that existed inside their heads and nowhere else. For a moment the cavalryman hesitated. But it would have taken more than this to hold him back, especially at the prospect of wine.

His knife thudded deep into the seasoned wood. With a grunt he worked its blade free, then tilted the barrel forward. The sickening stench as a mucus-like bile dripped from the barrel and splashed across the floor made him grit his teeth in nausea. A moment later his stomach rebelled on him. His hands slipped. With a crash the barrel hit the ground. The metal bands holding it together burst open and the barrel collapsed. Its contents gushed in a dark brown, rancid, fetid mess across the floor.

The cavalrymen's captain leapt to his feet. In the midst of the filth, a hunched skeletal wreck of a thing lay curled and twitching in a fetus-like ball on the ground. It looked almost human, though painfully thin, with a large, round, ball-like head that twisted round on the stem of a neck. Strands of hair hung in slimy locks from the grizzled dome of its skull, almost hiding what there was of its blurred features, all of it covered in cancerous lumps of diseased flesh.

Two cavalrymen stepped forward, less squeamish than their leader. Their swords soon put a stop to the movements of its limbs with well-aimed chops to its head and chest.

"Whatever it was," one of them said, as they wiped their blades clean, "should've died long ago."

With a belch of gasses the cracked skull collapsed into a bubbling, slime-like affirmation of the cavalryman's words. The men stared at it, while outside on the lone hillside, Salwayn moaned. Her

A Girl, A Toad And A Cask

body collapsed into the toad-like shape she had all but forgotten. "Aunt Lussa!" she called, but her words were lost in a frog-like croak.

POLYP BY BARBIE WILDE

In the deep, dark, softly pliable depths of shiny moist and mucky pink, brown and white, it was stirring. Slowly emerging from the dream years. Waking up for the first time and yet always cognisant of something. Waiting for its moment to come. Its hour upon the stage. Biding time, space, sanity. Waiting, waiting. Leeching nourishment from the Host. Sucking energy out of the stuff that came from above. Imagining what freedom would taste like. Hmmm. Freedom. It tasted of blood. And lots of it.

*

Vincent, a tall, nondescript, worried-looking man in his forties, waited for his colonoscopy appointment with a weary inevitability mixed with mild anxiety. He hated the whole rigmarole and yet, what was there to hate, really? It was a lifesaver, this procedure and that's how he should look at it, dispassionately and scientifically. But Vincent was not exactly the dispassionate, scientific type.

Not that a colonoscopy was painful, or even that unpleasant. After all, some people would pay big bucks to have a flexible tube with a camera at the end of it thrust deep up into their bowels, but not Vincent.

Polyp

Having a colonoscopy every year was a pain in the … ah, well, the jokes would come thick and fast if he ever told anyone about it, but it was too humiliating, too embarrassing. His body had let him down, genetically that is, and because of a pretty frightening family history of colon cancer, he had to have an examination every year. Luckily, he had a top gastroenterologist to do it, so the dire possibility of getting a perforated bowel from the procedure was remote. Still, having a man joke with you while he was threading an enormous tube up your ass was not exactly fun and games, was it? It verged on the pervy and Vincent was, if anything, not the least bit pervy, not the least bit exceptional, not the least bit an outstanding man of his immediate circle, which may explain to a small extent why he had to endure all of the worry and anticipation on his own.

*

First he had to prepare for a couple of days. Day One: a low residue diet consisting of white bread, white meat, no fruits or vegetables, no dairy products, no fiber whatsoever. (Basically, the diet that is killing off the Western World.) Day Two: after a breakfast of white toast and coffee, he had to fast and drink plenty of liquids until the procedure the next day. During the afternoon of Day Two, he was required to consume what felt like gallons of an osmotic laxative called Klean-Prep, a sweetly foul-tasting liquid that would turn anything harboring inside his intestines into a veritable Niagara Falls of shit. Diarrhoea for a day— so virulent that his butt felt like he'd been passing acid.

Vincent used to drink to get through the ordeal: vodka martinis (sans olives, of course, because of the fiber) or white wine, but he eventually realized that the booze just made him feel worse the day of the procedure, not better. So, he decided to look upon the regime like a brief spell in detox, something that movie stars and royalty would shell out thousands for. Of course, if he was a movie star or royalty, he'd be in some swanky drying-out clinic in the countryside, with beautiful babes giving him seaweed massages and gently caressing his temples, not sitting on an uncomfortable plastic chair in a dingy, urine-colored waiting room outside the Endoscopy Department of St. Stephen's Hospital.

His stomach was so empty that it almost made him feel sick and his colon grumbled noises of protest from the brutal treatment of the Klean-Prep experience. The magazines on the table were at least six months old and there was a large, hopeful-looking television in the corner, but it was resolutely off, daring some brave soul to turn it on. But Vincent knew that late morning TV horror (property shows, cooking shows, phone-in shows, talk shows) would be the last thing in the world to cheer him up on this particular day.

Then, after a wait lasting around half an hour, a nurse came in to escort him to a large room dotted with curtained-off hospital beds—all equipped with blood pressure and heart rate monitors. The tall, powerfully-built nurse—whose nametag proclaimed her to be Ewomi Abayomi Sullivan —brusquely told Vincent to strip from the waist down. This was the

Polyp

kind of invitation that he would normally obey with alacrity, but from someone like Ewomi, who looked like she was permanently chewing on a wasp, it was more an order that he had to follow, or risk severe consequences to his manhood. As she left, Ewomi pulled the curtains around his bed for privacy, but they never quite met—gaping holes meant that if they really wanted to, the other nursing staff could spy on him. But, then again, why would they want to?

The faded, flower-patterned hospital gown lay on the bed. (Why flowered-patterned? Couldn't they have found a more manly garment for him to wear?) He had his pants halfway down to his knees when Ewomi bustled in without apology, holding what looked like Baby Doc Duvalier's leftover Bermuda shorts. A fetching shade of turquoise and made of some kind of disposable, papery cloth material, Ewomi announced that these were Vincent's "Dignity Shorts", a new PC innovation to prevent people of certain religious affiliations from getting too embarrassed by the inevitable discovery that hospital gowns open at the back are prey to.

Vincent put on the "Dignity Shorts" and felt anything but dignified. Rather than a handy opening in the front for any necessary trips to the toilet, there was a slit up the back , which provided easy access for Dr. Stanson and his long black tube of joy.

Ewomi returned with a couple of forms and fired some questions at Vincent. They were all the usual suspects: did he have the human variant of Creutzfeldt-Jakob disease? (Like he would know?) Did he have any dental work that might get knocked out by a careless elbow of the medical staff? What medicine was he on? Did he still have his tonsils, etc., etc., etc. (Why ask the same questions every year? Couldn't they just file his answers away in a computer?)

Finally Ewomi left him in peace. Vincent lay down on the bed and placed his hand on his lower abdomen. It felt a bit weird down there, although it was hard to judge, considering what he'd put it through in the last couple of days. And if he was an alcoholic, maybe his colon was too—desperate for an invigorating Margarita or a nice glass of crisp and fragrant Chablis.

Then there was movement. Down there. As if a ferret was scuttling through the winding passages of his bowels. Vincent nearly levitated off the bed in alarm, but after the initial shock, he put it down to some kind of fart-fuelled spasm.

*

Nestling in Vincent's colon—an area the length of 20 meters and, if flattened out, the surface of a football field—it was building up to the crisis point. It didn't want to hurt the Host, so its first tenuous attempts at freedom were cautious. It gathered its intelligence from the hundred million neurons embedded in the "second brain", or the enteric nervous system that controlled the gastrointestinal system of Vincent's body. Although only containing one thousandth of the neurons residing in the human brain, the "second brain" was capable of operating independently of both the brain and the spinal cord. But whatever had evolved in Vincent's gut was beyond the wildest

Polyp

dreams of the most unconventional of neurogastroenterologists.

*

Colleen, the head endoscopy nurse—a cheerful soul with an Irish lilt and a charming manner—pushed back the curtains so she could roll Vincent's bed into Endoscopy Room 4. He lay back and stared up at the ceiling as it whisked past.

Dr. Stanson—movie star handsome and prosperous-looking—was already in the examination room and a couple of other nurses bustled around, getting the equipment ready. The nurses connected Vincent to the blood pressure, heart rate and blood oxygen level monitors and then inserted a nasal cannula: a thin tube with two small nozzles that protruded into Vincent's nostrils that delivered supplemental oxygen.

Colleen asked Vincent to roll over on his left side, with his right arm lying down his body, the palm of his hand facing upwards, so she could administer his procedural medication intravenously into a handy vein in his wrist: a relaxing cocktail of buscopan (an anti-spasmodic, 20 mg), midazolam (a sedative, 2 mg) and pethidine (AKA demerol, a pain-killer, 25 mgs).

As Colleen injected the sedatives, Vincent felt their effects swirl through his bloodstream, instantly melting away his anxiety. He didn't give a damn anymore and it was wonderful. He wished he could have the stuff on a permanent drip feed 24-7. The one time that he opted out of sedation—because he had an important presentation in the afternoon and needed his wits about him—was a pretty appalling experience. It wasn't necessarily the discomfort that remained burned into his memory, but the abject humiliation.

Vincent was facing a color monitor that was connected by a lead to the endoscope camera, so he could watch the whole thing on the screen if he wanted to. It felt like he was in a cheap version of *Fantastic Voyage*, colonically journeying through his own body, loosey-goosey with the drugs, daydreaming about Raquel Welch in that tight-fitting white bodysuit of hers—floating around in a tiny ship in his circulatory system.

Vincent was grateful he didn't have to see the freak show behind him, as his doctor skillfully threaded the Pentax Zoom Colon 18 Endoscope through his anus, up his rectum, then his colon: sigmoid, then descending, then the transverse and ascending colon, then the cecum, and ultimately ending up at the last junction in town, the terminal ileum.

The only pain involved was when the doctor gusted some air through the tube to distend his colon. From a camera's eye view, his colon looked as corrugated as an accordion, or his ex-wife's clothes dryer extractor tube. Hard to spot incipient fleshy growths—or polyps, as they were known—amongst the ruffled terrain of the colon that way, so the endoscope was equipped with air tubes along with a camera and a lighting device. It also was able to squirt blue dye up there, a most disconcerting sight, but it helped the doctor spot any polyps, which, if left

Polyp

to themselves, might go over to the dark side and become cancerous in the future.

Vincent closed his eyes and tried to drift away with the drugs, but was alerted by Dr. Stanson saying something about a polyp. He opened his eyes and was a bit shocked to see a prominent growth attached to the side of his colon displayed on the monitor. *How do the damn things grow so fast?* Vincent wondered. He watched as Dr. Stanson attempted to perform a polypectomy by lassoing the polyp with the cold snare electric wire device that was also contained within the endoscope. Dr. Stanson looped the wire over the polyp and tightened it. He gave a little tug, which normally would slice the polyp away from the wall of the colon, at the same time cauterizing the wound, but the polyp stubbornly held on for dear life.

Then something happened. The polyp was loose, but when Dr. Stanson tried to suck the fleshy growth into the endoscope for retrieval and later biopsy, it refused to go in. It seemed to expand, right there, on its own.

Vincent was watching the show on the monitor with a drugged fascination. He heard the puzzled responses from the staff behind him as they tried to figure out what to do. Then a pain shot through Vincent's bowels like a shard of broken glass. He cried out and tried to move. One of the nurses placed her arms over him to hold him down. "Easy, Vincent, easy," Dr. Stanson soothed. "It's just the air I've pumped in. Let it out if you need to."

"It's not the air!" Vincent shrieked, writhing on the table. Colleen hurriedly prepared more Demerol and shot it into Vincent's vein.

Then he heard one of the nurses scream. The pain in his gut became unbearable and he joined her. Colleen shouted, "Doctor, look at that!"

Dr. Stanson gave a startled yell, and that's when it got really weird.

Vincent felt something deep inside of him rise up (the only way he could describe the sensation) and move down... pushing the endoscope in front of it.

Dr. Stanson, meanwhile, was trying to understand why the endoscope was coming out of his patient's anus at high speed, nearly burning his rubber glove-encased hands, without any help from the esteemed doctor himself. Finally, the endoscope came shooting out of Vincent's rectum like a missile, whacking one of the nurses so hard on the forehead that she dropped to the floor as if she'd been pole-axed.

Then something else travelled down and blasted out of Vincent's ass, ricocheting around the room like a bullet, entering the bodies of the unfortunate hospital staff at abdominal level—causing everyone in the room except Vincent to come to a nasty and unexpectedly sudden demise.

The ripping pain and chaos of the scene was all too much for Vincent, who blacked out.

*

When Vincent finally came to and opened his eyes, the machines around him were still beeping contently. He had no idea how long he'd been unconscious. For a moment, he thought he must have had some midazolam-induced hallucination, but when he looked over his shoulder, he was horrified to see that

Polyp

the examination room was littered in blood and body parts. He sat up in bed and took in the eviscerated bodies of his doctor, the endoscopy nurse and the other nurses on the floor. Vincent turned and dry heaved over the other side of the bed.

He was still in pain, but it didn't feel life threatening. Whatever had done this didn't seem interested in him, but what had issued forth from his bowels to cause such mayhem?

Vincent carefully got off the hospital bed on the monitor side, not wanting to tread in the blood and guts slooshed all over the floor. He went over to the door of the examination room—but froze. Suddenly, he didn't want to open it, worried about what else he would find.

Reluctantly, he pushed the door open and peeked out. It was bad. Blood everywhere, bodies everywhere. Ewomi was lying on the floor near the nurses' station and he spotted her chest rising and falling fitfully. He walked over as quickly as he could and knelt next to her. Her uniform was soaked with blood and bits of mangled colon were poking out from her lower abdomen.

Vincent placed his hand on her forehead. It was feverishly hot. Her eyes popped open, she looked at him and screamed: "What did you do?"

He snatched his hand away and screamed back: "I didn't do anything!" Ewomi convulsed, choked, threw up blood and died right there in front of him.

Vincent stood up slowly. Everyone in the recovery room was dead. He walked over to the small cupboard where he'd placed his clothes, and quickly dressed. He didn't know what was going on, but one thing was for certain, hanging around in the Endoscopy Department of St. Stephen's hospital in his "Dignity Shorts" was not going to be good for his health.

Vincent moved through the eerily empty corridors of the normally bustling hospital. Blood was everywhere, bodies were everywhere, with entrails streaming out of their abdominal cavities. No one was left alive. His midazolam-fogged brain was trying to make sense of it all. Something very fucked up had just occurred. Was some rampaging polyp going nuts in the hospital? How the hell could something like this happen, especially to someone as unremarkable as him?

Vincent made his way down to the entrance hall. It was silent, with just the ringing of unanswered phones echoing throughout the building.

He stopped just as he was about to go through the revolving doors to the street, and turned around. The white walls of the hall were drenched in arterial spray, as if Jackson Pollock had been possessed by an alien and then gone mad.

Why was he still alive? Whatever had carried out this massacre could so easily have obliterated him, too.

Then he heard it. A sound. A sound like nothing he'd ever heard before, except maybe in some cheesy sci-fi film when he was a kid and his big brother had made him watch the black and white versions of *The Thing From Outer Space* or *The Day The Earth Stood Still*.

Polyp

Vincent could have turned back to the revolving doors and gotten the hell out of Dodge, but he chose not to. He could have called the police, but would they have believed him? ("I think a polyp just came out of my butt and slaughtered a bunch of people.") He didn't think so. This thing had come from him, so it was his problem to sort out. Maybe he had some kind of immunity—it could have killed him, but chose not to. Hold on a minute, a polyp making a choice? His screaming brain wanted to reject the thought as soon as it emerged. But something had butchered all these people and he knew in his gut—no pun intended—that it had come from inside of him.

Vincent followed the sound as best he could. It was a bit difficult to pinpoint its source, but as he walked down the corridor it grew louder: a sucking, slurping, slushing sound, accompanied by an almost Theremin-like whistling.

Vincent was walking past the Disabled Toilet when he realized the noise was coming from inside. He had never faced anything particularly dangerous in his life before. He'd always made a point of avoiding any conflict or confrontation, so he was literally quaking with fear. There was no question in his mind that he had to go in there and face it, whatever it was, however, Vincent was fervently hoping that his immunity theory wouldn't prove to be unjustified.

With his heart thumping like a Keith Moon drum solo, Vincent cautiously opened the door to the Disabled Toilet. The squelching sounds quieted down, but did not cease. He was relieved to see that the lights were still on. He slipped inside and spotted the polyp in the corner. It had grown terrifyingly fast and was at least 7 feet tall, slouching on the toilet like a disaffected teenager, human intestines piled up next to it. No features to speak of, just a huge, leech-like mouth containing a tripartite-jaw filled with hundreds of tiny sharp teeth that were busy masticating its unfortunate victims' colons. Vincent noticed some black spots just above the mouth that might be eyes. At the same time, the polyp noticed Vincent and swallowed the remains of its dinner.

And smiled at him…

Vincent felt like throwing up, but all he could do was gag. The smell of the thing was revolting—a vile combination of excrement and blood—and he wondered how long he could stay on his feet without fainting.

Then it spoke…

"Hi Dad, how's it hanging?" the polyp wheezed. Its voice had a strange, low-pitched, guttural, echoing resonance, as if the polyp had just had a laryngectomy and was using Esophageal Speech to burp out its words, like the now sadly deceased veteran actor, Jack Hawkins, in his later years.

Vincent's balls shrank to the size of peanuts and a chill iced his extremities.

"I… I'm not your father. You're a … m…monster. W-Why have you murdered all these people?" Vincent stuttered.

"Hey, a boy's gotta eat," the polyp burped cheerfully.

"How did this happen? What the hell are you?"

Polyp

The polyp reared back in what looked like a very human kind of annoyance: "Man, you want ME to explain to YOU what's going on? Geez, you must be insane in the membrane. I AM, that's what you got to get your head around. Forget about explanations. I exist and that's all that you have to worry about right now."

"Oh, shit."

"Hey, you're talking about the stuff I love," the polyp burbled. "Shit and blood and all these millions of neurons I'm ingesting right now. Making me smarter, making me high on serotonin, the so-called "happiness hormone". Did you know that more than 90% of the body's serotonin lies in the gut? I am eating. I am growing. I am smarter than you. I am happier than you. I am the "second" brain of your nightmares, Daddy dearest."

Vincent didn't know what to do. It was rather alarming to be talking to an enormous fleshy bump, especially when it kept calling him "Dad". He wanted to kill it, but he was being distracted by its personality. After all, no one, or no thing, had ever called him "Dad" before. And this polyp *was* a part of him. What would happen if the polyp died? Would Vincent die, too? What if it wanted to get back inside him, its former Host? It was too awful to contemplate.

Vincent pushed these thoughts from his mind. He didn't care what happened to him anymore. This monster—created in his gut somehow—had massacred dozens of people, so his course was clear. He had to destroy it.

Vincent turned and ran out of the toilet, then down the corridor to the entrance hall. Being forced to watch all those old Sci-fi movies back in his childhood, he knew that the most effective weapon against unknown creatures was fire. Of course, now that new regulations prevented any smoking in a public building, finding the required ingredients to burn the polyp to a crisp was challenging. By the time he'd found a fire ax, wrapped strips of cotton wound dressings around it and drenched it with rubbing alcohol, precious minutes had flown past. Finding a match or a lighter was the most difficult task, requiring him to rummage through the handbags and pockets of the corpses littering the entrance hall. Then he remembered that hospital staff were the worst offenders as far as smoking was concerned, so he concentrated his search on the bodies behind the information desk and was rewarded with a vintage gold Dunhill lighter.

Vincent dashed back down the corridor to the Disabled Toilet, armed with his makeshift torch. The slurping and munching noises had resumed, so the polyp was still in residence. Vincent squeezed through the doorway, just managing to hide the ax behind his back. The polyp stopped chewing and swallowed.

"You walked out in the middle of our conversation, Dad. That's really rude."

"Stop calling me Dad, you, you ... THING." Vincent felt the insult was pretty limp, but he was simply lost for words when confronting the creature.

"Hey, Polyp is the name, Daddy-O. I came from YOU. So get over it."

Polyp

The polyp leaned over and grabbed some more intestines with its mouth, snorfling up the disembodied colons like spaghetti bolognaise. While its attention was momentarily distracted, Vincent took the opportunity to light the rags on his homemade torch. The polyp, instantly alerted, spat out its food and growled. Vincent doused the creature with alcohol, threw the torch and then ran like hell.

He stopped twenty feet down the corridor and turned around. The sound emerging from the toilet was horrendous: a crackling, hissing, squealing, throbbing racket, accompanied by wisps of greasy, miasmic smoke curling from underneath the door. Then, totally unexpected, an explosion … blowing the door out so violently that it hit the wall opposite. Fire alarms began to wail and the sprinkler system kicked into action.

Vincent cautiously walked back to the toilet, wondering what he was going to find. Covering his mouth and nose with his shirt tail so he wouldn't have to breathe in the truly repellent smell of fried polyp, he peered around the doorway.

The polyp was still on the toilet, but the top half of it was gone, the other half sinking slowly into the bowl—scorched and blackened, heat blisters growing on the surface of the creature, steam caused by the water from the sprinklers gently rose up like a mist from a harbor town. But it was what was inside of it that made Vincent fall to his knees, overwhelmed by the horror of it all.

He'd made a mistake. A big mistake. He could see that now. But how could he have anticipated that the diabolical thing would explode?

From inside of the polyp, hundreds of new fleshy growths were squirming and moving, tiny at first, but as they devoured their creator, they grew fast. Some of the more energetic ones were already busily crawling down their progenitor, onto the floor, slithering determinedly towards Vincent like inchworms hyped up on crack cocaine.

Vincent turned and crawled on his hands and knees out of the toilet, weak with fear and horror. He managed to scramble to his feet in the corridor and stagger to the entrance hall, just in time to see two firemen dash through the door and make for the source of the foul smoke. Vincent tried to stop them, tried to speak, tried to warn them, but he was too shocked by what had happened to make any sense and just waved his arms around ineffectually. As one fireman helped him out of the building towards a waiting ambulance, he heard a distant echoing scream come from the direction of the Disabled Toilet.

As he lay on the gurney inside the ambulance, Vincent looked through the small window as first firemen, then policemen, then the army streamed into the hospital. An attendant gave him something to calm his nerves, but no one bothered to ask him what had happened. They were too busy fighting the Polyp Horde inside. He wondered if the humans would win.

Then he felt something. Inside of him. That scuttling feeling inside his bowels again. And Vincent knew that it wasn't over.

Polyp

Johnny Mains

THE CURE BY JOHNNY MAINS

"It's bad news,' the Doctor said, sympathetic eyes, mouth slightly turned down like a child who has been forbidden sweets for drawing on the wallpaper. 'The tests have come back and they reveal that you have Stage 2B bone cancer; a high grade which has grown through the bone wall. We need to start a treatment of aggressive chemotherapy before it progresses to Stage 3 and spreads to other parts of your body."

CANCER, CANCER, YOU HAVE CANCER AND YOU ARE GOING TO DIE.

She started to cry. The Doctor opened his drawer, pulled out a box of tissues and passed them across to her. He stared at Amanda hard, for the longest of times and then spoke again.

"I won't lie to you—this is bad," he said. "However, there is a treatment which has been developed in Sweden; highly controversial, ethically unsound and if news reaches the public there will be hell to pay for everyone involved. But, in the five tests that have been carried out in this last year, it has proven 100 percent effective. To be eligible for this test you have to be diagnosed with Stage 2B and you must also sign a contract between yourself and the treatment centre whereby you declare you will never, ever talk about what you see, hear or experience

The Cure

while in their care."

Amanda looked up. She had only taken in part of what the doctor had said, but it sounded like hope.

"One hundred percent effective? You mean a cure?"

The doctor nodded, then opened up his drawer. He pulled out a brown A4 folder and passed it across to her.

"All the information you need is here. Do NOT show this to anybody."

*

Amanda left the clinic and walked down the street. She reached a Vegan cafe where she had carrot cake and drank a cup of green tea without tasting either. Her bones felt hollow, her eyes seemed to shrink back into her skull. The cake felt like ash in her mouth and no amount of tea seemed to be able to wash it away. Her stomach felt heavy and bloated and her lymph nodes burned under her skin.

She phoned her mother and said that she was coming home. Mother seemed oblivious to any worry or near hysteria that Amanda might have conveyed in her voice and said that she would put some dinner on.

"Father will be really happy to see you. He's found a couple of books in a second hand shop for you."

Life goes on.

Nobody was there to pick her up when the trained pulled into Effingham station, but there was a taxi available. When it pulled up at the house she saw her mother in the garden. She got out, paid the diver and he took her small bag of luggage from the boot and handed it to her. All of a sudden it seemed impossibly heavy to carry. Her mother looked up, smiled and came to greet her. Then the world tilted sideways and Amanda went with it.

*

When she came to the faces of her worried parents peered down at her.

She was lying on the sofa in the front room, with no memory of getting there. She tried to get up, but she felt smothered by the blanket they had placed on her. It felt heavy and it was suffocating her.

"What's wrong bubblegum?" her father said, stroking her face.

She told them.

It wasn't easy on them, but then, it wasn't easy on her either.

Both parents were pole-axed by the announcement that Amanda was going to hole herself away in a treatment centre in Sweden and that they wouldn't be allowed to come and visit, only to send letters and phone. When her mother had asked why, she said that it was the only way she could do it—the only way she could be strong was if she did it on her own.

*

The next week Amanda arrived in Sweden and made her way to Ytterby, a small village on the island of Resarö. The medical centre was next to the church.

The Cure

She checked in at reception and was taken through to her room—it was comfortable, if slightly basic, with a single bed, sofa, TV and a fridge.

She walked a lot in those first few days, trying to empty her head from thoughts of her disease. Sometimes she felt as if she could feel her bones being eaten by increments.

On the fifth day she was called through to the office of her case doctor, a tall, blonde man called Stephan whose eyes were the bluest she had ever seen.

"You have read the literature," he said in a sing-song voice. It wasn't a question; it was a statement of fact. "You understand what has to happen here."

"Yes, I do," Amanda replied. "But this was a very hard sell on my parents. They think I've gone and joined some kind of cult."

"Of course, they will naturally be worried. You are their only child. I trust you have told them they can still phone and email you? Of course you can also talk on the web-cam if you wish, but you must never reveal anything below shoulder height. Nobody must know that you're showing."

Showing. He made it sound *so natural.*

"I just want to get better," she said softly.

Stephan smiled and held out a clenched fist. He opened it and revealed a single yellow and red capsule; it reminded her of the rhubarb and custard sweets of her childhood.

"Swallow it. It's all the medication that you need. Then we will move onto the next phase."

Amanda stared at the pill, half expecting it to combust in front of her eyes.

Is it really this simple?

She took it, popped it into her mouth and dry-swallowed. Stephan smiled.

"Very good. Now we can commence with the second part of the treatment. You've read the literature; you know what has to be done. And it has to be done soon. The window is very small, as you well know."

He got up, flashing a smile again. His teeth were very white.

*

Amanda stared herself in the mirror, carefully applying make up. Once she was satisfied, she walked the half-mile into town, found a bar and waited.

It didn't take long.

Jorge was very beautiful and very intense. She went back to his sparsely furnished flat and slept with him. The walk back to the medical centre was one of the longest she had ever taken. He had been nice, and it would have been fun to see him again.

That night her body screamed in agony with the pain from her exertions.

*

On the last day of her cycle she took a pregnancy test.

Stephan was happy with the result. Amanda was moved from the room to her own flat on the outskirts of town. Her food and other sundries were delivered to her twice a week. She went out for small walks, only to get some fresh air, nothing more. She phoned

The Cure

her family once a week and told them she was doing well. Her father asked her why her hair hadn't fallen out. He then broke down, begging her not to try any untested treatment.

"I'm your dad. I'm supposed to die first," he said through tears.

After that she stopped calling her parents as her stomach grew big with her pregnancy.

During the last month one of the nurses came to stay with her. By now she was barely eating, sleeping for twenty hours a day. Her thin frame and distended stomach gave her the look of a famine victim but Stephan seemed unconcerned.

"It will be fine," he said. "I've seen worse cases than this. You'll be fine."

*

Her waters broke and she was rushed to hospital. The pain was excruciating.

"Dad!" she shouted, but all she got were people in green scrubs with masks over their faces, their eyes giving away no emotion.

"Push," she was told.

And so she pushed. And pushed.

All of a sudden the pain was gone and she felt as if she'd been sucked up by a vacuum.

Stephan held up her baby. It looked little more than a dirty grey sac, flecked with blood. But she could see movement; the baby was pushing and kicking.

What's happening?

Stephan laid the sac on the table and cut it open with a single *slice* of a scalpel. Black liquid flooded out from the sac, splashing onto the table and floor.

He lifted the baby up, and Amanda started to scream.

There was no face, just a flat grey surface. The arms were devoid of hands and the legs had no tiny feet. But still the grey thing kicked.

Amanda's screams grew louder.

Stephan handed her baby to a nurse who rushed it out of the room. He placed a hand on Amanda's shoulder and smiled. His teeth were very white.

"Well done. You're cured."

The Cure

THE BIG ONE BY GUY N SMITH

"I'm afraid," Doctor Kemper glanced somewhat furtively at the big raw-boned man who filled the chair on the opposite side of his desk, averted his gaze. "The news is not good."

Out of the corner of his eye the balding doctor looked for a reaction. There was none, the other's expression was impassive. No matter how many times he had had to convey the worst possible news to a patient over the years it never got any easier.

"Give it me straight, doctor. Let's stop pussy-footing around."

"All right," he said with relief that he had not got to embark upon a lengthy rigmarole. "It's cancer of the most aggressive type. Mostly in the left lung but it has already begun spreading to the right. It's inoperable."

There was still no reaction from the other, his gimlet ice-blue eyes boring into the doctor.

"How long?"

"Well..."

"How long have I got?"

"Six months, maybe more, maybe less. There's a chance we can slow its progress but we can't put it in remission."

"I see." Carl Strickland scraped back his chair,

stood up to his full height. "Well, thanks for putting me in the picture. I won't take up any more of your time."

"Wait a minute," Kemper was somewhat taken aback by the other's cool reception of the worst possible news. "We can help you, make it easier for you."

"Make it easier for me to die, eh?" A brief half-smile. "Drugged up to the eyeballs, lying in a hospital bed. Thanks but no. I'll look after myself, doc."

"You...you're not going to…" the doctor licked his dry lips.

"No way. I don't plan anything like that, simply that I've got something to do in the time that's left to me."

"It'd help if you gave up those fags."

"Bit late for that, isn't it?"

"It might give you an extra few weeks."

Strickland laughed. "You know as well as I do what caused this cancer; a glancing blow from a charging Cape buffalo in South Africa a couple of years back. A chest injury that put me in hospital for three weeks. The cancer took time to grow. Now it has. I might've died out there if the bull hadn't had a fatal bullet in its heart. It dropped seconds after it hit me. Otherwise it would probably have gored me to death and I wouldn't be sitting here now listening to your forecast of a slow death. Might've been better but that's how it goes. I got a two-year extension of life for which I'm grateful. So I'll stick with my fags and make the most of every day that's left to me. They're a bonus."

Doctor Kemper sat staring at the wall for some

time after his patient had left. He wondered what it was that Strickland had to do in the months left to him. The other was the kind of man whom you didn't put those kinds of questions to.

*

Out in the street Carl Strickland lit a cigarette, inhaled deeply. A spasm of coughing had passers-by glancing at him in alarm. Right now the first thing he had to do was to phone Konrad Kumer in Mbeya. Time was not on his side.

The small terraced house was little more than a base for Strickland on those occasions when he was in Britain. The rest of his time was spent abroad in different countries. Hunting. He had the money to pursue such a luxurious lifestyle and he made the most of it. Last year he had hunted Polar bears on the ice off Baffin Island and then flown to Switzerland to spend two months in the mountains after *Moufflon*. Then it was back to Africa after the 'Big One', a mighty bull elephant which had eluded hunters for years. It had killed three, a Spaniard and two Americans, all of them with many years of hunting experience under their belts.

The 'Big One', the big prize, trophy tusks for which men had paid tens of thousands of dollars in vain hope. None had succeeded. Not as far as Strickland knew but his priority was to check that out.

Konrad Kumer was the only professional hunter on the Dark Continent who stood any chance of leading a client to success. Unless he had already done so but there had been no mention of it when

The Big One

Carl had attended the Shot Show in Last Vegas in January. It would have been the talk of the event if somebody had bagged that prized elephant.

Carl Strickland's fingers shook slightly as he picked up the phone. He had already forgotten his visit to Doctor Kemper. He had more pressing matters on his mind.

"Carl, how are you?" The hunter's gravelled tones were somewhat staccato on the line, a grizzled Colonial who had built up an enviable reputation as a PH. Whether you wanted buffalo, lion, leopard or elephant, he got you one. The only prize which had eluded him so far was the Big One. And Kumer wanted *that* as badly as every other hunter.

"I'm fine," Strickland lied.

"Good. Good. When are you coming back to Mbeya?"

"Depends."

"On what?"

"A chance at the Big One."

There was a long silence, then "Every hunter wants the Big One. In over ten years none have succeeded. Another was killed a couple of months ago. A German. Highly experienced. The big fella charged him, survived both barrels from a .500/416. The trackers took the German's remains back to camp in a bin liner."

That's excellent, Strickland thought. *That tusker's still around.*

"He must have half a ton of lead in his thick hide," Konrad Kumer continued. "He's tough and he's the most cunning elephant I've ever known. Maybe he'll end up dying a natural death long after you and I have gone."

"I'd like a go at him, Konrad," Strickland said. "Win or lose."

There was another long silence almost as if the veteran wasn't prepared to risk it. The toll of hunters was mounting.

"It'll cost you."

"That's no problem."

"Thirty thousand dollars for a start, then there's the licence and trophy fee."

"I'll go for it."

"I'm free in a couple of weeks, a gap between bookings."

"Book me in."

*

The Toyota pick-up bumped its way along the seemingly never-ending, tortuous track. On either side the scrub plains were burned brown by the relentless heat. Only the coming of the rainy season would save the vegetation. Somehow it always did.

Sam, the tracker, also served as driver, his powerful body hunched over the wheel, constantly glancing from right to left.

"Buffalo," he pointed. "There's a good bull with them."

"It's elephant we're after," Kumer grunted. "The Big One."

The Big One

"Not to be killed. No bullet will kill him. He kills hunters. He is the god of the Imbezi people. They get very angry with hunters."

"Then keep clear of them." A cigarette dangled from the professional hunter's lips, showered ash down his khaki shirt. He was lean of build, his skin wrinkled by a lifetime spent in the heat. It was impossible to judge his age. Strickland put him at somewhere between fifty and seventy. "We're not looking for trouble."

"Until we find the Big One." There was a tremor in the tracker's voice.

"Just find him." Kumer turned to his client. "Problem is that dammed elephant spends most of his time on the Lupa Reserve these days. He's cunning, knows he's safe there. We just have to hope that he ventures out and we pick up his spoor," he said, and shrugged his bony shoulders. "It's asking a lot, Carl. We might just be lucky. Or unlucky."

"Show him to me and I'll get him," Strickland answered, then gave way to a bout of coughing. "Man or beast, you have to die someday. Sooner, later, depends on your luck." He wiped his mouth with the back of his hand, noticed a trace of blood. That was how it was these days.

"We'll make camp soon," Konrad Kumer announced when the sun was sinking low in the sky. "Start out before daylight. There's a water hole about a mile beyond that clump of trees. Never dries up. Most of the wildlife hereabouts drink there. Could be the big fella fancies quenching his thirst and a bath to go with it. We'll find him tomorrow."

*

The early morning was bitterly cold. In an hour or two it would be unbearably hot.

"We'll make as much ground as we can before the heat of the day," Kumer slung his old Westley Richards double .450 on his shoulder. It was his duty to protect his client, a precise shot in a life-or-death situation. There had been many over the years; he had never failed. He did not relish this safari, and secretly he hoped that the Big One was on the reserve and would stay there.

*

Three hours later Sam picked up elephant spoor and further on some droppings. He scooped up a handful of the latter, nodded. "Fresh," he announced. "Sometime during the night. Maybe two, three miles ahead of us. They'll stop to rest soon."

Konrad Kumer licked his dry lips. "The Big One amongst them?"

"Maybe, maybe not," Sam traced an outline of one of the prints with his stick, mentally measuring it. "That one big. Maybe not big enough."

Strickland's feet were dragging; he wasn't breathing easily. He turned away each time he coughed, not wanting his companions to see the crimson spots on the hard ground. It was becoming harder than he had thought but he was determined to stick it out. There was nothing else left to him.

By nightfall they had not so much as glimpsed the elephants.

The Big One

"Travelling fast," Sam said as they prepared to camp out. "If they keep going through the night we will never catch up with them. Best to make for the water hole, get there before daylight. It's our only chance."

*

Strickland wondered how he was going to make it through the day. His double Holland & Holland .700 seemed to weigh a ton. Nevertheless he gritted his teeth and followed in the wake of Kumer and Sam.

Somehow they made it to the waterhole before dawn. As the sky lightened he saw that it was nothing more than an acre or so of mud. But there was moisture there and at this time of the year that was a scarce commodity out here.

"We'll lie up in those rocks over there." Sam indicated some scattered boulders, the only vestige of cover. He was edgy. So was Kumer. Strickland trembled for a different reason.

Daylight.

A bunch of warthogs came, wallowed noisily and left. An hour passed and then Sam's ear went down to the ground. Strickland glimpsed the other's expression when he raised himself up, one of momentary fear. Then it passed.

"Elephant," he whispered, "coming through the scrub jungle. Just one... *big*!"

Strickland unslung the .700, slid two shells into its breech, closed it with a faint click. God, it was heavy, seemed twice the weight it had been on his last safari. He was sweating heavily.

"I'll tell you when to shoot," Kumer reminded him. "And not until. Get it?"

Carl nodded. He would shoot when he judged he had a killing shot within his sights. Kumer didn't figure in his plans.

Now they could hear the elephant approaching, crashing through trees, uprooting some.

Like it's desperate to get to the water.

Then they saw it, a veritable behemoth emerging from cover, trunk and ears swinging.

"*It's him!*" Carl breathed.

Sam had backed away into the rocks, was nowhere to be seen. He had found them the beast, his job was done. Nobody hung around when the Big One was close.

Kumer loaded the Westley with trembling fingers. He hoped that he didn't have to fire it. Strickland was a bloody fool to think he could succeed where top hunters had failed. He, too, began to edge away. Carl Strickland was bad medicine in a situation like this, a kind of hoodoo that beckoned death.

The elephant came on at a steady trot, an old bull which had deserted the herd, was living his last days alone. *If* he ever died. The Imbezi believed he was invincible, would live forever. They could be right. Kumer began backing away. Strickland hadn't even noticed, he had eyes only for the Big One.

The elephant halted on the edge of the bog, uplifted its trunk and trumpeted. Almost like it knew the hunter was around and was challenging him. Its mighty tusks gleamed white.

Strickland lifted the heavy double rifle with

The Big One

considerable difficulty, used the rock in front of him as a rest. He took a sighting. Sweat was making his eyes smart, his vision was blurred. His hands were shaking.

The beast turned sideways on. *Perfect.* The hunter's dream, an ear shot where the solid bullet would penetrate, rip into the brain, destroying it instantly.

Strickland pushed the safety catch forward, his forefinger rested on the front trigger. This was it!

He took a deep breath, held it. Squeezed.

The report was deafening, the rifle's recoil throwing his weakened body backwards. He heard the £100,000 gun clattering on the stony ground.

Oh, Jesus!

It was all he could do to crawl to where it lay. He grasped it but he was no longer strong enough to lift it. It was as though his entire strength had evaporated with that shot.

But he didn't need the gun, He had shot the Big One, he couldn't have missed at that distance. It was lying dead by the waterhole. All he had to do was to crawl to where he could see its inert form. He asked nothing else. He had achieved his ambition.

Suddenly the Big One was towering above him, trumpeting its fury. It saw him with eyes that glinted sheer rage, Evil. Another human had dared to try to kill it. Now death was its prerogative.

A huge foot was raised, hovered over Carl Strickland, an executioner's axe poised for a beheading. Gloating, savouring every second.

It came down slowly, seemed to Strickland to be in slow motion, blotting out the sunlight. Darkness. It rested on his chest and stomach; he felt the pressure, his breath being expelled. Bones starting to crack.

He screamed and that was when the Big One went berserk. Its victim's body crushed, squelched; a morass from which arms and legs protruded.

The trunk encircled the human remains, lifted them aloft, swung them high and then dashed them on the jagged rocks. Again and again.

Finally, the Big One lifted the bloody remnants of Carl Strickland to the full extent of its trunk and flung them into the midst of that rocky outcrop.

One final trumpeting and then the elephant turned, ambled back to the waterhole. It took its time bathing in the thick mud, burrowing deep for water with its trunk. Only then did it return whence it had come, a triumphant victor leaving the field of battle.

*

It was maybe twenty minutes before a hunched, lean figure rose up out of the rocks, wide-brimmed bush hat pushed back on his head, rifle at the ready in case it was needed. It wasn't. Apart from a couple of vultures circling high above there was no sign of life.

Only death.

The Big One

Kumer saw the bloodied human remains a hundred yards away, fought off the desire to retch. Such 'accidents' were nothing new to him, he had witnessed more than his share over the years. There was no sign of the huge beast. It had wreaked its terrible vengeance and departed, probably back to the safety of the Reserve. Kumer breathed a sigh of relief, lowered the Westly double with trembling hands.

"Sam!" He cupped his hands, shouted. "It's safe to come out. It's gone."

The tracker stood up slowly, shaded his eyes and scanned the scrubland as far as the dense patch of jungle. He wouldn't take Kumer's word for it; he had to see for himself. Slowly he began to walk forward, his black features ashen. It might have been the dust. Kumer knew it wasn't.

For some minutes they stood there, not talking. Such happenings as they had witnessed take time to sink in.

"You'd better go and fetch the truck, Sam," he spoke at last. "There's some waste bags in the back. We'll need 'em. I'll stop here, keep the vultures off."

The other turned away, broke into a fast jog like he wanted to be as far away from this place of violent death as possible.

Kumer seated himself on a rock, rifle across his knees. He had a long wait ahead of him but that was fine. He knew that the big feller would not return.

It was strange Strickland missing at that range for the guy was a brilliant shot. He was a sick man, though, that much had been evident since they had left base camp yesterday morning. *If you ask me the guy was dying,* the PH told himself. Maybe the Big One had done him a favour, spared him from weeks of suffering.

At least it was quick.

*

Greg Mason had been head ranger at the Lupa Reserve for four years. Poaching was the bane of his life, the Imbezi were the worst but at least they only killed to eat. Gangs from further afield were only interested in ivory, left the carcass to rot.

Word reached him that there was a dead elephant by the lake and that tribesmen were already plundering the meat. Doubtless it was the work of the Imbezi and they had poached it.

"It's the Big One," his informant, who had run five miles to deliver the news, announced.

"In which case the Imbezi would not have killed it because the beast is a god to them." Mason was already striding to where the battered old Mitsubishi was parked in the compound. "Probably poachers from one of the other villages. They've nicked the tusks and left the body. I'd better check it out before there's nothing left of it."

The Big One

Two hours later he sighted the frenzy of butchering close to some trees by the lakeside, turned the truck off the rough track and bumped his way over ground that became a swamp when the rains came.

There were maybe fifty natives on and around the mighty dead beast. A huge cavern had been hacked out of its side. Machetes and knives were slashing and cutting, joints of flesh thrown out to women who were stowing them in baskets.

Greg Mason braked to a halt, sounded his klaxon. Men froze in their tracks, defiant and guilty stares greeting the newcomer.

"Stop!" Mason jumped down. "You!" He singled out the tribal chief, arms and legs awash with elephant blood. "Poaching carries a jail sentence and I guess the cells at Mbeya are going to be very crowded. So you have slain your god, eh?"

"No, boss," the chief squelched his way out of the beast's belly. "We no kill. Nor poachers. Elephant die and we find him."

"Try again, Goma," Greg shook his head. "That yarn won't wash with me."

"It's true," the chieftain pointed back into the stomach of the elephant. "You come, see for yourself."

"I suppose I might as well take a look even if only to prove you a liar," the ranger picked his way carefully through a morass of slimy intestines.

"See, boss!" Goma was pointing at the morass of lungs that the villagers had cut away, indignant at having his words doubted. "I tell truth. See for yourself."

Mason stared; saw a succession of growths on those huge lungs, the size of toy balloons ready to burst. Some had bled profusely before death had stemmed the flow.

He let out a long sigh, nodded an apology to Goma. "I guess you're right. This animal has been sick for a long time, getting worse day by day. Finally even his strength gave out so he just lay down and died. Probably in terrible pain. He's survived bullets but he couldn't beat the Big C."

He turned away, wiped his boots before he got back in the truck. The Big One had killed a hunter only weeks before. Konrad Kumer, the PH, had told the coroner's court that he believed that the guy hadn't had the strength to aim his heavy rifle because he was sick. An autopsy on the remains of the deceased revealed one of the most aggressive types of lung cancer. Now both man and beast were dead, both victims of the Big C. Life could be strange at times, Greg Mason reflected.

And so could death.

The Big One

CANKERMAN BY PETER CROWTHER

"Again?"

The boy nodded, his face tear-stained and screwed up as though at the memory of something unpleasant.

"Nasty dream," Ellen Springer said, stifling a yawn. It wouldn't do to appear unconcerned. She knelt down beside her son's bed and eased him back under the clothes. The boy shuddered as his tears subsided. A shadow thrown by the hall light fell across the bed and Ellen turned around to face her husband, who was standing stark naked at the doorway, scratching his head.

"Was it the lumpy man again?" he said to nobody in particular. The lumpy man was a creation of David's, and a particularly bizarre one. He had first appeared in the sad time after Christmas, when the tree was shedding needles, the cold had lost its magic and already a few of the gaudily colored gifts deposited by Santa Claus in David's little sack had been forgotten or discarded. Only the credit card statements provided a reminder of the fun they had had

Ellen nodded and turned back to finish the securing exercise. "There, now. Snuggle down with Chicago." She tucked a small teddy bear, resplendent in a Chicago Bears football helmet and jersey, under the sheets. Her son shuffled around until his face was against the bear's muzzle. "Alright now?" He nodded without opening his eyes.

Throughout January and into February David had woken in the night complaining about the lumpy man. He was in the room, David told his parents each time, watching him. He had with him a large black bag and the sides of it seemed to breathe, in and out, in and out. The man posed no threat to David during his visits, preferring (or so it seemed) to be content simply sitting watching the boy, the bag on his knees all the while.

"Okay big fella?" John Springer said leaning over his wife to tousle the boy's hair. There was no answer save for a bit of lip smacking and a sigh. "We'll leave the hall light on for you. There's nothing to be frightened about, okay? It was just another dream."

Stepping back, Ellen smiled at her husband who was standing looking as attentive as 4 am would allow, his right hand cradling his genitals. "Careful, they'll drop off," she whispered behind him.

John pretended not to hear. "Okay, then. Night night, sleep tight, hope the-"

"He's still here, daddy."

"No, he's *not* here, David." He recognized the first sign of irritation in his own voice and moved forward again to crouch by the bed. "He never was here. He was just a dream."

The boy had opened his eyes wide and was now staring at his father. "My... my majinashun?"

"Yes." He considered correcting and thought better of it. "It was your majinashun."

"He said he'd brung me a late present."

John Springer heard the faint *pad, pad* of Ellen moving along the hallway to the toilet. "He said he'd brought you a present?"

David nodded.

"What did he bring you?"

"He got it from his bag."

"Mmmm. What was it?"

"A lump."

"A lump?"

David nodded, apparently pleased with himself. "It was like a little kitten, all furry and black. At first, I thought it was a kitten. He held it out to show me and it had no eyes or face, and no hands and feet."

"Did he leave it for you?"

David frowned. "Let me see. May I see it?"

The boy shook his head. "I don't have it any more."

"Did the man take it back?"

Another shake of head and a rub of small cheek against the stitched visage of the little bear.

"Then where is it now?"

For a second, John thought his son was not going to answer but then, suddenly, he pulled back the bedclothes and pointed a jabbing finger at his stomach, which was poking out pinkly between the elasticized top of his pajama pants and a Bart Simpson T-shirt.

"You ate it?"

David laughed a high tinkling giggle. "No," he said between chuckles. "The man rubbed it into my tummy. It hurt me and I started to shout."

Cankerman

"Yes, you did. And that's what woke your mommy and me up."

David nodded. "You called my name, daddy."

John looked at him. "Yes, I called your name."

"It scared the man when you called my name."

"I scared the lumpy man?" He moved into a kneeling position on one knee only and affected a muscle-building pose. "See, big daddy scared the lumpy man."

David chuckled again and writhed tiny legs beneath the sheets. John felt the sudden desire to be five years old again, tucked up tightly in a small bed with a favorite cuddly toy to protect him against the things that traveled the night winds of the imagination. Then he noticed his son's eyes concentrating on something on the floor behind him.

"What is it?"

David shook his head again and pulled the sheet up until it covered the end of his nose.

"Is it something on the floor?" He turned around, sticking his bottom up into the air, and padded across the room to the open door sniffing like a dog. There was a smell. Over inside the doorway, coming from the mat which lay across the carpet join. It smelt like the rotting leaves which he had to clear from the outside drains every few weeks during the early fall.

There was a shuffling from the bed. "He went under the mat, daddy. Lumpy man hid under the mat when I cried."

David's father turned around and stared at his son who was now sitting up in bed. Then he looked back at the mat. Ellen wandered by towards their own bedroom and glanced at him. "Isn't it time you went back to sleep, too, Mister Doggie?"

John smiled and gave a bark. He lifted the mat and looked underneath. Nothing. He felt suddenly silly. He had looked under the mat more for himself than for David, he realized. It would have been easy to tell the boy not to be frightened; that a big man could not hide beneath a small rug. But, just for a few seconds, he had been frightened to go back to bed without investigating the possibility that there was... something... under the rug. But the smell...

"Has anything been spilled around here, Ellen?"

"Mmmm? Spilled? Not that I can think of, no. Why?"

"It just smells a bit off." Actually, it smelled *a lot* off. It stank to high heaven. He laid the rug carefully back in place and got up. "Nothing there." He turned around and snuggled David back into his sheets. "So, off to sleep now. Hoh-kay?"

"Hoh-kay," said David.

John wandered out of the small bedroom and swung back along the hall to the toilet. Within a minute or two he was back in bed, his bladder comfortably empty, with Ellen complaining about the coldness of his feet. He lay so that he could see into David's room. The little mat lay between them, silent as the night itself and, despite John's tiredness, sleep was long in coming.

That was the March.

David left them in the September.

Cankerman

The problem was a Wilms tumor, a particularly aggressive renal cancer which showed itself initially as an abdominal swelling on David's left flank. Ellen discovered it during bathtime. The following day the tummy aches began. At the weekend, David started vomiting for no apparent reason. By the following Tuesday he had shown blood in his urine.

The Wilms was diagnosed following an intravenous pyelogram, where a red dye was injected into a vein in David's arm. It was confirmed by a singularly unpleasant session on the CT 'cat' scanner, which looked like a Boeing's engine and hummed like the machine constructed by Jeff Morrow in *This Island Earth*.

The prognosis was not good.

David had a tumor in each kidney. He had secondaries in lung and liver. The kidneys were removed surgically but on the side which was worst affected they had to leave some behind because of danger to arteries. He went through a short course of radio-therapy and then a course of chemo. He felt bad but John and Ellen kept him going, making light of it all each day and dying silently each night, locked in tearful embraces in the hollow sanctity of their bed.

The tumor did not respond.

David's sixth birthday present was for the consultant to tell his parents that it had spread into his bones. It wouldn't be long now.

Morphine derivatives, Marvel comics and Chicago the bear kept him chipper until the end, which came just before lunch on the third of September in the aching sickness-filled silence of St. Edna's Children's Hospital. Both Ellen and John were there, holding a thin frail arm each. Their son slipped away with a sad smile and a momentary look of wise regret that he had had to abandon them so soon.

Ellen started back at school late. When she did return, she had been sleeping badly for almost two weeks.

The cumulative effect of the long months of suffering, during which a life was lived and lost, had taken their toll. And though the grass had already started to grow on top of the small plot in Woodlands Cemetery, no such healing process had begun over the scarred tissue of Ellen Springer's heart. On top of that, she had inherited a difficult class at school.

Their lives were undeniably empty now, though they both went to great efforts to appear brave and happy, affecting as close a copy of their early trouble-free existence as they could muster. David's room had been re-decorated, the Simpsons wallpaper stripped off and the primary colors of the woodwork painted over in pastels and muted shades with names such as Wheat and Barley and Hedgerow Green. The bed had been replaced with a chair and a small glass-topped coffee table and on many evenings Ellen would sit in there supposedly preparing for the next day's lessons though, in reality, she would simply sit and daydream, staring out of the small window into the tail-ends of the ever-shortening days. Another Christmas would soon be upon them and neither of them was looking forward to it.

The lumpy man and his black bag had been forgotten, though John still had the occasional nightmare. Ellen never mentioned David's dreams—in fact, she tried never to mention David—and John had never told her about his and David's conversation that long-ago night when the lumpy man had brought their little boy a late Christmas present.

The first night after the funeral had been so bad that they could not believe they had actually survived it. Despite a sleeping pill—which she had assured John she would be stopping 'soon'—Ellen had tossed and turned all night. She had told John that David had been in their room watching her. John had tried to reason with her. It was the healing process, he had told her, the grief and the sadness and the loss. David was at peace now.

She had cried then, cried like she had not cried since the early days following all their conversations with doctors and surgeons. How they had begged for their child's life during those lost and lonely weeks.

Ellen did not stop the sleeping pills, nor did John try to persuade her to do so. But her nights did not improve. Then, after five or six days, she had told him that it was not David who visited their room at night while she was asleep. It was somebody else. "Who?" he had asked. She had shrugged.

He had managed to get her into the doctor for a check-up. She had not wanted to go back into a medical environment but she had relented. Too tired to argue, he had supposed. Or just too disinterested. John had spoken to the doctor beforehand and had persuaded him to refer her to the clinic for a full scan. The local hospital agreed to let her through—despite the fact that there was no evidence to support any theory of something unpleasant—because of her traumatic recent history. She had taken the test on the Monday and they had the results by second post on the Friday. It was clear.

They celebrated.

That night, John had a dream. In his dream a tall man wearing dark clothes and an undertaker's smile drifted into their bedroom and sat beside Ellen. He stroked her head for what seemed to be a long time and then left. He carried with him a huge, old-fashioned black valise, the sides of which seemed to pulsate in the dim glow thrown into the house by the street-lamp outside their bedroom window. Soon, he seemed to say softly to John on his way out, though his mis-shapen lips did not move. John awoke with a start and sat bolt upright in bed, but the room was empty. By his side, Ellen moved restlessly, her brow furrowed and her lips dry.

The following two nights John stayed awake but nothing happened. During the days at the office he ducked off into empty rooms and grabbed a few hours sleep. The work was piling up on his desk but problems would not show up for a week or two. John was convinced it wouldn't take that long.

On the third night the lumpy man came back.

His smile was a mixture of formaldehyde and ether, which lit the room with mist, its gray tendrils swirling lazily around the floor and up the walls. His face was a marriage of pain and pleasure, an uneven countenance of hills and valleys, knolls and caves, a place of shadows and lights. And his clothes were black and white, a significance of goodness and non-goodness: a somber dark gray tailcoat and a white wing-collared shirt sporting a black bootlace tie which hung in swirls and ribbons like a cruel mockery of festivity and inconsequence. His hair was white-gray, hanging in long wispy strands about his neck and forehead.

Ah, it's time, his voice whispered as he entered, filling the room with the dual sounds of torment and delight. And as he listened, John Springer could not for the life of him decide where the one ended and the other began.

Feigning sleep, curled around his wife's back, John watched the lumpy man move soundlessly around the bed to Ellen's side and sit on the duvet. There was no sense of weight on the bed.

The man placed his bag on the floor and unfastened the clasp. There was a soft skittering sound of fluffy movement as he reached down into the bag and lifted something out. John felt the strange dislocation of dream activity, a sense of not belonging, as he watched the man lift an elongated roll of writhing darkness up onto his lap. He laid it there, smoothing it, smiling at its feral movements, sensing its anticipation and its impatience.

Not long, little one, his voice cooed softly through closed unmoving lips, and, leaving the shape where it lay, he reached across and pulled back the duvet from Ellen's body.

Ellen turned obligingly, exposing her right breast to the air and the world and the strange darkness of the visitor in their room. The man lifted the shape and, with an air of caring and gentility, lowered it towards the sleeping woman.

John sat up.

The man turned around.

And now John could see him for what he really was, a bizarre concord of beauty and ugliness, of creation and ruin, of discard and harmony. There were pits and whorls, folds and crevices, warts which defied gravity and imagination and thick gashes that seeped sad runnels of loneliness. *Go back to sleep.* His voice echoed inside John Springer's head.

No, he answered without speaking. *You may not have her.*

John sensed an amusement. *I may not?*

No, John answered, pulling himself straighter in the bed. *You have taken my son, you may not have my wife.*

The man shook his head with a movement that was almost imperceptible. Then he returned his full attention to Ellen and continued to lower the shape.

No!

Again he stopped.

Take me instead.

The lumpy man's brow furrowed a moment.

Surely it cannot matter whom you take, John went on, sensing an opportunity or at least a respite. *You have a quota, yes?*

The man nodded.

Then fill it with me.

For what seemed like an eternity, the lumpy man considered the proposition, all the while holding the shifting furry bundle above Ellen's breast. Then, at last, he pulled back his hand and lowered the thing back into his bag.

John felt his heart pounding in his chest.

Cankerman

The man stood up from the bed, his bag again held tightly in his right hand, and moved around to John's side.

John shuffled himself up so that his back was against the headboard. *Who are you?* he said.

I am the Cankerman, came the reply. He sat on the bed beside him and rested the bag on his lap. *And you are my customer.* John licked his lips as the lumpy man pulled open the sides of the black valise and pushed the yawning hole towards him. *Choose*, he said. John looked inside.

The smell that assailed his nostrils was like the scent of dead meat left out in the sun. It was the air of corruption, the hum of badness and the bitter-sweet aftertaste of impurity. Gagging at the stench which rose from the bag, John still managed to hold onto his gorge and stared. There seemed to be hundreds of them, rolling and tumbling, climbing and falling, clambering and toppling over, pulling out of and fading into the almost impenetrable blackness at the fathomless bottom of the Cankerman's valise.

All were uniformly black.

Black as the night.

Black as a murderer's heart.

Black as the ebony fullness that devours all light, all reason, all hope.

Cancer-black.

Choose! said the Cankerman again.

John reached in.

They scurried and they wobbled, squeezing themselves between his fingers, wrapping their furriness around his wrist, filling his palm with their dull warmth, their half-life. They pulsated and spread themselves out, rubbing themselves against him with a grim parody of affection.

Big ones, small ones, long thin ones, short stubby ones. All human life is there, John thought detachedly. And he made his choice.

There, deep within the black valise, his arm stretched out as though to the very bowels of the earth itself, his fingers found a tiny shape. A pea. A furry pea.

He pulled it out and held it before the grisly mask. *This is my choice*, he said.

So be it, said the Cankerman, and he closed the valise and placed it on the floor. Taking the small squirming object from John's outstretched hand he allowed himself a small smile. *No regrets?*

Just do it.

The Cankerman nodded and, leaning towards him, placed the black fur against John Springer's right eye... and pushed it in.

Pain.

Can you hear a color?

Can you smell a sound?

Can you see a taste?

John Springer could.

He heard the blackness of a swirling ink blot, smelt the noise of severing cells, and saw, deep inside his own head, the flavor of exquisite destruction.

Goodbye.

When John opened his eyes the room was empty. He lay back against the headboard and felt exhaustion overtake him.

Cankerman

Ellen's hand brought him swimming frantically from the deep waters of sleep into the half-light of a smoky fall morning.

"I let you sleep," she said simply.

"Mmmm." He licked his lips and squinted into her face. "What time is it?"

"After eight."

He groaned.

"Hey, I had a good night."

John looked up at her and smiled. "Good," he said. "I told you: nothing lasts forever."

"You were right. But it'll take me some time." She stood up and walked over to the wardrobe.

"I know." He watched her sifting through clothes. On impulse, he closed his left eye and saw her outline blur. "Love you," he said... softly, so that she might not know how much.

X FOR HENRIETTA BY STEVE DUFFY

Towards the end of Farnsworth's tour of the facility, the laboratories began blurring into one, a bewildering succession of well-lit rooms filled with gleaming stainless steel and calibrated glassware, watched over by earnest young scientists in white nylon coats. Perhaps sensing this, Kleinjean the facility manager became even more animated as they approached the last of the labs.

"So, here we come to the jewel in our crown right now," he told Farnsworth, ushering him through the door marked "Project HeLa". "Ground-breaking work being done in here. Major income stream, we envisage. Now, here's our ace researcher, ha-ha— that's, um, Jacob, ah, Needleman? Jacob, this is our new head of sales from Atlanta, Mr Evander Farnsworth. Ha-ha." Kleinjean's laugh was like a nervous tic: it had nothing of spontaneity or of genuine amusement in it.

Farnsworth advanced with hand outstretched towards the bearded man in the skullcap sitting at a large, expensive-looking microscope. "Mr Needleman."

"Doctor, actually," said the scientist, not bothering to look up from the eyepiece of the microscope. "Doctor Needleman." His tone was quite neutral, which in itself went sufficiently against the grain of the day for Farnsworth to find it faintly offensive. Accordingly, he kept his hand exactly where it was and raised the volume of his salutation: "Doctor Needleman, well, of course. My apologies, *Doctor*."

Perhaps the scientist caught the nuance in his reiteration: Farnsworth wasn't sure. Needleman adjusted the focus wheel slightly, gave a brief snort of approval, then straightened up and removed the glass slide from the viewing stage. "Mr Farnsworth." He looked at the chief executive's hand. "They ought to have told you by now not to shake hands with any of us scientists. Don't you know the sort of things we keep in these test-tubes?"

"Ha-ha!" Kleinjean and his false laugh came too late to forestall the antipathy that seemed to have sprung up, from nothing it seemed, between the two men. "I was just telling Mr Farnsworth, Jacob—you're our main man on the HeLa project, isn't that right? We're all very excited," he said parenthetically to Farnsworth.

If Needleman was very excited, he was doing an excellent job of hiding it. He placed the glass slide into a white polystyrene case, which he closed and sealed with tape before locking it away in a glass-fronted lab freezer at his rear. Turning back towards his visitors he held out, somewhat to Farnsworth's annoyance, his hand. "Gentlemen. Yes, the HeLa project is definitely something else, as the kids say nowadays."

"We were hoping you could, ha-ha, talk us through it, maybe?"

Needleman regarded Kleinjean for a second, as one might glance at a noisy air-conditioning unit, then turned back to Farnsworth. "You'd like to hear about our little project? I'm flattered. We don't often get visitors from boardroom level down here at the research facility."

"Well, I'm still familiarising myself with the various branches of the business, Doctor Needleman. Now this thing of yours, Mr Kleinjean tells me it's set to be a real moneyspinner for the company."

Needleman seemed unenthused by the prospect of what might or might not accrue to the company. Instead, he picked up a stoppered flask from the desk in front of him, held it out to Farnsworth and said, "Well, there you have it."

Farnsworth tilted the flask this way and that. So far as he could see, it contained a slightly sedimented pinkish liquid, something like the melt-water that runs off a frozen joint of meat. "I do?"

"Oh, yes. Know what that is?"

Farnsworth shook his head, holding it up to the light as if the answer might thereby be revealed.

"That's living tissue from a dead woman."

Farnsworth was very careful not to let the flask drop to the bench, or to betray any feelings of surprise or disgust. Instead, he gave the contents a little shake and said: "Living tissue from a what now? I'm afraid you'll have to explain that one for me, Doctor."

"With pleasure," Needleman said expressionlessly. "Well. Let me see. Perhaps it's best if I go back to the beginning.

X For Henrietta

"You see, I used to work at Johns Hopkins in Baltimore, in the Tissue Culture Laboratory under Dr Gey. Around that time—early 1951—we were knocking our heads against a wall trying to propagate human cell tissue in the laboratory. Every time it was a bust—every culture we prepared, nothing ever took, and we were left with a bunch of dead cells in a Petri dish. We didn't have idea one. Was it the culture? Were the nutrients not right? Was it the ambient storage conditions? Was it just a flat-out impossibility, growing cells outside the body? No one knew. And then, one day, a fresh tissue sample from the wards came down to the lab.

"We didn't do anything out of the ordinary, just the standard processing. That is, we drew off some fresh chicken blood, prepared a culture dish, and macerated the sample—chopped it up, ground it down fine, mixed it in with the blood. Then we sat back and waited for it to die.

"Except this time, it didn't. When we checked the culture, we found the cells were alive—they were growing and dividing, right there in the glass. Bingo." He leaned forward and tapped the flask in Farnsworth's hand gently with his forefinger. "The first human cell line, right there."

"What, *this* is the actual sample?" Farnsworth looked confused. "But, 1951, that was almost twelve years ago—"

"It is, indeed," said Needleman. "And yes, it was." He smiled, as if to himself. "Like Topsy, it just growed."

"I don't understand." Farnsworth continued to turn the flask this way and that. "You hit upon some new way of preserving it—"

"Didn't I just say, we didn't do anything out of the ordinary? No, these cells are the only extraordinary part of it all. These cells, and the woman from whom they were taken. 'Helen Lane', we called her, because the original paperwork on the cell line referred to it as HeLa and we needed a person's name to tie it to, so no one would know who the real donor was. In the Tissue Culture lab, we knew better: we knew she was really Henrietta. Mrs Henrietta Lacks, a black woman around thirty-one years old at the time of admission."

"A coloured…"

"A Negro, yes. A woman of colour, as I think the expression has it."

Farnsworth once again took care not to betray his instinctive distaste by letting go the flask. Instead he asked, "And how precisely did you come by these extraordinary cells, Doctor Needleman?"

"They were harvested from a cancerous tumour on her cervix," Needleman said, and this time Farnsworth was unable to disguise his repulsion.

"Watch out!" Needleman deftly retrieved the flask. "Wouldn't want you to let it smash. That stuff gets everywhere, you know."

Farnsworth strove to recover his poise, while surreptitiously wiping his hand on the leg of his pants. "So they're actually cancer cells?"

"Not in the sense you probably mean," Needleman said, placing the flask on a stand. "In one sense, the most literal sense, yes—they were taken from a tumour, therefore they're cancer cells. But you don't mean that, do you? You mean, 'if I'd dropped that flask just now, would we all have caught cancer', isn't that so?"

Despite himself, Farnsworth nodded.

"Well, no. Those tests were actually carried out on prisoners in a penitentiary. HeLa cells were injected into their arms, under the skin. The worst thing any of them got was a benign lesion."

Farnsworth relaxed slightly. "I see. So this is cancer research you're doing here? Do we—pardon me, but do we do that sort of work at Yoyodyne?"

Again Needleman smiled that dry, unenthused smile of his. "Far from it. See, cancerous tissue doesn't come from outer space. It's not some bug you catch off the lavatory seat or the door-handle. It's regular human tissue, just out of control at a sub-cellular level. The fact that HeLa was derived from a tumour doesn't make it any less Henrietta."

"So?"

"So, if you forget for a moment about the whole cancer angle, think of it as merely a bunch of human cells, then this *living human tiss*ue is of *enormous* scientific interest, scientific *value*." Needleman emphasised the words with scholarly taps of his forefinger on the flask. "Its point of origin doesn't matter in that way. We can use it for anything. Anything we'd like to do to a human being, but can't, for reasons of ethics or propriety... I don't know, squeamishness. Qualms."

There was an odd quality to Needleman's voice. Had Farnsworth picked up on it, he might have identified it as something almost like sadness.

"New brand of mascara? Worried about allergies, side-effects? Test it with HeLa, and sidestep a class action lawsuit under Rule 23. Got a polio vaccine? Want to see if it'll kill you or cure you? Try it out with HeLa in a test-tube. That's what Jonas Salk did, and they gave him a tickertape parade. Shame about Henrietta, though. No tickertape for her. She died on the ward, six months after we started growing her cell line in vitro. The cancer had metastasised throughout her entire body.

"I went up to see her, you know. After she'd been re-admitted for the last time. She was asleep, the drapes were drawn around her bed. I just stood there by the bedside for a little while, then went back down to the lab. Beautiful woman," and now there was no mistaking the sadness in his voice. "Really, a remarkably beautiful woman, still, after all the pain, after all the wasting away in a hospital bed."

There followed a moment's pause, during which Needleman gazed at the flask on its stand, seemingly oblivious to the other men in the room, and Farnsworth tried to get his head around the implications of what he'd just been told. Unbeknownst to him, his hand was still rubbing spasmodically at the spotless material of his suit pants.

"I still don't really understand. In what sense is the stuff in that flask 'alive', now?"

"In the same sense that anything is," Needleman said, "Cellular mitosis. Regular and uninterrupted replication of cells." He paused again. "In fact, there's a sense in which the HeLa cell line may even be more alive than you or me."

X For Henrietta

Farnsworth suddenly realised he wanted to be out of the laboratory. He really didn't care for Needleman, let alone the weird and outlandish things he was telling him. "What's that supposed to mean?" he asked, a trifle brusquely.

"Okay." Needleman seemed to have shrugged off his short-lived melancholy. "There's a function of the living cell that we don't as yet fully understand. It's to do with somatic cell division—how many times a cell can divide, which as I've explained is what we're talking about when we're talking about its growth, about it being 'alive'. There's a guy named Leonard Hayflick put in a lot of work on this at the Wistar Institute up in Philly. See, in the normal course of events cells flourish for a certain time, and then they fade away, stop dividing, die. The thing is—" he paused again—"the thing is, we're not seeing that fading away with the HeLa cells. The little buggers keep on dividing, keep growing."

"What, you're saying they could be immortal?" Kleinjean had all but faded into the background during the course of the conversation, and now he blushed bright scarlet as both men looked round in surprise. "Sorry, sorry. I never had it explained to me in this level of detail before. Sorry. But, doctor—you mean they'll keep on growing forever?"

"Well," Needleman said, "forever is a pretty long time. As of this year they've outlasted three members of the original HeLa teams, at Johns Hopkins and at Yoyodyne, and frankly I expect them to outlast you and me. Which I guess you'd have to say would be one up to Henrietta."

Steve Duffy

*

Speedwalking back to his chauffeur-driven Lincoln, the facility manager prattling in his wake, Farnsworth felt as if several planks of the platform on which his sense of reality had hitherto been established had turned worryingly creaky all of a sudden. Worse than that, he was still smarting from his conversation with Needleman. The doctor, he felt, had got the better of him, somehow; had scored off him in some indefinable way that was irritating out of all proportion.

Dismissing Kleinjean with a shoo-fly gesture as he climbed into the back of the limousine, Farnsworth finally hit upon what he ought to have said in the lab—what he would say, next time his path crossed that of Needleman. "Oh, and one more thing," Farnsworth mouthed the words to himself, relishing their tang, "I'm new in town, Doctor Needleman, and I was wondering—do you know of any good golf clubs hereabouts?" He smiled. Golf clubs. Ha. That ought to remind Doctor Needleman what was what.

He relaxed a little, and gradually began to take in his surroundings again. He'd been stressed out, running on auto-pilot, since leaving the lab, so thoroughly had events conspired to discomfit him. Now, settled in back of the Lincoln, he found its factory-fresh luxury—the leather upholstery, the chromium trim, the smooth-purring hum of the engine—delightfully conducive to a mellowing of his mood. Almost without thinking, he fished out his pocket handkerchief and set absent-mindedly to wiping his hands, front and back. You couldn't be too careful in those sorts of places.

Thus occupied, he glanced up in time to notice a little knot of pedestrians heading towards the main gates up ahead. The Lincoln had sped past before Farnsworth could really form an impression of them. Were they employees? Visitors? He didn't know. But among them, standing out from the rest, had been one face in particular that had caught his attention. Not bowed in courteous deference to rank or class or colour, not gazing in naïve admiration at the black coachwork of the company Lincoln, but staring directly at him, for all the world as if at an equal. The face of a woman, a negress…

Farnsworth hit the intercom button. "Hold up there," he told the chauffeur, in a voice a little higher than usual. "Who's that? Who's that by the roadside?"

"'Scuse me, sir?" The chauffeur pulled over by the gates. "You mean those people we just passed there, sir?" He rolled down his window and called to the uniformed gate attendant, an aged black man. "Hey! Who those people back there?"

"Why, those will probably be employees, sir," the gate attendant said, directing his attention not to the driver but to Farnsworth, who by now had rolled down his window and was craning to look back at the approaching pedestrians. "Yoyodyne people like myself and your own self, sir. It's come the end of their shift, I guess—"

"Whoa there, boy," the outraged chauffeur interjected. "That's Mister Farnsworth you talkin' to! He's senior management, understand? High-powered executive. You and he, you ain't no fellow employees or nothin'. You're two different things in this company, you get it? Two different things altogether."

"Yes indeed, sir." The gate attendant looked suitably mortified " That's right."

"So what you say now?"

"Well, I would like to apologise, sir," said the attendant humbly. "You know I didn't mean nothin' by it, sir, not the slightest thing. You and me, why we are two separate things, two entirely separate things, 'coss we are. I open the gate, is all, and—"

Farnsworth could put up with no more in this superlatively trying place. "Then why don't you quit yammering and just open it?" he said, and jabbed hard at the window button till the smoked glass slid back up again. By the time he thought to look, the pedestrians had already passed through the gates and boarded a bus by the roadside.

Was the rest of his day to be filled with such petty annoyances? Back at the hotel, the desk clerk took forever to answer his peremptory ringing of the bell, loitering instead in the corridor beyond talking to a figure in the shadows; a chambermaid it seemed, whose half-glimpsed face seemed familiar—though why this should be, Farnsworth hadn't the slightest idea. Adding further insult to injury, the elevator attendant took forever to get the doors closed, a job he was presumably paid to undertake only two or three hundred times each day. Farnsworth frowned and tutted, and eventually reached for the old-fashioned inner grille, just as the attendant managed to jerk it loose. For a moment the two became farcically entangled.

"Oops," said the attendant. "Pardon me, sir." He raised his hands high in apology, but Farnsworth had already recoiled as if from a JD with a flick-knife. "I don't rightly know how that grille got jammed so—"

"Look at that, now," Farnsworth snapped. There was a smear of black grease all the way up the back of his hand and over the cuff of his silk shirt—the attendant's fingers must have been oily from the elevator gates. "Look here, what you've done, you damn incompetent. This shirt cost more than your month's wages, you know."

"I am most truly sorry, sir," said the attendant, and hauled out his handkerchief to make amends. Before he could touch him, Farnsworth had retreated to the farther corner of the lift. "Just work the damn controls, will you?" he snapped. "And try not to get any more of that mess on me." All the rest of that brief yet uncomfortable ride up to the top floor, Farnsworth rubbed away surreptitiously at his soiled hand.

Frustrated, soiled and wounded in his very essence, Farnsworth sequestered himself in the antebellum luxury of his penthouse suite and ordered dinner in his room. Before and after mealtime he spent long minutes in the bathroom, scrubbing his hand clean with soap and pumice till the skin on the back came up in a red weal. Late into the evening he paced, unaccountably restless, up and down the room, staring out over the city lights as if trying to remember something, then turning again to the opulent anonymity of his suite, before realising, with a little start, that he was still itching away at the back of his hand.

Steve Duffy

Sleep was a long time coming, but once under, he seemed to slip directly into a vivid, neurotically comprehensive dream, set in a place he recognised instantly as the Alabama of his youth, the family tidewater mansion and the town that bore his forefathers' name. As is the way with dreams, the details were skewed by just enough to give the whole an indefinable air of the weird, but some things—the sweep of lawn down to the riverbank, the dusty road that led towards town through woods of loblolly and pitch pine, catalpa and swamp cyrilla, all fragrant and shady in the lengthening shadows of dusk—were photographically accurate. As was the fear he felt, there in the dream: that breathstopping, onrushing mixture of terror and exhilaration that quickens the greatest and gaudiest of our youthful misdemeanours.

For he was out late, against the expressly given orders of his elders: his mama, reed-fragile on her sickbed yet still somehow so implacable; his terrifying grandfather, Bible-fierce, inflexible as a ramrod. Don't go out, they'd said; don't be on that Drewry road come sundown. And he always minded his mama, and he went in mortal fear of his grandpa's word, which in his childish mind was all mixed up with the word of God from the brassbound bible that stood open on a lectern in the library, open at Isaiah, whose voice was the voice of an old Southern general in his cups: "And they shall go forth, and look upon the carcases of the men that have transgressed against me: for their worm shall not die, neither shall their fire be quenched; and they shall be an abhorring unto all flesh." And that was the fate of the transgressor. And yet here he was, little Ev, Evander Farnsworth

X For Henrietta

III of Farnsworth's Landing, snuck over the wall and creeping through the gathering dusk.

Away over to Darktown there was a clamour, he couldn't tell whether it was panics or celebrations. Voices, raised high in the country stillness, carrying through the trees on the cooling air. He didn't know whether to feel afraid or alive, didn't know if the one wasn't just the same as the other once you stripped all the rest of it away. He shrank into the shadows, back against a high old pine, catching his breath as the first of the torches lit up the night.

Once in his very early childhood, he remembered torches; the night his father had taken ill for the last time and Doc Ralston had been sent for, all the servants strung out along the drive, holding lit brands against the cloaking evening mist that crept in off the Alabama River. Was this the same thing? Had someone fallen sick down in Darktown, and the people were lighting the way?

No. Not tonight. For one thing, there was no mist—it was a clear cool night, and the stars were coming out above the treetops, eternally familiar and endlessly remote—and for another, he knew what was happening, anyway. Knew without being told, it seemed. Maybe the secret lay in the land itself, how it lay so hushed and still as if in waiting; maybe its very stillness gave that secret away. Or maybe it was a murmur in his blood, his blood that now raced in his veins and roared to fill his eardrums, so that only when the torches were almost upon him could he hear the shouting, the white men shouting, what they were saying: the same thing he'd heard whispered in the chambers of his heart.

Because he was only a child still, he had no way of knowing whether these men were happy as they tramped on down the road in their ramshackle procession, or whether they were angry, or whether it was some peculiarly adult variety of excitement that moved them so. All he knew was, they were making a lot of noise, and it seemed to him that anything that could animate a body so, would probably fall foul of one or another of his mother's abundant prohibitions. And yet in the midst of all this clamour, these whooping red-faced country folk with their overalls and plaid flannel shirts, there was one man who seemed not to be part of the entertainment.

Which was strange, for he was in the van of the procession. There he went, pressed and helpless in the flood of townsfolk, the slumped Negro in his field clothes; his head bowed, his face invisible to little Ev, held up by men on either side of him, buoyed on the wave of general intoxication and yet not touched by it.

Now he couldn't help it; now he too was cheering. He realised it only when the Negro raised his head—his battered, swollen head—and looked in his direction, as the crowd came level with his hiding place that was now no concealment at all in the flaring torchlight. For a second their eyes met, the bleeding beaten man and the spoilt little rich kid, and in that moment Evan heard only the sound of his own voice, as if all the bawling and hollering had died away, and there was nothing else astir in all that fierce and flaring night but the high, clear voice of a child singing out "Lynch him! Lynch the dirty nigger!"

X For Henrietta

And in that instant, he felt a hand clamp down upon his own, and he turned around, and in the moment before waking—the moment before the forty-three year old Evander Farnsworth III awoke in a screaming snarl of sweating formless terror—in that moment, he sensed more than saw the towering figure of his grandfather, stern and soldier-straight behind him, close enough for the odour of bourbon and Havanas and something less definable, something rank and ruined and putrid at the gut, to fill his nose. Close enough so that, when he finally turned in fear and trembling to face the old man, the blazing of the patriarch's ice-blue eyes seemed a fire set to cleanse his very soul.

*

Later, when sorting through their impressions, his colleagues all agreed that Farnsworth had seemed a little distant from the get-go. They spoke of his moodiness, his absent-mindedness, his habit of losing the threads of conversations and apologising, the way he seemed almost "elsewhere". Some, perhaps with an air of bitterness, spoke of a peculiar habit he had of talking, not to you, but slightly over your shoulder— "as if," said one aggrieved department head, "as if he was looking to see was there someone more important whose ass he could be kissing, once he'd gotten tired of having you kiss his own." Others, maybe the more observant, felt it was less to do with the ass-kissing hierarchy, and more to do with a basic, some said all-consuming, nervousness. "I always thought he looked scared shitless, to be honest," said one of the advertising managers, "as if he was waiting for the axe to fall, you know." But who knew? It may have been nothing more than hindsight on his part. All, however, could hardly help but notice the sticking-plasters that habitually covered the back of his right hand, stretching some days all the way up inside his immaculate shirt cuff.

And over and above these sundry snapshots and artists' impressions, one colleague in particular—well, hardly a colleague, perhaps, but still one of that select group introduced to Farnsworth on his first day at the facility—one man, Dr Jacob Needleman, remembered being woken from sleep one night in the dead pit of three a.m. by the insistent ringing of the telephone. With that slow molasses dread we reserve for all calls that reach us past midnight, Needleman picked up the receiver and said "Who is it?" into a silence he at first mistook for a dead line.

"Who's there?" Needleman said again, wondering for a second if the anonymous hate calls they'd got after first moving south had begun once more. And then there came a voice, so weak it was barely audible, a voice that might have belonged to some lonely astronaut patched through by relay from his Mercury capsule on the nightside of the world: "About the body…"

"What? Who is this?" Needleman asked once more, feeling vulnerable and foolish in his pyjamas and bare feet, staring into the darkness outside the undraped windows. A pause, then the voice came again: "The body. The body of the… woman. Did they bury it, or just burn it?"

X For Henrietta

"Is that—are you the man who came to my laboratory the other month?" Needleman thought so, but he couldn't be sure. This seemed the voice of a smaller, less confident version of that man—maybe even younger, if such a thing were possible.

"I need to know. Did they burn the body, or bury it?"

"What body?" asked Needleman, more certain of his ground now. Mentally he was already composing a letter of complaint to his superior. They didn't pay him enough to deal with this meschugge, in his home, in the middle of the night already.

"The nigg—the woman. The woman you had in a glass. Her body." It was scarcely louder than his wife's regular even sleep-breathing, across the other side of the bed. Carefully, so as not to disturb her, Needleman said:

"They buried her. The family claimed the body, took her back to… I can't remember. No, to Virginia it was," remembering despite himself, despite his wish for the crazy man to get off the line, "Clover in Virginia. They buried her on family land, they called it Lacksville. Like the family name, Lacks."

"Family land," said the voice, and there followed a noise that might have been laughter, laughter from which all trace of spontaneity and enjoyment had been expunged. "So she's in there, in the soil. The body."

The pause that followed was so long Needleman had little choice but to say "Yes." Immediately after, as if angered at having to repeat himself, "Why do you ask? What's so urgent at this time of night?"

"I needed to know," the voice began, and then broke horribly over the next words, as if whatever came next had hands and was strangling them unspoken. After another pause it resumed: "I need to know, is it dead?"

"Well, of course, she's dead," Needleman said angrily. His wife stirred a little, and he continued more quietly, but with no less vehemence: "I told you, she died of a particularly aggressive form of cervical cancer, late in 1951." He was in no mood now to play metaphysical games over the HeLa cell line.

"But you have her, alive," came the reply. "You have her in your lab there," and for some reason shivers broke out over the totality of Needleman's hide, head to toe palpitations, so that he almost dropped the phone.

"Those are her cells," he told the voice, after composing himself. "Those are the cells we took from her when she was alive, from her uterus. That's not the same—"

"How do you *know* it's not the same?" The voice was still remote, unnaturally so, but the agitation was plain to hear. "Have you been to see? The worm shall not die, and the fire shall not be quenched, and have any of you people been to that grave, and dug it up, and taken a little look-see what those goddamn fucking cells are up to *right this second*?"

"No," said Needleman, wondering where the hell this was all going. "No, we haven't. It doesn't work like that."

X For Henrietta

"How the *fuck* would you know how it works?" The voice was unrelenting. "You came right out and told me you haven't got the first idea what's going on with those dirty things. You don't know how it's alive, you just know it is alive. And what I'm saying is, suppose when they put her in the soil, those cells were still alive inside her? Growing, multiplying... suppose it survived? Suppose it isn't dead? Suppose it isn't even in there any more—"

"Okay," Needleman said, cutting in on the other's rising panic with decisiveness. "Okay, that's it, now. You've had your ten cents' worth, and that's it. It's nowhere in my contract that I have to talk crap with drunks at this time of the night, let alone scientifically illiterate drunks with no sense of shame or decency or god knows what. And another thing: how the hell did you get this number? This is not in the listings, it's my private home number, and if you went into my personnel records and used that information just to wake me up with some stupid cockamamie—"

The voice on the other line said something under its breath that knocked the wind out of Needleman's sails, brought his righteous ire to an abrupt halt. "Excuse me?" he said, hardly believing his own ears. "Excuse me? What did you say just then?"

"Ikey-kikey, big fat Jew," said the voice, distinctly this time, and then it began laughing. Needleman's furious rejoinder was stopped, more than anything, by the volume and shrillness of this laughter, which within a few seconds had ascended the scale to become almost a scream, and not the scream of any sane person. For the best part of a minute Needleman held the ear-piece of the receiver cupped inaudibly in his hand, uncovering it only for the briefest of intervals, glancing as he did so at his wife. The screams showed no signs of abating. Finally, Needleman replaced the phone on its cradle as quietly as possible, then reached down and unplugged it from the wall.

This was in the early hours of a Saturday morning. At eight, room service came knocking at Ev Farnsworth's penthouse suite with his regular weekend treat, eggs Benedict. No reply. By half nine, there it was in the hallway still, untouched.

When the desk manager with the master keys finally came to investigate, Ev was discovered slumped naked up against the bed, with the empty container of Drano at his side. Not many people (confided the ambulanceman who sheeted him, laid him on the stretcher and helped carry him out via the service elevator) manage to kill themselves outright by swallowing household caustics. Most often, they suffer the torments of hell for weeks, even months at a time—some poor souls even survive it, and are wrecked internally for life. "This guy, looks like he got the whole can down," the ambulanceman said, with what sounded for all the world like admiration. "Imagine that! Musta burned all the way through the poor bastard's innards, clean out his ass and down through the floorboards."

"Clean is right," confirmed his unimaginative partner, as they negotiated the little knot of Negro chambermaids clustered in the corridor, waiting to clean up the considerable mess attendant upon Farnsworth's demise. "I mean, how dirty could a man feel?"

X For Henrietta

"You saw his body," the first ambulanceman said, elbowing the elevator call button. "Damn, it looks like he tore all the way through to his own guts from the outside, with his own goddamn hands as well. Was that the Drano, you think? When he felt it kicking in?"

"They was old wounds too," said his companion. "Healed-over scars, lots of 'em, opened up again."

"Well, whatever. I never seen such a godless mess. I mean, the guy was all over blood! It looks as if some dame put the fingernails to him but good."

"Dames," the second ambulanceman said, as from the depths of bitter experience. "You don't want to be messin' with any of that."

"You got that damn straight," said his partner. And the elevator doors closed on them, and on the mortal remains of Evander Farnsworth III, shortly to be heading back in a sealed coffin to Farnsworth's Landing and the family plot. Reflected in the polished outer veneer of the doors, the face of a black woman—one of the chambermaids, maybe—was caught in the act of turning away. A moment, no more, and it was gone.

BITTER SOUP BY GARY MCMAHON

(For Barry J. House)

"Pass the bottle, would ya, shit-stabber?"

Jonesy took another large mouthful of whisky before handing it to his friend, Banko, and enjoyed the slow burn as the liquid made its way down his throat. "Go steady. It's the last bottle, and then we're back on the paint thinner."

Banko smiled. His blackened teeth glistened in the darkness; the firelight failed to reflect from their tarry surface.

"Ugly bastard," said Jonesy. He snatched back the bottle and tipped it towards his lips.

"I'm off to make a tape," said Banko, struggling to his feet. His legs were aching and his ankles were swollen to twice their normal size. It had been a hard day scavenging, and for little reward. The only items of interest the two men had managed to retrieve from the ocean of refuse was a partially burnt computer motherboard and some broken costume jewellery. Pickings were slim these days. It seemed as if people had stopped throwing things out—indeed, the garbage trucks had become less frequent in their deliveries. Banko could not even remember when the last one had come—was it a week ago, or even longer than that?

Biter Soup

"You and your frigging tapes," muttered Jonesy. "Always talking into that damn machine, but never saying anything of use."

Banko stuck up two fingers. "Up yours," he said, before stumbling off towards the entrance to their lean-to hovel.

He walked inside, shutting the door behind him. The dump was quiet, especially at night, but Jonesy had a habit of singing rugby songs when he got too drunk.

Stepping carefully over the piles of rubbish they'd collected, he made his way to his corner of the dwelling. There were pictures stuck to the wall next to his bed—a nude young woman, circa the late 1950s, a drawing of a hovercraft, an architectural plan showing the exterior of a large building in London. Just random stuff he'd found out there, in the mile upon mile of rubbish, memories plucked from the cast-offs of the city.

Banko sat down at his little toy desk, pushing his legs under the desktop. His knees scuffed against the wood, rattling the flimsy piece of furniture and causing the items in the drawers and balanced on the lid to shake.

He picked up the small cassette recorder and pressed the play and record buttons with his first two fingers. The antiquated machine stuttered into life. His fingers moving like insects across the cluttered desk, Banko then snatched up the microphone. Its long lead resembled a thick piece of liquorice.

"Hmmm. Day five-hundred and seven," he said into the head of the microphone. "Night." He paused for a moment, chewing his bottom lip, and then continued. "Pissed again. A bad day out in the waste: nothing to be found and nobody around to talk to. Even the birds seem to have fled. Saw many dead rats, their eyes glassy and foam at their mouths. Dead. Everything's dead."

He switched off the tape recorder and sat staring at the wall and the curled photo of the nudie model who must surely have died decades ago. He felt like crying, but the tears refused to come so instead he spat into the palm of his hand and used it to clear some of the grime from his cheeks.

"Fuckers," he said, not even knowing who he meant, just needing to express vulgarity.

When he went back outside Bella had arrived.

"Hello, you old sod." She smiled as she said it, and her eyes glittered like cheap paste diamonds through the dirt on her face.

"Aye, how are you doing?" He sat back down by the fire. The flames were spluttering, threatening to die, and Jonesy had not even bothered to put on more fuel.

"Not bad," said Bella, sitting down opposite and staring at him through the short blue flames. "Been wandering about, looking for signs of life. Where is everyone these days?"

"Nobody here but us pigeons," said Jonesy. He belched and drank from the bottle he was clutching tightly in one hand.

Biter Soup

"Shut up, you tosser." Banko threw some wood onto the fire and watched the flames catch, spitting a little. He watched Bella's thin body, feeling a warmth that never seemed to reach him from the fire.

"I did find something else, though," Bella said. "When I walked out to the west-end of the dump." She leaned forward, pressing her open palms towards the fire. "Up past the wrecker's yard, beyond those screens of car shells, there's a big patch of earth that's been all torn up."

Jonesy farted.

"What do you mean, 'torn up'?" Banko tilted his head so that he might hear her better.

She shivered, wrapping her arms around her midriff. "It looks like someone's ripped it all up with a bulldozer, or something. Big chunks. Or maybe an earthquake—the ground looks like it's heaved. Turned into weird shapes, like animal sculptures and stuff. I could've sworn someone was watching me, too, except there's nobody left around here to spy on me. Nobody but you." She smiled again. Her two front teeth were missing, but she still possessed a frail kind of beauty.

Banko stretched out his legs. "How deep were these holes in the ground?"

"Very," she said. "Deeper than you could dig with a shovel: I couldn't see the bottom."

"And the sculptures? Who do you think made them?"

She shook her head. "No...*sculptures* isn't right. It's the wrong word. They looked too natural, like part of the landscape. Not man made."

They sat in silence for a while after that, passing the bottle—once they could prise it from Jonesy's hands—between them. The drink tasted old, stale. It smelled unpleasant.

Banko could not take his eyes off the landscape, the jagged outlines of the tall trash mountains, the runs and valleys which had been carved between those grotesque humps. He could have sworn that he kept glimpsing movement, like the slithering motion of tiny landslides, but could not be certain. He was old, it was late, and he was getting drunk.

*

The next morning the sky was brown and patchy, as if someone had thrown shit at the horizon. Banko rose from his bed fully clothed, as usual, and went to the sink under the window. The plumbing was rudimentary, but they had access to cold water in the hovel. He took a drink, cleaned his remaining teeth, and then walked over to Jonesy's bunk. The younger man was still sleeping; he was cuddling a moth-eaten old teddy bear, something he'd salvaged a long time ago.

"Silly sod," Banko said, softly, almost lovingly, and then he walked outside. The sky looked no better from this vantage point, so he bent over the remains of the fire, trying to catch a ghost of warmth.

It felt like ages had passed before he moved again, and when he straightened up Jonesy was stepping out through the doorway. "Morning, old-timer," he said, snorting yellow snot into his hand and examining it. "Ready to go?"

Biter Soup

Banko nodded. "Not too far today, though. I'm worried about what Bella told us."

"Don't you think we ought to take a look, then?" Jonesy spat on the floor.

"Not today. I feel...I dunno, a bit unsure. Let's see what she says next time she comes over. She said she was going back to check it out herself."

The two men trudged across the uneven ground, examining the hills and mounds of rubbish. Their eyes scanned the landscape, never missing a thing, not even the omnipresent gulls and pigeons hovering above and perched upon the stacks of household waste. They walked for a while, beneath the hazy sun, and spoke little. They reserved their energy, keeping it for the activity rather than wasting it on empty words.

After about an hour Banko finally spoke. "Can you see it?"

Jonesy nodded. "Of course I can, you arsehole. Been seeing it for about twenty minutes. What is it?"

Banko scanned the horizon. "Dunno. But it isn't right. It's following us, but at a distance. It isn't a man, that's for certain."

"Wild dog?"

"Maybe." But he wasn't so sure. Whatever had been following them, it never looked the same whenever he caught sight of it. Perhaps there was more than one thing following. Maybe there was even a herd. But none of them resembled each other; they all looked different somehow. They all looked *wrong*.

"What's that? Up ahead?" Jonesy stepped up the pace, moving in front of his companion. He always liked to be the first one to examine a find.

"Be careful. It might be…" Might be what? Banko did not even know what he was saying, what he was afraid of. All he knew was that there *was* something here to be feared.

Overhead, a gull cried out, flying low over their heads before swooping inelegantly away. The sound of its wings was like paper speedily folded and refolded by a maniac.

"Christ almighty." Jonesy was standing over whatever he had found, his face creased in disgust. He poked at it with a long stick.

Banko looked down. It was a grubby white plastic bag, with what looked like words stencilled on the side. The ink had faded, so he could not make out what they said. There was a large black hazard sign above the corroded text. "Don't," he said, but it was too late.

Jonesy's stick had already sunk into the plastic, splitting the bag. The contents spilled out onto the ground, thick, red and ropy, coated with light skeins of a white webby substance.

"It's medical waste," said Jonesy, retching loudly. He put his hand over his mouth.

Banko took a step backwards, away from the stench; rotten eggs mixed with spoiled meat. "Fucking hell." The remains—if that's what they were—did not look human, nor did they belong to any animal Banko had ever seen. There were small, thin bones, perforated like flutes, and the flesh that clung to them was like pink scallops—rubbery, almost appealing.

Biter Soup

"Are they guts? Intestines?" Jonesy jabbed with his stick and unfurled a long string of what looked like purple-veined sausages.

"Come away," said Banko. "It isn't natural. Isn't right."

Jonesy did not need telling twice.

The two men left the shredded bag where it was, and set off back to their dwelling. They spoke even less than they had on the outward journey, preferring to remain tied up in their own thoughts.

Banko kept thinking about Bella, and the things she claimed to have seen: weird earthen sculptures, but unlike anything that was ever formed by human hands. His senses turned inward, looking for something inside him that he could use to protect himself against this horror. But he found nothing, only the wounds he had carried around with him for decades: the beaten parts of himself that he could never touch, not even with a pointed stick.

*

He made another tape that afternoon, sitting at his undersized desk and staring at the nudie photo:

"Hmmm. Day five-hundred and eight. Found something odd out in the waste. A plastic bag, looked like it might've been from a hospital. It was full of some kind of offal, an organic matter that didn't seem even remotely identifiable. I think something's wrong, and not just out here, among the rubbish heaps. We haven't seen anyone in days. The trucks have stopped coming. In the distance, the city seems to be sleeping...or dead. There aren't any lights at night, not even street-lamps. No distant traffic sounds. Nothing."

He switched off the recording machine and put his head in his hands. They smelled of the stuff from the plastic bag, even though he had not touched it. He tried to remember a time before all of this, when he had a real life, but nothing came. His memories were buried beneath a landfill of regret; his past was nothing but dust and ashes. He was unable to reach the pictures stored at the back of his mind. They were lost to him now, like so much else he could hardly remember.

*

When Bella returned she was wearing a dusty bowler hat with a torn rim. She was limping, so they saw her coming a long time before she actually reached them.

"What's wrong with her?"

"How am I supposed to know," said Banko. Unfocused anger filled him, washing out everything else. He had to pause, take a deep breath, and try to find his centre. "Maybe she fell, or something."

Jonesy said nothing. He was already put out, in a mood because of the way Banko had spoken to him.

"Good evening, gents," Bella said. Her voice was muffled, as if she were wearing a scarf over her mouth. When she got closer, Banko saw that the entire bottom half of her face had slipped off the bone.

"God…what happened?"

"God didn't happen, but something else did. Maybe the devil." Her smile did not even look like a genuine human expression. The movements of her lips were wrong; her teeth had gone crooked in their gums. He was surprised that she could even speak at all.

"What happened to you?" Jonesy could do nothing, it seemed, but repeat the same question.

"I went back. To the western sector. It was different—things had changed. Those shapes I told you about, they were moving, as if they were alive. Swaying about. They didn't even look like earth, not any more. They looked like flesh. All red and slimy, like internal organs."

Banko recalled the bag; the medical waste inside and the way it had poured out when Jonesy had burst the plastic. A strange thought occurred to him.

Had it simply been oozing out of the splits in the bag, or was it trying to escape?

"I touched one of them," said Bella, raising her left arm. The bones of her hand had knotted together, forming something like a boxing glove but with the veins showing through the partially flayed skin. "It doesn't hurt," she said, still trying to smile.

"Your face…what about your face?" Banko could not help but ask.

"I was itchy. I kept scratching it. With this hand." She waved the boxing glove in the air. Blood flew from it in a light spray, painting the ground at her feet. "I didn't know what I was doing…"

When she walked towards them, heading for the cold, dead fire, both men backed away at the same time. They turned to face each other, but neither man could meet the other's gaze.

*

It took Bella three hours to die. It happened just before midnight, when the cloudy, jaded eye of the moon had reached its zenith. She had stopped talking almost two hours earlier, and by then her face was so deformed that she was unable to mobilise her jaw. Blood had begun to seep from her tear ducts and her teeth had fallen out.

She did not seem to be in much pain, but when she slumped forward, her head on her knees, Banko heard a splitting sound like seams being torn.

"What do we do? Bury her?"

Banko shook his head. "I'm not touching her. Not ever again."

Jonesy moved towards her remains, one hand stretched out away from his body, like the stick he'd used on the plastic bag. "We can't just leave her. She needs some respect." When he pushed her shoulder with his fingertips she canted sideways, her guts flopping out like dried fish. Spores rose in a gentle puff of cloud through the gaping hole in her abdomen. Her internal organs had dried out, withered, turned to dust.

"Keep back," said Banko, but it was too late. The spores had drifted over to Jonesy, and he had breathed them in, taken them inside, and absorbed them into his system.

Biter Soup

They both knew that his days were numbered.

Banko grabbed a shovel from the hovel and started to dig a hole. When he broke a few inches through the stubborn crust, he stopped working and turned around. Jonesy was sleeping soundly, his long chin resting on his narrow chest. Bella's corpse had vanished, as if the ground had opened and swallowed it up.

*

They set off towards the west early the following morning, two tall, thin men in long black overcoats. Jonesy was using a dented tubular metal crutch to walk, and Banko refused to even touch him. "I'm sorry," he said, keeping his distance.

"It's okay, shit-stabber," said Jonesy. "It was my own fault. You told me not to touch her." His hand and lower arm already looked like some kind of sea anemone; suckers and tentacles, tight little bunches of blind eyes, and rows of nodules running along the inside of his forearm. His skin was dry and rough, like emery paper.

"I don't know why we're doing this. She told us what we'd find, and there's nothing we can do to stop it." Banko strode ahead, taking the lead. He wanted to make sure the way was clear of obstacles, so that his friend would not lose his footing and fall over. If that happened, Banko knew that he would be unable to bring himself to help Jonesy to his feet.

"Yeah, but I want to see it for myself before I die. I want to stand beside what killed me, see what it is, where it came from. What it's made of."

Banko could not argue with this logic: it seemed sound, if a little desperate.

They walked for another hour or so, following the pale sun as it limped across the low, dull sky. The air was cold and smelled of decay. The heaps of trash reared up beside them, growing higher the further they travelled. There was not a single bird in the sky, or sitting on the rubbish heaps. Soon the men passed the old wrecker's yard, an area populated mostly by the burnt out shells of old cars and motorbikes. Then they hit open ground, before encountering a dip in the earth that had not been there the last time they had walked in these parts. It looked as if the ground had slumped, too tired to support even its own weight.

"Here we go," said Jonesy. "Any last-minute doubts?"

Banko looked up at the sun, its pathetic wan light, and then shook his head. "What else is there? Let's just get on with it, shall we?"

The wounds in the earth were terrible, scouring the soil as the men descended at an angle along the side of the depression. There were great holes and gouges, along with smaller, possibly even deeper, slits in the ground. The earth itself had formed strange patterns, and in places tendrils of dry, fleshy matter had thrust out of the rifts to sway in the air like groping limbs.

And something was stalking them beyond the rows of rubbish. They could sense it as it made its way along their route, keeping hidden, staying out of sight. Occasionally they heard the gentle clatter of its passage; a tin can falling into a crevasse, a plastic bin bag whispering as it was brushed aside, the chatter of empty plastic bottles.

"Won't be long now," said Jonesy, ambiguously. "Not too long to go, you old bastard."

The wounds in the earth were widening; the disease had taken hold. They could hear the tectonic wailing of plates as they shifted heavily beneath the strata, while unseen things forced their way to the surface. The entire area was now covered in fleshy growths and spores, like exotic hothouse flowers. They twitched when the men drew near, as if they were alive and sensed the approach of strangers.

"This cancer of the world," said Banko, feeling like a stranger in his own skin. "It's spreading. Everything we ever internalised, pushed inside to decay, has broken through the earth's crust to take control."

They reached a flat area, right at the centre of the basin. The ground seemed to writhe and contort beneath them, as if underground fault lines were following their progress, keeping pace with them from below.

"Look at that one," said Jonesy. He pointed towards a bright purple neoplasm that was even now flowering into bloom. It reached out of a rent in the earth to lean towards them as it grew into a massive tumour in the shape of Bella, hollowed out, her legs fused together sprouting from the earth like a thick stalk. She leaned forward, opening her red-rimmed toothless mouth. When she lifted her arms there were sheets of pale flesh attached to her sides and triceps, forming rudimentary wings. Her body shuddered, still rooted to the ground, and her belly popped soundlessly open, releasing tumours and abscesses that rolled down her conjoined thighs to curl up at the place where her feet should be.

Her eyes were empty. She looked beautiful, like some glorious angel of the metastasis watching over her young.

"Shall we rest for a while, shit-stabber?" Banko indicated the flat ground nearby. He was not afraid; he was interested to see how this would end. There were no holes, no wounds where they stood. Not yet. But the new-born tumours blossomed and crowded around them, growing like hideous blooms to obliterate the landscape and turn it into something new, something endlessly hungry: a garden of carcinomas.

Calmly, the men sat down to watch the sunset.

Banko took out his tape recorder and set it on the ground. He picked up the microphone and pressed the play and record buttons.

"Hmmm. Day...no, I don't know what day it is," he said, staring at his friend, looking directly into his fast-dimming eyes. "But I do know it's almost over. This is the last." He paused for a moment before continuing, taking in the sights of a corrupted New Eden. "My best years are behind me, but I wouldn't want them back."

Then he ran out of things to say.

Biter Soup

FROM THE EDITOR

AN AFTERWORD

Cancer is a devious bugger. It hides, it lurks, and it pounces when you think it's down and defeated.

Cancer is a monster.

It has been a presence in my life for as long as I can remember. I first came across it in the late Sixties. My Gran's brother came back to town to die with his family. I was fascinated by this man, so thin as to be almost skeletal, wound in clothes that were many sizes too large for his frame, his skin so thin that I could see his blood moving... not pumping, for it had long since stopped moving enough to keep him alive long. He rarely spoke, just sat by the fire as if trying to soak up heat, his eyes frequently wet from tears, not of sadness, but of pain. He lasted for months in that condition until it finally took him and I knew then that cancer was a monster.

Since then it has taken others, both friends and family, a young mother with two pre-teen children, a cousin who was like a big brother to me, and a girl I never got to know for she was taken before her twentieth birthday. Other family members are still fighting.

And so am I.

The first indication that the monster had found me was when I had a tennis ball-sized tumor removed from my guts back in 2019. At the time they said they got it all out of me and I didn't need any follow up. I felt good and strong after recovering from the surgery and went about my life.

On the 4th of August 2023 I didn't feel well, took myself to the docs... and later that day found myself in hospital. I had a gall stone, a big, nasty one.

But that's not the subject of this horror story... the monster had only been lurking, and now it had once again crept out of the shadows. While treating me for the stone, the docs also discovered I had liver cancer... a tumor, a huge tumor, on over half of my liver. I had an op to try to remove the gall stone. That failed. Another op a few days later also failed so they decided the stone would have to stay where it was and I needed a bile duct bypass. I also needed something done about the liver...

Three weeks after being admitted I was sent home with a bile-drain in to wait for a date for the big surgery...

Finally got that arranged and on 16th November went in for surgery.

I was on the table for over ten hours (the surgeon was knackered by the end of it). They cut me open from between my nipples down to above my right hip and got to work. They cut out fifty percent of my liver and bypassed my bile duct. When I came to I had a lot of pain and an enormous scar, but was told I was on the mend. After a week recovering...

during which I also caught COVID… I was sent home.

Ten days later I felt ill again. Back to the docs, and got rushed to ER…the surgical wound had got infected. They drained 3 pints of noxious puss out of my body, pumped me full of antibiotics, left a drain in to keep the puss from building up… and again I started recovering.

Another week later I got home, in time for a quiet Xmas.

It was slow and steady going into late January when I had a chat with the surgeon, the puss-drain finally came out, and a CAT Scan showed that I appeared to be all clear… they thought they'd got all the tumor and my liver seemed to be healing nicely.
Meanwhile recovery continued. After the drain came out I immediately started feeling better and stronger and I was able to get about a lot easier, meaning I got more trips out of the house, more driving got done and things were approaching normality.

And it's been all good news from the first checkups since the surgery. Another CT scan shows my liver is recovering nicely, there are no signs of any cancer, and my blood work is all clear. Blood work every 4 months from now on, CT scans once a year.

So here I am, more than fifty pounds lighter, still tiring a bit too easily for my liking, but a whole lot stronger both mentally and physically.

And most definitely still here.
Cancer's arse?
Kicked.

But it's still a monster. And I can't fight it for people.

As a writer and as an editor there is something I can do. A while back I rallied up some friends, and friends of friends, and asked them for some stories. They responded brilliantly. We put them together in this wee book, and the proceeds are going towards cancer research.

You're doing your bit too by buying it.

These stories are our reward to you.

Karōshi Books

ACKNOWLEDGEMENTS

All profits from this book will go to the Beatson Cancer Research Institute.

The Editors would like to thank the cover artist and the contributing authors for giving over their stories freely for this charity book.

A big thank you to Willie for pulling it all together and his editing skills. My own father died of cancer when I was 11 years old and I know the devastating effect that had on me then and for the rest of my life. If the money raised from this saves even one person from losing someone they love it will be well worth the effort.

Peter Mark May

The Unspoken

Karōshi Books

Karōshi Books is run by the award-winning editor Johnny Mains, Peter Mark May of Hersham Horror Books and Cathy Hurren, a production editor at Routledge.

The Unspoken

Polyp copyright © Barbie Wilde 2011
(Previously published in The Mammoth Book of
Body Horror, ed. Paul Kane & Marie O'Regan.
Constable and Robinson/Running Press 2012.)

Foreword. Signs in the Air © Ramsey Campbell 2013
Just Breathe © Tim Lebbon 2013
Photographs of Boden © Simon Kurt Unsworth 2013
The Last Gift © Steve Lockley and
Steven Savile 2013
Where the Market's Hottest © John Shirley 2013
Pages of Promises © Stephen James Price 2013
Underbelly © Anna Taborska 2013
Heal Thyself © Scott Nicholson 2013
Harbinger © Stephen Laws 2013
The Unfinished Basement © William Meikle 2013
Alien Love © Nancy Kilpatrick 2013
A Girl, a Toad and a Cask © David A. Riley 2013
Polyp © Barbie Wilde 2013
The Cure© Johnny Mains 2013
The Big One © Guy N Smith 2013
Cankerman © Peter Crowther 2013
X for Henrietta © Steve Duffy 2013
Bitter Soup © Gary McMahon 2013

Printed in Great Britain
by Amazon